CROWN OF CINDERS

ALSO BY EMILY R. KING

The Evermore Chronicles

Before the Broken Star
Into the Hourglass
Everafter Song

The Hundredth Queen Series

The Hundredth Queen
The Fire Queen
The Rogue Queen
The Warrior Queen

The Wings of Fury Series

Wings of Fury

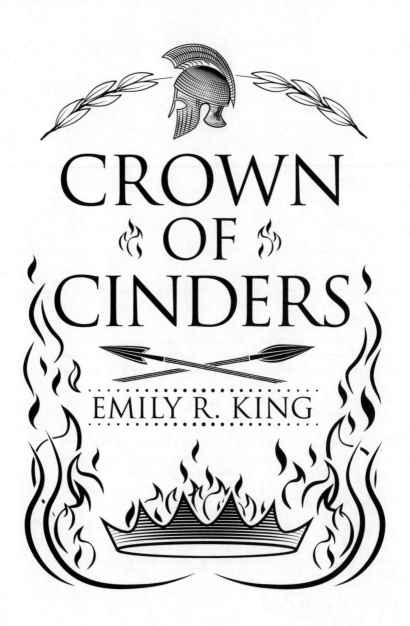

CROWN OF CINDERS

EMILY R. KING

47NORTH

Published by 47North, Seattle

www.apub.com

Amazon, the Amazon logo, and 47North are trademarks of Amazon.com, Inc., or its affiliates.

ISBN-13: 9781542023740
ISBN-10: 1542023742

Cover design by Ed Bettison

Printed in the United States of America

For Stacey, Sarah, and Eve,
Sisters forever

A tale is told that only women know.
For when the men of the Golden Age passed down
Their stories of victory and sacrifice,
They did not think to ask the women theirs.

But a goddess sworn to uphold heroes,
Whispers to the heart of every soul,
Of warriors long ago buried in ash,
That their glory may outlast the shifting stars.

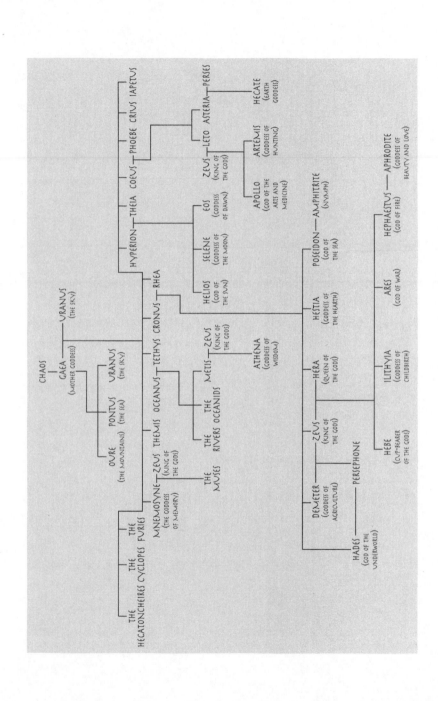

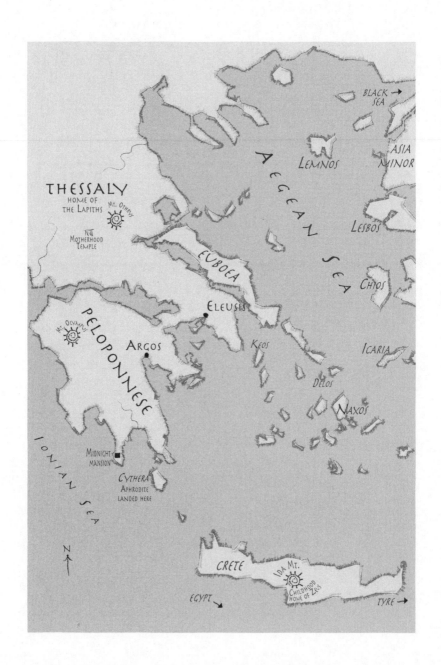

PROLOGUE

Mama often said that within every soul lived a story. Like the shape of each soul, every story was a unique creation, and no one else could truly tell a person's story.

I thought of our mother as my older sisters and I prepared supper. Bronte, thirteen, hummed to herself as she set the table. Cleora, the oldest at fourteen, stirred the bubbling pot of chestnut soup, her cheeks pink from the heat of the fire. I swept the floor with a bundle of straw as tall as my eleven-year-old frame. Gentle amber light poured through the windows, casting a cozy glow throughout our one-room shack. The mighty Helios was finishing his daily journey across the sky. A sunset this glorious was a signal to all that he was thankful for his great domain. When the gods were happy, all were happy.

As sundown surrendered to twilight, I closed the shutters and lit the candles. A shuffling noise came at the front door, followed by a faint knock. Bronte rushed to open it. Our mother, Stavra Lambros, stepped in from the noisy city street. Her modesty mask, her velo, gleamed bronzy in the candlelight. Mama removed it and pushed her hair out of her face. Even after a long day's work at the Aeon Palace, her beauty shone like moonlight on the sea.

"Evening, girls," she said, closing the door. She surveyed the room and found what she expected: a tidy home and washed children. But she didn't seem to notice the pile in the cedar chest in the corner, the accumulation of a week's labor.

Cleora set the pot of soup on the table and ladled portions into our bowls. My stomach grumbled eagerly as we all sat down. I reached for the basket of flatbread. I was hungry, but mostly I wanted to finish so we could get on with our plans for the evening.

Bronte lightly tapped my hand. "Althea, wait."

My mother, sisters, and I joined hands and bowed our heads.

"Dear Gaea," Mama said, "we give thanks for another day in this world of your creation. We ask that you watch over us, and over all thy daughters seeking guidance and protection. Divine day."

"Divine day," I murmured in chorus with my sisters.

Mama passed each of us a flatbread. "How was your day, my shining stars?"

"Good," Bronte said, her mouth full of soup.

Cleora ate daintily, tearing off pieces of bread and dipping them in the soup. I swung my feet back and forth and glanced at the wardrobe chest, hardly eating. Bronte nudged me with her foot, and I kicked her back.

Mama drank from her wine cup and sighed. "I can eat during the play, if you'd like to begin?"

It was difficult to tell which of us stood faster, Bronte or me, but in an instant, we were both rushing to the wardrobe chest. Mama stayed at the table while Cleora hung a bedsheet across the center of the room, concealing our side.

Bronte and I donned our costumes. We had outdone ourselves, away from Mama's view. We had sewn stars all over her navy cloak, and for my emerald robe, we had wired on twigs and leaves. My hands ached from splinters and pinpricks. Bronte was Uranus, the sky god, and I was Gaea, the earth goddess. The most impressive part was our masks. Made from linen and plaster, they had taken days to mold to our faces in layers and dry. Mine was a rounded woman's face with a long, straight nose; holes for the eyes and mouth; and a crown of lines to mimic hair. Bronte's mask was simpler in design with strong, angled lines. We wore our velos for modesty, but these masks were worthy of any theater actor.

"Girls?" Mama asked, somewhat distracted. "Are you ready?"

I peered out from behind the hanging sheet. She had finished eating and gone to the window to check the street. Women were not permitted to sing, dance, or act, among other things. Despite the penalty of a hefty fine or prison time, in the privacy of our home, we took the risk. We did not tell the traditional stories of the Almighty, the ones celebrated across Thessaly. As his name implied, the God of Gods did not favor any tale that did not center around him. Like most powerful men, he was vain.

Mama sat by the door to guard it as though expecting someone to burst in. Her unusual lack of composure concerned me.

"Althea," Bronte said. "It's time."

I stepped onto the cot—our stage—and Bronte hid low to the floor by the chest. Cleora, our narrator, stood off to the side with her lyre. I posed—arms overhead, palms touching, mimicking the peak of a mountain—and then Cleora tugged on the sheet, and it fell to the floor.

Mama's eyes turned watery. "Oh, girls. Althea's costume is perfect."

I lifted my chin, preening. The sores on my hands were well worth her reaction.

Cleora strummed the lyre. "We begin our tale before the dawn of time, when Chaos reigned, a raw and undivided mass, naught but a lifeless bulk with the warring seeds of ill-joined elements compressed together. Though there were land and sea and air, on the land, no foot could tread, no creature swam in the sea, and the air was lightless. Nothing kept its form, and all objects were at odds. Cold essence fought with hot, moist with dry, hard with soft, and light with things of weight. In this strife, the land boldly severed herself from the sea and sky." I threw out my arms, directing the sea and sky to divide from me. "The fiery, weightless force of heaven's vault flashed up and claimed the topmost citadel."

Bronte came rushing forward in her robe and mask as Cleora strummed the lyre in a cascade of notes. Mama grasped her hands together in delight.

"The thick and powerful earth held up heaven's weight." Bronte and I pushed against each other in a choreographed struggle until I kneeled on the ground and she loomed over me. I braced her weight, which felt heavier than in rehearsal. Cleora strummed the lyre and went on. "The land rounded herself into mighty curves, then bade the sea extend and rise under the rushing winds, encircle the earth, and gird her shores. When all had calmed to peace and harmony, the land called herself Gaea."

A rap sounded at the door. We all jumped.

Mama stood slowly. "Who is it?" she called out.

"Palace guards. We need to speak to Stavra Lambros."

Mama's eyes widened. Bronte tore off her cloak and mask, and I began to peel off my robe, but my hair became tangled on the twigs and leaves. Cleora tried to tug my robe off.

"Ow," I said.

A louder voice. "Open up!"

Bronte joined Cleora, and together, the three of us pulled off my costume, yanking out more than one strand of my hair and leaving bits of twigs and leaves in the rest. As I held the sheet over myself, the door banged open. A lanky guard stepped inside, armed with a long sword and a sneer. Behind him stood a taller, bulkier figure. The second guard ducked to enter, his shoulders brushing both sides of the doorframe. His bald head nearly reached the ceiling.

"Are you the handmaid Stavra?" the tall one asked.

"I am," Mama replied.

"Rhea is missing. Do you know where she's gone?"

"I don't."

The lanky guard began rummaging through our cabinets and cupboards. Cleora shuffled Bronte and me into the corner and held us out of the way.

The bigger guard strode to the pot of soup, picked up the ladle, and slurped it. A stream of stock dribbled down his chin. He spoke between sips. "A servant told us you packed a bag for Rhea before she disappeared."

"I did as she ordered," Mama replied evenly, maintaining her poise. As a personal handmaid to the Almighty's consort, Rhea, Mama would be someone to ask about her disappearance. "Rhea didn't say what it was for, though she did order a slave to send it to the docks. Is her trireme there?"

"It's still moored."

The lanky guard found our theater masks on the floor and picked mine up. "What's this?" he asked.

"My daughters make and sell them to street actors," Mama answered.

He tried it on, but it was too small for his face. The larger guard set down the ladle, took the mask, and tried it on. Again, too small.

"Street actors, you say?" He crushed the delicate linen in his huge hands and stamped his foot down on Bronte's mask, flattening it. He dropped my balled-up mask, picked up the pot of soup, and carried it to the door. "Don't leave the city. The general may wish to speak with you."

He ducked out the doorway. The other guard stepped purposefully on Bronte's already squashed mask as he ambled out after him.

Mama's shoulders rose and fell. I peeled away from Cleora's grasp and picked up my ruined mask. My robe had not fared much better; it was torn from taking it off so quickly. The bigger loss was our stolen pot, the only one we owned. Our performance was over, and our evening ruined.

Our mother's voice reached out to us, quiet yet firm. "Who made order out of Chaos?"

Cleora frowned. "Pardon, Mama?"

"Your play," she replied, a fervor shining in her eyes. "Outside these walls, people will tell you Uranus pinned Gaea down and placed his throne above hers, but without her firm foundation, he would have had nothing to set his throne upon. Every living thing is born from Gaea."

My sisters and I glanced at each other questioningly.

"Mama," Bronte said, her tone careful. "The play was supposed to make you happy."

"We didn't mean to upset you," Cleora added.

"You didn't upset me," Mama replied. "I'm sorry our evening was cut short."

"It's all right," I said. "It's not your fault."

Mama gave a sigh of disagreement. "I need you three to always remember who you are. The shape of your soul, the very essence, is without equal. Don't let anyone convince you their story is more important than yours."

"Yes, Mama," I replied, still confused.

"Clean up and put yourselves to bed." She grabbed her cloak. "I must go out."

Mama often left during the night without telling us where she was going or what she was doing. Each time, we would lie awake, worrying and waiting for her return as the moon's silver light shone over the echoing hills of our mountaintop city and into the wooded valleys below. Tonight's wait felt like it would be even more unbearable than usual.

"Must you go?" Bronte asked.

"Yes. Someone needs my help."

"Is it Rhea?" I asked, rising on my tiptoes in anticipation.

Mama fastened her cloak. "Don't fret about it, Althea."

I wanted to ask why the Titaness needed Mama's help. Or why Mama would risk the Almighty's wrath to help his consort, but I doubted she would answer.

Mama kissed the top of my head and opened the door. "Don't wait up."

I closed the door behind her and sank to my heels.

Cleora began clearing the table. "Help us, Althea."

Then footsteps approached the front door again. Mama was back? I threw the door open to find the big palace guard.

"Where's Stavra?" he asked.

I rested a hand over my stomach and repeated the lie I had rehearsed. "She's gone to fetch a tonic for my upset belly."

He squinted at me.

"I haven't been well," I said, feeling genuinely sick to my stomach from anxiety.

"That's why we made chestnut soup for supper," Bronte added, stepping forward to stand with me. "It helps calm the belly."

The guard mashed his lips into a line. "Send Stavra to the palace immediately upon her return."

"We will," Cleora answered. She shut the door behind him and rested her back against it. I wondered if I appeared as frightened as she did.

"Do you think we should find Mama and warn her?" Bronte asked.

"No," Cleora replied flatly. "She will be all right. Let's clean up and get ready for bed."

We went about our chores, but our nightly routine was hardly a distraction. As I washed dishes and readied for bed, I thought of all the falsehoods that had been told this evening—the biggest being Cleora's unfounded faith that Mama would be all right. I tucked myself into our lumpy cot between Cleora and Bronte. My sisters slipped their hands into mine. Usually, we took turns telling each other a story before we fell asleep. That night, it was my turn, but the worry grinding away at my gut was all-consuming. My sisters didn't prod me. None of us was in the mood.

The hours rolled on, pushing the moon onto her lofty midnight throne. I listened to every noise outside our door, waiting for Mama, and kept telling myself she would come home soon and everything would be all right. I was the last one still awake, tethered to my inner platitudes, my sisters' sleepy breaths surrounding me, when I realized that my mother was right: people are made up of stories. We *are* stories—and our truths form us as much as our lies.

1

A knock sounded at midnight when the crescent moon stood guard over the slumbering world. The moon goddess, Selene, entered Theo's and my bedchamber. The pearly glow of her pale skin and luminescent robes chased the shadows into the corners. Her voice, like fingertips dancing across the strings of a lyre, entered my mind.

I bring word about your missing brothers.

"You found them?" I asked, sitting up.

One of them.

Theo rested a hand on my back and waited for an explanation. The goddess had spoken to my mind only. She could not project to more than one person at a time.

Wake your sisters and meet me at the stables, Hera. I will lead you to your brother tonight.

Selene floated out before I could correct her—*My name is Althea.* It had been six moons since I learned that Cronus, the tyrant ruler of the Titans, was my father. Hera was the name of his daughter, a Titaness and goddess whose birthright was nobler than my humble mortal upbringing.

"What is it, Althea?" Theo asked.

"She located one of my brothers." I got out of bed and began dressing. Theo got up as well. "You should go back to bed," I said.

He stopped with one arm through his tunic. "You don't want me to come?"

"You're safer here."

As a former officer in the First House's army, Theo was experienced in battle, and as a half Titan, he had more strength than a regular man. But Cronus had survived my hurling him into the sun, and he had gone into hiding. He could be anywhere, but his followers were everywhere, and they were actively searching for us. We had hardly left the mansion these past six months for fear that we would be found. Cronus would not be lenient with us for destroying his palace and challenging his authority. Capture meant an eternity in Tartarus, the same punishment he gave Uranus after dethroning him.

Theo fiddled with my arm cuff. "Come back soon." His tone held a compelling lilt. His inherited Titan strength was his voice. When used with real intent, his voice could be very persuasive, even influencing another's behavior.

"Is that a command?" I asked.

"A plea." He kissed my forehead, his lips lingering so long my fingers were drawn to his warm chest. "I love you."

My throat clamped shut. He had said it so often in recent weeks, and I had yet to reciprocate.

After a long pause, he said, "Be careful."

"I will."

I stepped out onto the balcony and put on my helmet. Cleora had one crafted for Bronte, herself, and me. Mine was a lion's face, Bronte's a dragon's, and Cleora's supposedly mimicked a bee but resembled a wasp. Each represented the shape of our soul.

The quiet waves striking the shoreline serenaded the night. Perched on the cliff of a secluded coastline, the Midnight Mansion was Helios's home. In recent months, it had become our haven. No one except our cousins Helios, Selene, and Eos—also second-generation Titans—knew we were here. Selene and Helios helped us search day and night for our missing brothers, while Eos, the goddess of the dawn, drew maps of where they had not been found. The first-generation Titans mostly aligned with Cronus, but Hyperion, our cousins' father, remained neutral. Hyperion had, however, agreed to take in my half sister, Delphine, and Theo's mother until we could be with them. I had tried to send Theo to Hyperion with his mother, but he wouldn't go.

I stretched my feathery wings out behind me. They manifested from my lion-shaped soul, more popularly known as a griffin. I was still adjusting to my wings, but I enjoyed the thrill of launching into the sky.

"Althea?" Bronte called from below.

I wasn't surprised to see her roaming through the garden. Her key Titan strength was to grow plants, and she had done that, producing fruits and vegetables for us. Consuming ambrosia and nectar, the food of the gods, was like living off only wine and cheese. We needed other sustenance as well.

Bronte opened her reptilian wings and flew up to the balcony, landing beside me. "I saw Selene arrive. What's going on?"

"She found one of our missing brothers."

Bronte's green eyes lit up. "When do we leave?"

"As soon as we collect Cleora."

"I don't think that's a good idea," Bronte replied.

Cleora had not been herself since Mnemosyne, the goddess of memory and a counselor to Cronus, altered her memory of our mortal upbringing and his tyranny. Our two missing brothers had also been raised among mortals. We had been searching for them since General Atlas, the new head of Cronus's army, placed a bounty on our heads. Sell swords—mercenaries—were hunting us. We had to find our brothers before they did.

"We cannot leave Cleora behind," I said. "We may need her."

"All right," Bronte exhaled. "I know where to find her."

She leaped into the sky with a grace that caught my breath. I stepped off the ledge and threw out my wings to catch me. Bronte hovered beside me, her tawny hair glossy in the moonlight. The shape of her wings gave her slim hips and bosom a sinuous curvature that was dragon-like in magnificence. We swooped down over the garden and around the mansion to the outdoor kitchen, where Cleora tended a fire in the massive hearth. The firelight flickered across her slender face and wavy red hair as her amber eyes were mesmerized by the flames. She could often be found here, kneeling at the foot of a fire, her fingers stained with ash and her chiton blackened with spots from sparks.

As we landed, Cleora dipped her fingertips into the fire. Her skin appeared normal but had an impenetrable barrier, like an exoskeleton. She tugged a tendril of flame out and let it squirm between her fingers before it dissipated to smoke. Bronte made an *I told you she's lost her mind* expression.

"Cleora, Selene found one of our brothers," I said over the crackling fire. "We're leaving to fetch him. Would you like to come along?"

"I would, but I need to get up early to bake bread, or the matron will be cross."

"The matron? Cleora, we no longer live at the Mother Temple. Don't you remember?"

She stood away from the fire. "Of course I do. We're at the Midnight Mansion."

"That's right," I said, but I wondered how much she truly understood anymore. She never spoke of the time Cronus had held her captive. Perhaps she didn't recall, but ever since, her mind had been foggy, and the mere mention of his name caused her to shudder.

Cleora brushed soot off her hands. "Is Zeus coming?"

"I hope not," Bronte replied flatly.

"Selene only mentioned us," I said. We trained daily at dusk, when Helios and Selene could both guard us from their positions on high. Zeus, whom Rhea referred to as her stormking because of his ability to drive the clouds of heaven, had a harder time training with his thunder and lightning without being seen, so he was less experienced.

"We should at least ask," Cleora pressed. "He's our brother."

He was also a husband now. Zeus and Metis had been married just a fortnight, and I didn't relish the thought of barging into the bride and groom's bedchamber, but he deserved to know we were leaving.

"I'll see if he's awake," I said. "I'll meet you both at the stables."

Cleora spread her waspy wings and took off. Bronte muttered something about patience—a quote from her favorite Titan philosopher, Prometheus, no doubt—and left too.

I flew to a grand balcony on the far side of the mansion. Tiptoeing up to the cracked doubled doors, I whispered, "Zeus?"

Someone made a shushing sound, then footsteps padded in my direction. Zeus tied the sash on his robe and swung the door open. His curly raven hair hung messily around his face. "Bored with Theo already?" he purred, batting his sky-blue eyes. Behind him, a large lump lay on his bed, hidden under the blanket.

"I'll leave you to your bride," I said, then noticed a slave's drab robes on the floor. "Zeus?"

"Mmm?"

"Who's in your bed?"

The covers flew up—Jacinta, a kitchen slave. I clucked my tongue in disapproval.

Zeus stepped outside and closed the door behind him. "Why are you here so late, Althea?"

"Our sisters and I are leaving," I replied coolly. "Selene located one of our brothers. Go back to bed, and we'll—"

Zeus threw both doors open and tramped inside. "Leave me," he said.

Jacinta wrapped the bedcovers around her and scurried out. Zeus rummaged through his wardrobe and began to dress. I stepped inside, picked up Jacinta's robe, and dangled it away from me.

"You're bedding slaves days after your wedding?" I dropped the robe back on the floor. "Where's Metis?"

13

"Off somewhere having another one of her visions, I suppose."

She was probably avoiding her husband while he diddled the slave. Metis *was* the goddess of prophecy, after all. She must have seen this coming.

"Why did you get married if you intended to be unfaithful?" I asked.

Zeus put on his armor. "You'll understand when you're married, for the rest of your very long life."

"I'm never getting married."

"Does Theo know that?"

"He knows I've no interest in being a wife."

Zeus walked into the shadowed corridor and lowered his voice. Helios's bedchamber was the next room over, and he needed rest after his long day. "If you ever change your mind about getting married," Zeus said, "I suggest you find a groom more fitting of your station. Theo may be half Titan, but he's still below a goddess."

"I don't recall asking your opinion." I sped past him, but Zeus matched my stride.

"For someone so adamant about not marrying Theo, you're awfully offended at me for supporting your decision. You know I will never lie to you, Althea. I always tell the truth."

"Do you always tell Metis the truth too?"

"I don't lie to my wife. She hears what she wishes to hear."

Chastising Zeus did no good, so I walked even faster to put this portion of the evening behind us. Zeus kept up but said nothing more. I hoped our two missing brothers were less headstrong.

Our sisters were at the stables with Selene. At the sight of us, the moon goddess's countenance shifted, and her voice entered my head.

Oh. He's *joining us.*

As Metis's cousin and long-time friend, she wasn't fond of Zeus or his wandering eye. Nor did she hold much faith that Zeus would over-throw Cronus and rise as our next ruler. I believed in him because the oracles told me the prophecy in person, but the longer I knew my little brother, the more certain I was that he would not prevail on his own.

Selene mounted her winged steed and took off into the sky. Cleora handed the reins of a second winged horse to Zeus. The glorious animals, which also pulled Helios's carriage, were bred by Hyperion in the east. Like my sisters and me, Zeus had his own wings that resembled the shape of his soul, an alabaster eagle. Wide, sleek, and white feathered, his were arguably the prettiest, but he was awkward in the skies. I suspected he was afraid of heights.

He took his time mounting the saddled horse.

"This was a bad idea," Bronte muttered.

"'Every tree begins as a seed,'" Cleora said, citing a well-known aphorism of Prometheus's. Cleora and Bronte opened their wings and launched into the heavens.

Zeus kicked his heels, and his winged horse took off. I lifted after them, and we soared. We had not strayed far from the mansion since going into hiding. Venturing out into the world, where Cronus could be hiding anywhere and sell swords were after us, was daunting.

Principal stars shone out around the moon, humming at me. It had felt magnificent to cup their buzzing light in my hands. I hadn't needed to call them again since weaponizing them against Cronus, yet knowing they were there was reassuring. Not only had the Almighty survived being struck with stars and tossed into the sun but his allies had rebuilt his palace for him, practically overnight and even bigger than before. I couldn't pretend to trust the prophecy about Zeus without also recognizing the enormity of the task ahead. We would need every Titan ally, every Titan strength, every mighty weapon we could gather, to bring the God of Gods to his knees.

2

Selene led the way northeast along the Peloponnesian coastline. The five of us banked away from the mainland and flew out over the Aegean Sea—Oceanus's territory. The banished brother of Cronus was a recluse, and the location of his home, Fort Admiral, was a well-kept secret. Metis, one of his Oceanid daughters, didn't even know where Oceanus and her mother, Tethys, dwelled. The god of the sea was the only Titan capable of mending the minds of those whose memories had been altered. I had hoped to ask him to heal Cleora, but Metis's parents hadn't attended her wedding.

Selene's steed guided us down to an island, and we landed on a rocky hillside fringed by beaches. A faint foot trail led northeast, inland, where an unnaturally thick silence crouched in the night. Not an insect buzzed or cricket chirped over the waves lapping against the shoreline below. I wondered if we might have discovered the edge of the world.

"Where are we?" Cleora asked.

"The island of Keos," Bronte replied, then shrugged at my curious glance. "I've been studying Eos's maps."

Zeus dismounted and stretched his legs. Selene did not dismount.

"Are you coming?" I asked.

This is as far as I go. I promised my father I wouldn't get more involved. The alliance between him and the Almighty is tenuous, and General Atlas grows impatient to find you. He and a band of Titan warriors visited my father earlier today to ask about your whereabouts.

General Atlas, the leader of the First House's army, was known for his towering Titan height, and his brutality. Selene and her family were risking much by helping us.

Take this trail northeast. Beyond that, I cannot see the path. A curtain of nothingness blinds me from the heart of the isle. Selene glanced at the heavens suspiciously, as though the stars were unreliable spies.

"How do you know he's here?" I asked.

Your mother informed me.

Rhea. I had never met the Titaness, but Zeus had, and he thought she was a good mother. We had differing opinions.

"Althea, what is Selene saying?" Zeus asked.

Bronte shushed him.

Selene's winged mare whinnied. She gave a pacifying hush, and then her silvery gaze intensified on me. *I hope you find your brother, Hera. I would do anything for my siblings. Be careful, and may Gaea be with you.*

She bid farewell to the others and rode into the sky until her light faded into the crescent moon.

"She loathes me," Zeus griped.

"You're never going to be her favorite," I agreed, patting his winged mare. "Go lie down."

The mare trotted off into the underbrush and bedded down to wait for us. I headed northeast up the foot trail in the scraggly grass, but in the dark, I kept losing the faint path. Frustrated, Cleora snapped a branch off a tree and bent over a shrub. To my astonishment, she drew out the plant's life force, a pale-blue light, leaving a withered stub. The light glowed in her hand like a large firefly. She lit the end of the branch with it and held up the torch.

"There," she said. "Now we can see where we're going."

"What—what did you do?" I stammered.

"Gaea placed a piece of her soul in every living thing. I took it to give us light."

"You stole the plant's *soul*?" Bronte asked, bending over the shriveled plant. "Oh, you poor thing." She coaxed it back to life. The shrub wasn't as robust as before, but its shoots were green again.

Cleora shoved the torch at Zeus. He held it at arm's length as she drew the soul out of another shrub, withering it. She offered me the bluish light. "Try holding it. A soul is no different than a star."

"I think they're very different," I said.

Cleora frowned. "You summon stars to use as weapons."

Bronte gaped at her. "Stars aren't *alive*."

"How do you know?" Cleora tossed the light at me, and on instinct, I caught it. The soul was warm yet cool, and unlike the stars I had held, it wriggled like a living thing.

I quickly passed it back to her, and she added it to the torchlight.

Zeus shoved the torch at me and sidestepped away. I understood his trepidation. Cleora had never drawn out the soul of a person, that I knew of, but that didn't mean she couldn't . . . or wouldn't.

Bronte fell into step beside me as we followed the path up the hillside. The torchlight shone before us as we walked ahead of Cleora and Zeus.

"She's not herself," Bronte said.

"She's still discovering her Titan strengths, like the rest of us."

"None of us are sucking out souls."

I couldn't yet fathom what Cleora had done, but we had the journey ahead to concentrate on. "We'll discuss this later, after we find our brother."

Bronte growled something under her breath, but she let it go.

The farther we walked from the shoreline, the quieter and thicker the murkiness. We followed the trail to a forest choked with dense and thorny brambles. We paused at the tree line and peered into the misty woodland.

"Do you hear that?" Bronte asked.

"I don't hear anything," I replied.

"Precisely." She examined the brambles. "We should find another path. These are crow's-feet briars. They are very poisonous to mortals."

"What about a Titan?" I asked.

"A single scratch would give us a headache. More than one would cause drowsiness. Too many and we could fall asleep and never wake up." She squinted into the shadows. "Crow's-feet are an aberration. This forest is cursed."

"By what?"

"Sorcerers."

A burst of flames shot up a dozen or so steps down the tree line. The blast of heat hit us, pushing us back a step. Cleora lowered her torch into the brambles again, more flames ignited, and the fire began to spread into the dense greenery.

I ran to Cleora and pulled her back. Her skin was icy cold. "What are you doing?" I demanded.

The spreading flames held her in rapt stillness. "Do you see him?"

"Him who?"

"Him."

I drew my sword and scanned the trees. For a heartbeat, I thought I saw three women in the inferno. They wore goat masks and stood very still as the fire raged around them. The oracles? I hadn't seen them since they appointed me to find Zeus on Crete. I coughed on the thickening smoke, and they disappeared.

The forest fire raged through the deep glens, crackling dry from the summer heat. Cleora continued to glare at someone I could not see. The intensity of her disdain was alarming. I believed she saw someone, but who?

"What is it, Cleora?" I asked.

"Father."

I aimed my sword at the fire and searched again. "Where . . . ?"

"I see him from time to time. He won't touch me again."

Was she delusional? Cleora was not one for making up stories, and she never spoke about Cronus willingly. She began to wobble on her feet. I realized she was going to faint, so I sheathed my sword and caught her before she fell. Her forearm was scratched and bleeding. Bronte ran over, and we dragged Cleora away from the flames. Zeus joined us, and I showed them Cleora's scratches.

"It's not so bad," Bronte said. "She should wake up eventually."

"Should?" Zeus replied.

Thunder crashed and lightning sliced across the wine-dark sky. A storm was gathering.

Zeus shrugged. "It isn't me."

A louder clap of thunder shook us, punctuated by lightning, and then the clouds began to dump rain in blinding sheets. In seconds, the ground was soaked and muddy.

The fire began to shrink, dispersing hissing smoke into the air, and the rainwater collected into quick streams running downhill. The lightning made flying too dangerous, so Zeus hefted Cleora up onto his shoulder, and we dashed across the slippery field for higher ground. Above us, a copse of trees grew along an outcropping of boulders. Their wide branches would offer shelter.

As we climbed, my footing slipped in the surging water. Bronte grabbed me, and we were both swept backward. We got up, drenched, and saw five figures armed with spears up ahead. Swathed in cloaks, their hoods shielded their faces from view. As we got closer, I saw that the strangers stood inside a great invisible dome that stretched high above them and toward the center of the island. The wall between us would have been invisible if not for the rain running down the outside.

We clambered through the water now rushing down at us. Cleora was still passed out, hanging limply from Zeus's shoulder. At the top, I pounded against the transparent wall. One of the hooded figures waved his hand, and a doorway opened between us. We scrambled through, sopping and breathless, and the opening sealed shut behind us. Inside was warm and dry. We were outside an oak forest, devoid of brambles. The storm petered off. With the noise of the rain lessening, I could hear cicadas and nighttime birdcalls. The cloaked figure in the middle edged forward.

"I'm Chieftain Megalesius of the Telchines tribe," he said. "Who are you, and what brings you to our isle?"

"We're here for someone," Zeus said.

"And who would that be?"

"We were told our brother was here," I answered.

The chieftain removed his hood. While his arms were raised, his sleeves fell to his elbows. Black tattoos of manta rays surrounded his wrists. His long ivory beard and hair were braided, streaks of green woven into the braids like stripes of seaweed. I had never heard of the Telchines tribe, though given the dome shielding them from the rest of the world, that wasn't much of a surprise. "I know you now," the chieftain replied. "You're the children of the Almighty. You there . . . You must be Zeus, the boy of prophecy."

"You've heard of me?" Zeus asked, perking up.

Bronte elbowed him in the side. "Everyone's heard of you."

The chieftain addressed me next. "And you're Hera."

"Althea," I corrected. "I still go by my mortal name."

"You look like your mother." Chieftain Megalesius waved at one of his companions. "Bring them, Lycus."

"Yes, Father," said the man on his right, the biggest of the five. Lycus approached us with his spear pointed at the sky. "Lay down your weapons, godlings."

I tried but was unable to open my wings. An unseen power bound my soul. I saw similar confusion on Bronte's face. I tried summoning a star, but nothing happened. I could no more call to the heavens than a mortal could reach the moon.

Zeus drew his sword. Chieftain Megalesius waved a hand, and Zeus's arms twisted behind him at an unnatural angle, bound by an unseen force. He strained against it.

"I wouldn't resist." The chieftain waved again, and Zeus's arms bent so far back, I heard his shoulders pop. My brother quit struggling, and Megalesius released him. Zeus folded forward at the waist, panting. He popped his shoulders back into their sockets one at a time, groaning loudly.

Bronte and I dropped our weapons and raised our hands. Lycus disarmed Zeus and then removed the short sword from Cleora's unconscious body. Two other men bound us. I tested the strength of the rope and noticed Zeus doing the same. The rope held. It could not be normal rope, or we would tear it apart with our Titan strength.

We were led about forty paces away and directed to climb into the back of a cart drawn by shaggy-faced oxen. They laid Cleora down beside us.

"Althea," Bronte said. "Do you think they know where our bro—?"

"Silence," Lycus barked, thumping her on the head.

Bronte sucked in a deep breath and held it. I doubted he hurt her. She was holding back her temper.

The cart began to move, the wheels creaking as we entered the woods. The men with torches went first, and then the chieftain led the oxen by its yoke. Lycus and another man followed closely on foot, no more than an arm's reach from swatting any of us upside the head. Lycus bore a deep, mangled scar across his upper lip that ran up to his left nostril, which was missing a chunk of flesh, an old injury that suited his mean, squinty eyes. The other man was stout and bald, with a neck so thick that his head seemed to rest directly on his shoulders. They sneered at us repeatedly, discouraging us from moving or speaking. From the front of the group, I heard a cheerful melody that sent gooseflesh tingling up my back.

Chieftain Megalesius was whistling.

3

As the night fell into its quietest hour, the cart stopped before a waterfall. Cattails and blooming hyacinths, violets, and yellow crocus surrounded the banks of the pond's rippling surface. The night was scented with jasmine, and fireflies darted over the water hole, casting their miniature reflections across the surface like dancing starlight. Lycus hauled us from the cart one by one and threw Cleora over his shoulder like a sack of grain.

"Take them to the tank and meet me in the village," Chieftain Megalesius said. "We have more to discuss." He studied me ponderously, then clasped his hands behind his back and departed into the woods.

Lycus and the other three men removed our helmets, tossed them in the back of the cart, and blindfolded us. They led us alongside the pond through the rushes. As we approached the waterfall, a billowing mist dampened my arms and face, and the cacophony of rushing waters grew louder, muffling most other noises and disorienting me. The ground sloped, and then I felt water lap against my sandaled toes.

"Get in," Lycus ordered. He shoved me forward into cool water. I went under, still blindfolded with my hands tied in front of me. My feet found the bottom, and I stood, sputtering. My arms were dragged over my head, and my bindings were strapped to something that lifted me out of the water until my feet no longer touched the bottom. I dangled there, my head above the waterline. Occasionally, a wave swept against my chin. I tilted my head back and thought about Theo's calming voice. More splashes sounded behind me, followed by Bronte's grumbling. Finally, I heard Lycus.

"Let's go."

"Shouldn't one of us stay?" asked another man. "This is a lot of godlings . . ."

"We're needed in deliberations, Scelmis, to convince Father to do what's best for the tribe."

Their footsteps boomed away, but I couldn't be certain they hadn't tricked us and left a guard behind.

"Zeus?" I called.

"This water is *cold*," he replied. "Have they no consideration for a god's sensitive parts?"

"They should have hung you upside down so we wouldn't have to listen to your harping," Bronte said. She began to sing softly to herself, her way of self-soothing. She wasn't fond of being in water.

"Where's Cleora?" I asked.

"I hear breathing beside me," Zeus answered. "I think it's her."

Images of my unconscious sister gradually drowning threw me into a panic. "Cleora!"

"She's sleeping," said a male voice in front of me. I did not recognize him. He had a lisp, and he didn't sound like any of our captors.

"Hello?" I asked. "Is someone else here?"

"Another captive?" Zeus asked.

"What I wouldn't give for a cup of amber wine and a piece of wheaten bread," the stranger grumbled.

"We cannot see you," I said.

"I can unblindfold you, but you'll have to put your head underwater."

Bronte snorted. "I don't think so, stranger."

"What do you think he's going to do?" Zeus challenged. "Drown us?"

"Yes," Bronte responded slowly. "That's precisely what I think he might do."

I needed to evaluate Cleora's condition. I didn't trust our prison mate, but at present, my sister's safety was more important than mine. Taking a deep breath, I dunked my head underwater. At first, I only noticed the cold, and then a sensation akin to fluttering tentacles skimmed my jaw. I nearly lifted my head out again, but the watery tentacles moved higher, and my blindfold slipped off. I raised my head and blinked water from my eyes.

We were indeed behind the waterfall. The tank, as the chief had called it, was a large pool with an eddy in the middle. The glistening cave walls were shrouded in ivy. Long ropes hung across the ceiling, like the rigging on the sail of a ship. Some had hooks attached to the ends, which our bindings had been set in, so we swayed in the stirring waters. I dangled between Zeus and Bronte, and on the far side of the pool was Cleora. Her head leaned back so her mouth and nose were clear of the rippling surface. Beside her, with his vivid blue eyes locked on me, hung a deep-chested young man about my age. His blue mane of long curls floated around him like tentacles, and he wore a silver collar around his neck. It was hard to see much else of him in the dim.

"Althea?" Bronte asked.

"Cleora is here," I said, "and another prisoner."

"He sounds cagey. Does he seem cagey to you?"

The young man smirked. "Put your head underwater and I'll unblindfold you next."

"Bronte doesn't like the water," I explained.

"Then she has never been in it with me."

"I'll do it," Zeus said. "I like to know to whom I'm speaking." He put his head underwater. Seconds later, he rose with his blindfold off. "Stars alive, that's cold. Thanks, stranger."

"My pleasure," the prisoner replied.

"All right, all right, all right." Bronte begrudgingly put her face in the water and resurfaced, sputtering. Her blindfold floated beside her. The stranger had not moved or changed his expression.

"Who are you?" I asked. "What can you tell us about the Telchines?"

"They're an ancient tribe of sorcerers known for inventing the art of metal-making. They're credited with crafting Cronus's infamous adamant sickle."

Cronus had pricked my sisters' and my heels with that sickle when we were newborns, divesting us of our Titan strengths. Through the power of the adamant, he had absorbed our godly traits until we cut him with the same sickle and released them.

Bronte narrowed her eyes at the prisoner. "How did you get here?"

"I grew up on Keos, with the tribe." His blue, blue eyes pierced me. "Who are you? Why have you come?"

"I'm Zeus." My brother puffed out his chest. "These are my sisters, Althea, Bronte, and Cleora."

"You're Cronus's youngest child," the stranger answered evenly. "These are your sisters? I was told their names were Hestia, Demeter, and Hera."

"Those are their Titaness names," Zeus replied. "They go by their mortal ones."

Sometimes I suspected that Cleora and Bronte wished to take on their Titaness birth names—Hestia and Demeter, respectively—though they had not expressed so.

"I'm Poseidon."

"Odd name," Zeus replied.

"My mother gave it to me."

"Your mother?" Bronte pressed.

"Rhea."

At last, we found one of our missing brothers! If I squinted, I could see the deep indents of his cheekbones and wide forehead. He was classically handsome, like Cronus.

"Mother hid me here from our father," Poseidon explained. "She told me my strengths were restored because of your bravery."

"You're welcome," Bronte answered pertly.

"Do you see Rhea often?" I asked.

"Often enough," Poseidon replied. "She told me about all of you."

"What did she say about me?" Zeus asked eagerly.

"She called you her 'stormking.'"

Bronte guffawed. "Because like a storm, people run away when they see him coming."

Her voice carried a hint of jealousy. Rhea had never visited my sisters and me, but she had visited Zeus and Poseidon and hadn't hidden the fact they were gods from them. Cleora and Bronte were more forgiving of this. They had worn the laurel crowns that Rhea had sent as gifts to the wedding party for Zeus's nuptials. I had not. Then again, I never took off my arm cuff, which had initially belonged to Rhea. For years, I thought it was Stavra's because she had given it to me without citing that it belonged to my birth mother. I wore it in Stavra's honor, not Rhea's.

"Why, if Rhea entrusted the Telchines with your guardianship, are you their captive?" Zeus asked.

"When the tribe learned about General Atlas's bounty, Megalesius's sons came for me in the middle of the night and put me in this collar. They want to turn me in for a reward, but they don't seek riches. They want adamant, which is only mined in the underworld."

"What do they want adamant for?" I asked.

"Lycus and Scelmis wish to craft a weapon." Poseidon arched his head. Every time he swallowed, his throat rubbed against the collar. "This collar is Lycus's invention. He built two. When they first put me in the tank, they made me wear both until Megalesius told them to take one off. The collars aren't crafted from pure adamant. They've been experimenting. These were forged with other metals tainted with sorcery. The Telchines think their next weapon could be greater than Cronus's sickle."

My mouth went dry. A weapon like that in the hands of Cronus would be disastrous, but in the hands of one of his enemies . . .

"Who will they craft the weapon for?" Bronte asked.

"Megalesius didn't say. For his sons, it is a matter of pride and reputation. They wish to reestablish the tribe as the greatest smithies in the world, beyond even the Cyclopes toiling away in Tartarus. They feel Megalesius has lost his verve for their true purpose. You see, long ago, the Telchines built the adamant sickle as a gift for goddess Gaea. Cronus stole it from his mother, to wield against his father, and never gave it back."

Zeus's brow furrowed. "That's not how he tells it. Cronus says he was the only one courageous enough to pick up the sickle and attack Uranus."

"Stories can be twisted to serve almost any purpose," Poseidon replied.

"What do you think the chieftain will do?" Bronte asked. "Will he turn all of us in or let us go?"

"Megalesius considers me a member of his tribe, but he will not put me above blood kin, and the three of you are of no consequence to him."

Bronte popped a brow. "*We're* not wearing collars. Maybe we can get out of here."

"The ropes binding our hands were made with sorcery as well," Poseidon replied. "Even if you break free, the interior of the island is shrouded by an enchanted barrier that keeps us in, and others out. Only the Telchines can open it. They've never shared the key word with me."

It didn't sound as though Poseidon was ever a welcome guest here. He had always been the tribe's prisoner, and now we were too. The isle's enchantment explained why Selene had not been able to see the interior. This place was hidden from her sight, as were we.

"How long until the tribe decides?" I asked.

Poseidon shook his head. "They could deliberate for another hour or for several more days."

"Days?" Bronte sputtered. "I'm not staying in the tank for days."

"And Cleora needs help," I added. She had still not awakened or shown any sign of healing.

"I think I can get her down," Poseidon said.

I tried to open my wings to break free, but I could not call to my wings or to the stars. "I'm typically more useful than this," I muttered.

"None of us are especially impressive right now," Poseidon remarked. "The enchantment over the isle affects a Titan's strengths adversely, each in different ways. I retained mine because I'm also considered a member of the tribe, but the collar suppresses it."

"So can you or can't you help Cleora down?" Bronte asked.

"I can try."

I squinted at him. "If you can do that, why don't you free yourself?"

"I was working toward that before you arrived," Poseidon replied. "I had conserved my strength for breaking loose. This seems more important."

He closed his eyes. Bronte and Zeus made dubious faces at each other, and then the water around Cleora began to rise and take the shape of a horse. The steed lifted Cleora high enough that her bindings came undone from the hook. She fell limp on top of the water horse. Poseidon had not moved except for his flaring nostrils. The water horse carried Cleora to the shore, where it crashed, ebbed away, and left her on her side. Poseidon slumped forward, his breathing hard, and the surface of the pool calmed.

"Cleora?" Bronte asked. "Cleora, wake up!"

Our sister roused. "Where am I?" She sat up, then groaned and lay down again. "I had the strangest dream. There was a fire—"

"Rest," I said.

"Poseidon, that was riveting," Zeus remarked. "I've never seen a horse made of water before."

"I'd applaud if I could feel my hands," Bronte added wryly.

Poseidon's wide smile jolted me. He resembled Cronus more when he was pleased with himself.

Footsteps approached, and Lycus and the bald man with no neck entered. The Telchines must have finished deliberating, and by the bundles of ropes they carried, identical to the ones around our wrists, their decision was not in our favor.

4

The guards dropped the ropes and rushed forward when they saw Cleora on the ground. Lycus aimed his spear at her, and the bald man drew his short sword. They hefted Cleora to her feet. She wobbled, still too drowsy to resist.

"How did she get down, Scelmis?" Lycus demanded.

Baldy shook his head. "I secured her, brother. I swear. Is she the one?"

"Her hair is the wrong color." Lycus let go of Cleora, and she sank back to the ground. He scanned the pool, skimming over Bronte to me. "That one. Father said she has the darkest hair of the lot. Bring her in."

Scelmis pulled on the rope attached to my hook, dragging me toward shore. I twirled through the water until my feet skimmed the bottom of the pool, but he hauled me too fast to find my footing. I stumbled to a stop, and Lycus snapped a silver collar around my neck. A heaviness pulsed from the metal, straight down to my ankles. I crumpled to my knees. How had Poseidon used his Titan strengths while wearing his collar?

Scelmis ran a finger down my cheek. "This is Hera? She doesn't seem intimidating."

"Don't underestimate her," Lycus replied.

Cleora tried to get up on rickety legs. "Don't touch her."

"Or what?" Lycus asked. "You're under our dome. You have no dominion here, goddess."

"And where is *here*?" she shot back.

"The heart of Keos, the land of the Telchines tribe. We were granted special defenses from the goddess Gaea, overseen by her son Oceanus, to guard our precious smithy from the rest of the world . . . in particular, the gods."

"You are mere godlings," Scelmis said, his fingertip on my other cheek now. I tried to rise, but the weight of the collar could have been the moon on my back. Scelmis drew his finger down my throat, to my collarbone.

Cleora leaned against the wall for balance. "Did you hear me? I said: Do not lay a hand on my sister."

Lycus arched a bushy brow and chuckled. "I heard you, woman. You don't present yourself like a godling or a Titaness."

"Appearances can be deceiving," Bronte called out from where she hung.

Lycus and Scelmis looked at her, and Cleora leaped at the hook above me. Holding on to it, she flung around and kicked Lycus in the chest. He flew backward into Scelmis, and they landed in a heap.

Zeus lifted his lower half and wriggled his bindings off his hook, splashing into the water. He swam to Poseidon and tried to remove his collar, but it wasn't budging. I reached for Lycus's spear while he was still down, but my tied hands frustrated my grip.

"Your bindings could hold Hecatoncheires," Lycus said, fighting me for his spear. "I enchanted them myself. Only my command can release you."

A big wave crashed into us, jerking us apart, slamming Lycus into the wall, and pushing Cleora away from me. Poseidon sloshed out of the tank and tackled Scelmis while he was trying to get up. Zeus swam to Bronte and unhooked her from the ceiling. They plunged into the water together. I crawled to Lycus's dropped spear, the collar weighing me down, and aimed it at him.

"Release us," I growled.

He snorted. "You can barely lift your head."

"Turns out that's all I need." I speared him in the shoulder. He sank forward, grasping at his bleeding wound.

The ground began to tremble. Cleora and I stayed low as a piece of the ceiling broke and fell. It missed Poseidon and landed on Scelmis's bald head, knocking him out. Lycus broke the spear and tossed it aside, then picked up his brother's sword, grabbed Cleora, and put the blade to her throat.

"We only want you, Hera," he said. "Come with me, and your siblings go free."

"Hurt my sisters, and I will strike you with lightning until you're a pile of ash," Zeus snarled, wading to shore with Bronte.

"You're all useless under our dome." Lycus pressed the blade tighter to Cleora's throat, his shoulder bleeding badly. Cleora was still held by the bindings, her wrists pinned together in front of her at an awkward angle.

"Perhaps," Cleora said with deadly quiet. "But until recently, my sisters and I lived in the world as mortals and dealt with plenty of men like you."

Lycus's lip curled, the mangled portion tugging up his notched left nostril. "You've never met anyone like me."

"You have that backward." Cleora reached her bound hands up, hooked him behind the head, and flung him forward over her shoulder. He landed on the ground with a crack, his head hitting the rock. She disarmed him and lowered his sword to his gullet. "What were you saying?"

"You're no goddess. On our land, you're like any other woman, made only for wedding and bedding." Lycus ran his hand up her bare calf and sneered.

Cleora pressed on the blade, breaking skin.

"Stop, Cleora," Bronte said.

"He needs to learn his place," Cleora snapped.

"Althea, we cannot let her kill him," Poseidon said. "Lycus is the only one who can release us from our bindings."

"Who are you?" Cleora asked, glaring at Poseidon. "You look like *him*."

"I'm your brother Poseidon." His lisp was more pronounced when he was nervous. He stepped forward, his cool blue eyes on her. "Let him go."

"He won't change. Men like him never do."

"She has a point," Zeus replied. He was standing over Scelmis, who was still passed out.

Poseidon glanced above Cleora's head, as if considering letting loose some more rocks.

"Poseidon, don't," I said. "Cleora, see Lycus? He's been punished enough."

Cleora noticed her handiwork then—the blood pouring down his neck and the gurgling noise bubbling from his throat. She did not let up. "After he releases us," she said.

"Lycus," Poseidon pressed.

Lycus's dry lips formed quiet words. "Oceanus's pearls," he rasped.

The bindings around our wrists fell to the floor, and the collars around Poseidon's and my neck unclamped and hit the ground. I massaged my neck and sucked in a deep breath, straightening to my full height. The crush of weight was no longer on my shoulders.

Cleora let go of Lycus as if throwing away a rotten piece of fruit. He slumped over, and his eyes rolled shut. "Are you all right, Althea?" she asked.

"Am *I* all right? Are *you*?"

She rubbed at the scratches on her arms. "I think so."

Poseidon examined Lycus's wounds. "He's alive, but we need to get him to the village healer." He hoisted him into his arms.

"What about Scelmis?" Bronte asked.

"I'll carry him." Zeus threw him over his shoulder.

My lips twisted. Cleora had been carried into the tank in that very same position, and thanks to her, we were all walking out. I regretted any doubt I had about bringing her along and looped my arm through hers. She grasped on to me and tilted her head against mine.

Bronte picked up the sword, and the three of us followed our brothers out from behind the waterfall to a well-worn path through towering oak trees. Dawn in her saffron robe shone down upon the woodland floor. The path led us to a village along a marshy inlet. Smoke curled out of the chimneys of the rock huts mudded with clay, and fishing boats bobbed along a wooden dock. A few terraces extended out over the marshland, overlooking the lazily flowing water. High tide tugged against the shoreline and the wooden pilings. The sea was out of sight, farther down the firth.

The chieftain and a small group stood outside a temple. Near the front was a statue of a Titan I had never seen worshipped—Oceanus, god of the sea. My sisters and I hunkered down in the foliage, and Zeus followed Poseidon out to meet the chieftain. They stopped a fair distance away, faced sideways so I could clearly view both parties. Zeus slung Scelmis to the ground. Poseidon set Lycus down carefully.

Chieftain Megalesius called out to them. "Where is Hera? I must speak with her."

The little hairs on the back of my neck stood up.

Zeus ticked his head to the side. "Why?"

"I have news about your father."

"Since when?" Poseidon asked.

Megalesius's green eyes blazed. "I don't converse with traitors."

"These people are my *family*."

35

"*We* were your family." Megalesius waved at his sons on the ground. "Your siblings should do well to take notice of your treatment of 'family.'"

Poseidon locked his jaw.

"What do you wish to tell Hera?" Zeus questioned.

"I speak to her only." Megalesius boosted his chin and scanned the forestlands. "Come out, Hera. Let us meet face to face."

"Do you think he really has news about Cronus?" Bronte asked.

I was worried that the mention of the Almighty might upset Cleora, but she was lost in thought, her focus inward.

"I don't know why the chieftain would lie," I said.

Bronte chewed her lower lip. "I suppose it does no harm to hear him out."

Rising from the underbrush with the spear in hand, I joined my brothers. "Megalesius?" I said by way of greeting. "This best be worth my time."

His lips spread in a toothy grin. "Hera. The Titaness who cast the God of Gods into the sun. I hear you can summon stars with your bare hands."

"I didn't come forward to talk about me. What do you wish to tell?"

"Your father has recovered from his injuries and resides at the rebuilt Aeon Palace in Othrys. He's accompanied by his brothers Iapetus, Coeus, and Crius. They retrieved his adamant sickle for him. The lot of them are gathering allies against you as we speak. They're preparing for a war of the gods."

"War?" Zeus asked. "How do you know this?"

"I will answer Hera's questions only," the chieftain replied.

Zeus set his foot on Scelmis's back, standing on him as he would a roped prize calf. "Your sons spoke to us that way too."

Megalesius's tone remained impassive. "They're intelligent boys, if not overly ambitious. Surely you can appreciate that, Zeus."

"Who gave you this information?" I inquired.

"Just because the outside world cannot see us does not mean we don't see them." Megalesius cut a side-glance at Zeus again. "Be wary of this one, Hera. He would throw you to the dogs for his own glory. Cronus made apparent which child he was the most intimidated by when he set the bounties on your heads. Yours is the lowest, Zeus."

Gaping, Zeus removed his foot from on top of Scelmis. "What was Hera's?"

"Three times more than the next in line."

I was not flattered, nor did it make sense. Zeus was the god of prophecy, fated to overthrow Cronus. Everyone knew that.

"Who has the second-highest bounty?" Poseidon asked.

Megalesius answered, maintaining eye contact with me. "Your other brother, Cronus's last hidden child."

Poseidon and Zeus spoke at the same time: "Where is he?"

Megalesius paid them no mind. He stared at me incisively, as though his next words could cut me wide open. "You really do remind me of Rhea. Even your name is like hers. 'Hera' is the letters of 'Rhea' reordered." He gestured at my arm cuff. "You also wear her symbol, the lioness."

My heart banged wildly. "Are you loyal to Rhea or Cronus?"

"We're loyal to whoever allows us to live in peace. Rhea has done as she promised, keeping the outside world at bay, but most Titans care only for their own happiness, and the world pays the price. You will come to understand this better in the decade to come. Mankind will pay for the gods' war in blood."

Scelmis woke from his black swoon. He tried rolling over, but Megalesius waved a hand, and his son stayed facedown.

The chieftain went on. "You're aware of the oracles' prophecy."

A statement, not a question.

"They recently visited me," he said. "They told me Cronus would not fall unless all of his children united against him."

I had glimpsed the three sister oracles in the burning woods, but I thought I had been hallucinating. "Did they say anything else?" I asked.

For the first time, I saw more than haughtiness in Megalesius. "No, but wisdom says their prophecy will come to pass. Not even the stars hang in the sky forever. Eventually they, too, fall."

His absolute conviction drove a warning into my bones.

"We're leaving," Poseidon said. "Give us the key word to open the gate."

"I thought you would have figured it out by now," Megalesius replied, with an impatient sigh. "The key word to release you is what has held you here all these years."

After a prolonged stare, Poseidon blinked. "Let's go. We can reach the nearest gate out of here by boat." He waved for our sisters, and he and Zeus headed for the dock. Bronte and Cleora strode toward our brothers, and Poseidon readied a fishing boat. My sisters gave the chieftain and his men a wide berth, but especially Cleora, who glared at them hotly.

"Hestia has fire, but it does not hide that her mind is unwell," Megalesius said, his tone touched with pity. "She must be whole before you face Cronus."

"I was told Oceanus can heal her. Do you know where to find him?"

"The god of the sea is all around us. Cast an offering into his divine waters, and he will hear you."

Scelmis tried to get up again. Megalesius held him down with his invisible power and spoke over his groan. "You must go now, Hera. The world needs you. Do not forget my warning: Zeus is too much like his father to entrust with our futures."

"I trust no man with my fate, god or otherwise."

Megalesius made a "hmm" noise deep in his throat. "I believe you will try to do what's best for everyone, but ultimately, what transpires will be beyond your control."

His lack of confidence in me was somewhat insulting, but I did not need to prove myself to him. I offered a farewell and walked to the docks. Everyone was on board the fishing boat except for Bronte. She chewed her lower lip in consternation.

"Do we have to go by water?" she whined.

"The nearest gate is at the other end of the inlet," Poseidon replied from where he sat at the stern. "This is the fastest way out."

"All right," she grumbled. We climbed in together, and she quickly sat between Cleora and me.

"Where are the sail and the oars?" Zeus asked.

"We don't need them." Poseidon put his fingertips in the water, and the vessel sailed forward.

Sea spray speckled us as we cut a path across the sunlit water. Straight ahead, where daylight touched the horizon, a rainbow prism glistened in the sky, revealing the outline of the dome. Poseidon slowed us to a stop, and we drifted up to the wall. Though blurry, the ocean was visible beyond.

"The village fishermen use this gate," Poseidon said. "I know it's here somewhere . . . Ah." He rested his hand against a rectangular section outlined in a gold haze and whispered the key word so softly that I missed it. The golden rectangle sparkled away, and Poseidon propelled the vessel through the gate.

Outside, Bronte opened her wings, accidentally whacking Zeus in the face.

"Careful," he said, and then gave Poseidon directions to where we first arrived on Keos and left the winged mare.

A little while later, I leaned close to Poseidon, and asked, "What was the key word?"

"Family," he said, a lump visible in his throat.

Megalesius had said the thing that would release Poseidon was what had held him there all that time. "You stayed as their prisoner for us?"

"You've been asked to make sacrifices too. Yours was not to know your true heritage until you were ready to receive it."

I hadn't yet accepted my heritage, but I doubted he would understand. Poseidon had always known he was a Titan. He had not made plans or dreams outside of that fate. I had desires that had nothing to do with acquiring a godly domain, but I did value those who performed their duties faithfully.

When no one was paying attention, I removed my arm cuff and tossed it into the sea.

"Oceanus," I whispered, "if you're listening, please help us. We need to find you."

The surface of the sea didn't change, yet as we neared our location, stronger winds swept at us, and storm clouds choked the morning sky. Bronte held on to the bench with her eyes shut. Poseidon concentrated on navigating the choppy surface, but the surf closer to shore grew so rowdy, I was certain we would capsize.

Poseidon moved to the bow and yelled, "Get down!"

I crouched next to Zeus. Bronte and Cleora held each other. Poseidon stood and extended his arms, his long hair whipping in the wind, and unfurled his wings. They reminded me of a winged horse's— feathery and sleek, only bluish, like his hair.

The sea before us grew placid, and then waves rose beneath us in the shape of horses. Poseidon clicked his tongue, and they charged us toward shore ahead of a massive wall of waves raging behind us. The water horses rode right to the beach, and our boat jolted as the hull scraped over pebbles and then to a stop.

"Please let that be land," Bronte prayed, her eyes still closed.

Poseidon held the seething sea at bay as the wall of water grew taller. Outside of the bounds of his strength, waves crashed against the steep shore. We abandoned ship and ran up the embankment. Poseidon's arms shook as the tidal wave towered over him. Once we reached higher ground, he jumped out of the boat and sprinted. The swell broke loose and barreled after him. As he neared us at the ridgeline, I caught his hand and pulled him up. The sea pummeled around us, drenching us and sending the fishing boat crashing into boulders. Our vessel was smashed to pieces, and the debris swept away with the receding water. I leaned against Poseidon, both of us soaked and winded.

"Well"—I panted—"done, brother."

A bang of thunder shook down on us. The storm roiled overhead, its winds shrieking like a murder of crows.

Cleora clasped hands with Bronte and Zeus. Poseidon and I joined the line, and then we spread our wings and took to the angry skies. A blast of wind shoved us toward the cliffside. Zeus was the weakest flier, and Cleora was still depleted, but we worked together to push back and fly to the hillside above.

From on high, the view of the thunderheads was frightening. A barrage of lightning bolts struck the sea, unrelenting in their brilliant violence.

This was no regular storm. We were in a tempest.

I whistled for the winged mare. Straightaway, she trotted up. Though I was certain they had never met, she went straight to Poseidon and nuzzled his shoulder with her snout. As he petted her, I glimpsed the shape of his soul—a flying horse.

A roll of thunder rumbled ominously for three heartbeats, and then the skies opened and heavy rain poured down. Rushing gales pushed raindrops into our faces, pelting us. The flight back to the mansion would be dangerous, but this tempest was not natural, and Megalesius's warning about an impending war worried me. I couldn't wait for blue skies to shine once more.

"Poseidon, ride with Cleora," I said. "Zeus, I'll help you fly. Bronte, you lead the way."

Cleora and Poseidon mounted up without complaint. Zeus stepped close to me, face to face, and slipped his arms around my waist.

"Don't enjoy this too much," I said.

His warm breath caressed my ear. "Oh, I will."

I pretended to ignore him. "Hold on tight."

"We both know you've no need to tell me that."

Bronte spread her wings, signaling us to go. I followed suit, and the wind immediately slapped me back. I caught my footing and launched us into the sky. Zeus weighed more than I had wagered, and his grip meandered a little too low, near to my backside, but I ignored it, climbed higher, and trailed Bronte out to sea.

My eyes saw stars from the endless flashes of lightning, and they streamed tears in the fierce winds. Each inhalation was like trying to breathe with a pillow over my face, and every clap of thunder sounded closer and crosser, as though the tempest was hounding us. I kept near to Bronte and the mare, but occasionally, a blast swatted me sideways.

Without warning, the slashing gusts of rain lost some of their bite.

Zeus's arm was outstretched as he fought back the tempest, alleviating the gales. I could finally fly straight and draw in a full breath, but his weight was still taxing. As we soared toward the mainland, pillars of smoke spewed up from a seaside village, and worry set in. Big cracks snaked across the hillside, and fields had been utterly decimated by sinkholes.

The devastation continued to the next village, and the next. We stayed along the coastline to avoid the smoke, but slices of the cliffs began sliding off and plummeting into the surf. A mighty gust pushed us toward the cascading rocks. My reaction time was slow from fatigue, so Zeus opened his wings. I held on as he dodged the landslide and flew us higher.

Father of stars. What is happening?

Ahead was the point of the peninsula where the Midnight Mansion was located. My heart tumbled to my toes. More smoke and flames rose from the immense structure, which hours ago had shone like the inside of an oyster shell.

Theo.

5

Zeus let go, and we sped side by side toward the mansion. I circled the wreckage of Helios's abode. The roof blazed red, the top floor had collapsed, the front pillars had crumbled, the kitchen was in shambles, and even parts of the lush grounds were aflame.

Landing in the garden among a copse of burning palm trees, Bronte, Zeus, and I took in our surroundings in a daze.

Bronte stomped out the flames on a tomato plant and moaned. "My poor darling."

The rest of her garden was in no better state. Every vegetable was either on fire, buried under soot, or charred to a stub. Big flakes of ash drifted down around us. Some pieces glowed red with the last breath of cinders. I brushed one out of my hair.

Poseidon and Cleora landed on the winged mare and dismounted. Bronte rushed to the groundskeeper's lean-to near them. The storage hut had collapsed under a smoldering pile of palm fronds and now leaned too far for use. She sorted through the remains, dug out a pouch of seeds, and tucked it away.

Zeus pivoted toward the mansion. "Metis," he breathed, and ran.

I took off after him, and we arrived at the catastrophe at the same time. What yet stood of the ivory exterior was charred. Pockets of fire still burned gluttonously in the debris.

"Theo?" I cried.

"Metis!" Zeus shouted.

The thick smoke made flying overhead for a bird's-eye view a waste of time, so we prowled along the perimeter to the front entrance. An aftershock trembled the ground, sending rubble bouncing around us.

Zeus kneeled on the buckled terrace where his wedding nuptials had taken place. "Metis!"

His panic gave voice to my own. "Theo?" I called. "Theo! If you're out there, make a noise!"

Someone groaned in the rubble straight ahead of me.

I dashed into the debris, scrambling and slipping on ash. I kept going until I found a slave half buried under a stone column. Her hair was singed, and her face and arms were covered in gruesome burns.

Zeus caught up to me and groaned. "Oh, Jacinta."

She was so disfigured I hadn't recognized her.

He sat beside her. "What happened here, Jacinta?"

"Titans," she rasped. "The quakes began in the night. Then they came . . . they came for you."

"Who came?" I asked.

She arched her back and gritted her teeth. Our other siblings joined us and congregated around her.

"Can you do anything, Bronte?" I asked.

Her grim expression was discouraging. She had the closest Titan strength to healing but was far from a healer.

The ground shuddered again. Jacinta began to breathe fainter.

Bronte kneeled beside her and took her hand. "Don't fear," she said. "I hear the fields of asphodel in the underworld are splendid." Bronte kissed her forehead as Jacinta exhaled her last breath, and then my sister bowed her head. "Gaea, please welcome your daughter beyond the gates of the sun and into the land of dreams."

My lungs stung from the smoke. Only Cleora appeared unaffected by the fires.

"They came here for us," Zeus said, his eyes bloodshot.

Bronte balled her hands into fists and rose. "Spread out. Keep an eye out for survivors."

She, Cleora, and Poseidon began combing through the ruins. Zeus stared vacantly at the horizon. I couldn't bring myself to move either. All I could think of was that I might kick over a piece of stone and uncover Theo's handsome bearded face.

Sunbeams broke through the thunderheads and spotlighted the smoldering mansion. The rays grew brighter as Helios rode down in his golden chariot, drawn by a team of winged white horses. He landed in the garden, and we all rushed to greet him.

The sun god's fine robes were sooty, his usually perfectly coiffed auburn hair a windblown mess, and his jaw was set. His usual molten amber eyes were bleak.

"Cousin," Zeus said, embracing him heartily. "Where's Metis?"

"And Theo," I inserted.

"They're safe," Helios replied tiredly.

The tightness in my chest abated. I could finally breathe without the aching worry.

"What happened?" Cleora asked.

"Pallas and his crew brought their hunt here." Helios twisted at his earring, fiddling with it as he explained. "When they searched the grounds, they found Theo, surmised that Hera had been here, and took to destroying the mansion. In the chaos, we got away. Selene and Eos fled to the Coral Mansion to be with our parents. Metis and Theo aren't welcome there, so I took them to Prometheus."

Theo was with his father.

Bronte's jaw fell agape. She had worshipped the god of forethought since she was a child.

"Unlike most Titans, Prometheus doesn't support Cronus." Helios blinked at Poseidon, as though noticing him for the first time. "You must be the brother they went to Keos to find. Welcome to what was once my home. It was more impressive yesterday."

"Helios," Zeus said. "We're so sorry."

"I knew the risks when I took you in," Helios replied, though his sorrow was palpable.

Another aftershock pulsed up from the earth.

Poseidon lowered to one knee and pressed his palm to the ground. "The quakes are coming from far away. Who . . . ?"

"The Almighty made a declaration at dawn," Helios said. "He asked that his six children turn themselves in, or mankind would suffer."

"But we cannot," Bronte said.

"Of course you cannot," Helios agreed. "He's intimidating you."

Poseidon rose. "This is a brutal form of intimidation."

"His terrorizing has only begun," Helios replied. "But you cannot, under any circumstances, turn yourselves in. It will require all of us to—" His head whipped around, out to sea. "No . . ."

He strode quickly to the cliff's edge, and we all followed. The thunderheads cast a bitter gloom over the water, where a fleet of triremes dotted the horizon, heading in our direction.

"Great gods," Zeus breathed. "The First House's armada."

Every ship in the fleet appeared to have come, more than three hundred, so numerous they peppered the surface of the sea.

Down the cliffside, four warriors in full body armor crested the top of the rise. This was the band of Titan warriors that General Atlas had commissioned to find us. Pallas, god of battle and warcraft, led the group. With him were his brother, Perses, god of destruction, and their cousins, Menoetius, god of violent anger and rash actions, and Lelantos, god of the unseen.

Pallas rode a griffin—a massive winged lion with a full mane and mighty feathered wings. Its shiny tan coat was sleek, and its huge paws threatened long, sharp claws. The beast's yellow eyes monitored us, its prey. A Titan renowned for wielding a spear with a leaf-shaped head,

Pallas's very pale hair was thin and short, and he wore no beard. With his equally pale skin and protruding front teeth, he resembled a mole rat. He was the only warrior rider.

His brother, Perses, was smaller but had a similar bulky build. Perses was by far the more attractive of the two, with his blond beard and tresses, though he still had the appearance of a varmint, perhaps a beech marten. He carried a *kopis*, a curved sword plated in gold, and a coiled whip. The sword reflected the sun, glinting so brightly it hurt my eyes. It was not gold plated; the material was more like a piece of the sun or an arm of a star.

Menoetius was the largest god of the group, with a fat neck and high, flat forehead. Long red hair hung down his hulking back. He carried a short sword in each meaty hand and stalked like a bull preparing to charge. With his reputation for having a short temper, he was the god most often associated with rashness. It was rumored he could drink multiple barrels of nectar before he passed out.

Lelantos, his brother, stood off to the side. The thin, lean Titan with furry, fulvous hair floated in and out of sight, as though blinking in and out of this world. In addition to his short sword, he carried a shield studded with spikes. His gear was made of another material I did not recognize. It was shiny and reflected everything around it. Even odder, his uniform and weapons flickered in and out of sight with him. He moved lithely, with intense purpose. If Menoetius was a bull, Lelantos was a mangy coyote.

"Look at the pretty sun god," Pallas declared, grinning wickedly. "Helios, you're dingier than a tarnished coin."

"I've had better days," Helios admitted. "Would you make my day better by leaving?"

"You know we cannot. We're under orders to collect the Upstart Gods, and we're to cut down anyone who stands in our way. Fly away, cousin. Make your day easier on yourself."

Helios drew his longsword and answered wearily. "I don't wish to fight you, Pallas, but I cannot let you have them." All four of the opposing Titans lifted their weapons. "I will not turn a blind eye to Cronus's tyranny any longer."

"You were accused of treason, of ripping apart our family," Pallas said, aghast.

"*Cronus* tore us apart when he divested his own children of their Titan strengths to protect his throne," Helios argued. "Don't think he won't do the same to any of us."

Pallas and his team of gods stalked closer.

"Step back, Helios," Menoetius growled. "I don't wish you harm, but I will do what I must."

Helios spoke under his breath to us. "Go to Mount Olympus. Prometheus lives outside the village at the north base of the mountain."

"What about you?" I asked.

The god of the sun responded slowly. "I will join you later."

The Almighty's armada sailed closer. I didn't like leaving Helios, and I wasn't certain Prometheus was trustworthy. General Atlas and Menoetius were Prometheus's brothers. But if Theo was waiting for me at Mount Olympus, I would go.

Helios aimed his blade at Pallas, and it lit on fire, becoming a flaming sword. Pallas lowered his spear and clicked his tongue, and his griffin charged. Helios jumped high and spun, cutting down at Pallas in midair. Their weapons clashed, and Helios landed behind him in a crouch. Menoetius and Perses ran at Helios, weapons out. Lelantos disappeared, flickering from sight. Then something struck Zeus in the back, and he fell to the ground. The same invisible force flung Poseidon. They tried to get up and were thrown back down.

Pallas charged at my sisters and me, his griffin clawing the ground as it ran. Bronte, Cleora, and I took off into the sky. The griffin extended its large tawny wings and launched into flight after us. The beast swiftly caught up. We stayed close together and banked north toward Mount

Olympus like Helios had told us to do. Pallas aimed his spear at me, and a light burst from the leaf spearhead. The blast struck my left wing, singeing me. I pinwheeled down and landed in the ashy remains of the vegetable garden. Pallas shot bolts of light at Bronte and Cleora, who also tumbled to the ground.

Pallas's griffin landed on top of me, pinning my upper body and snapping at my throat. A clap of light burst across the garden, and the griffin screeched and crouched away. Bits of light floated in my eyes, and then Helios stood beside me. He was on fire, glowing so brightly I thought he was the sun itself. Menoetius ran at him, ramming him in the center and throwing them both onto the rubble.

Cleora got up, panting. She was barely on her feet when something slammed her back down. Lelantos was mostly invisible, but when Helios's light reflected off him, it revealed the god's outline.

Zeus fought off Perses, then spread his wings and took to the sky. Pallas was right after him on the griffin, leaving Helios to take on Perses. Poseidon threw open his wings and took off too. My sisters lifted into the sky, and I bent into my knees to take off after them, but someone grabbed me around the neck. A voice filled my left ear.

"Divine day, Hera. I've heard a lot about you and your Upstart Gods."

"Upstart Gods?" I croaked.

"That's Cronus's name for his children." Lelantos's arm tightened around my gullet. "As ruler of the Titans, Cronus assigns us our domains. Every godling matures into the god of something, but he's decided none of you will receive that honor."

"I don't want it." I gripped Lelantos's arms and threw him over my shoulder. He landed somewhere on the ground in front of me with a thud.

I took flight and dived down the cliffside toward the beach. Bronte and Cleora had soared out over the sea. Pallas pursued them, his griffin roaring. The triremes at the front lines of the armada had reached the coastline. Several loud bangs went off, then nets whirled around us, launched from ballistae mounted on the deck of the ships. Two missed, but a third wrapped around Bronte, and she dropped from the sky into the whitecaps, where the weight of the net dragged her below the surface.

Poseidon dived after her. As I dodged the claws of Pallas's griffin, someone howled. Cleora hovered behind Pallas, fluttering her insect-like wings, her short sword deep in his shoulder. Pallas struck her in the face with his fist. She reeled backward through the air, crashed into the wall of the cliff, and tumbled to the rocky beach.

Lightning flashed overhead. This time, it was summoned by Zeus. The bolt struck Pallas's griffin, sending the beast free-falling into the water in a haze of smoke.

Poseidon resurfaced with Bronte, untangled from the net, and carried her toward shore atop a horse made of water.

A trireme armed its ballistae with heavy stones and fired at them. I sailed out over the water, drawing its fire. Big stones whizzed past me and splashed into the waves. One clipped my wing and spun me around. I righted myself and heard shouts of alarm. A trireme was tipping over as a sinuous fin rose beneath it.

A sea dragon.

The scaly deep-blue serpent with the horrifying maw reared up out of the water savagely, capsizing the trireme, and then dived headfirst into another. The second vessel rolled on its side and spilled crew members into the sea. As the gigantic sea dragon resurfaced, I spied a rider seated high on its back.

"Styx?" Zeus said, dumbfounded. "She's Metis's sister."

Another daughter of Oceanus. She had not attended Zeus and Metis's wedding either. She also happened to be married to Pallas.

The god of battle and warcraft spotted his wife from his position onshore beside the wounded griffin. His mouth fell open as the sea dragon gave a gut-shaking roar. Styx waved at us, but not in greeting. She was telling us to go.

Standing high on the cliff, Menoetius yelled, "Upstart Gods!"

The bull-like Titan held Helios by the hair. The god of the sun kneeled unarmed before the brute. Both of Menoetius's swords protruded from his back. He held Helios's own flaming sword to his throat.

"Turn yourselves in, godlings," Menoetius cried, "or Helios will be sentenced to Tartarus where he belongs!"

Zeus hovered in the air, his wings flapping furiously. The storm sizzled around him. "Never!"

"Then our cousin is Cronus's." Menoetius pushed the flaming sword closer to Helios's throat and shoved him onto his own chariot, and then he rode it out to the largest vessel in the fleet, landing the chariot on its deck. A warrior in brilliant golden armor pulled Helios off the chariot and threw him to the ground. He was almost double the height of anyone around him, including the giant Menoetius.

Zeus darted to me. "Althea, we must retreat. We cannot win this battle."

"I think that's General Atlas," I said. "He's bigger than all the others. That has to be him."

"Then we really should go."

The general's trireme released the ballistae. One stone hurtled between us. Zeus rose to dodge the next. General Atlas shouted something, and the ballista adjusted their aim toward Styx and her sea dragon. The Titan general picked up one of the massive stones himself and tossed it at Styx. It knocked her into the water, and the dragon roared as it was struck repeatedly by the ballistae. Atlas pulled Menoetius's swords out of Helios's back and threw his flaming sword overboard. Helios stayed down, even as the Titan general stepped on his injured chest.

My blood boiled. I could not let Atlas take Helios without a fight.

I reached for the midheavens. My fingertips buzzed and my palm warmed as I pulled at the universe. Almost immediately, a star blazed across the sky. Atlas and his crew sighted the glittering trail headed toward me. The general took his foot off Helios's chest, picked up another stone, and heaved it at me with such force that the trireme rocked.

I caught the star and backflipped, dodging the stone. Chest heaving, I tucked my wings behind me and dived at the general's trireme like a comet. Before I dive-bombed the deck, I reopened my wings, and an updraft pulled me back. I made eye contact with Atlas and flung the star.

His eyes went wide. "Abandon ship!"

His crew bailed into the sea. Menoetius picked up Helios and leaped overboard. The star struck the center deck, decimating it. A tidal wave swelled outward from the force, rocking the other ships sideways. Styx had remounted her sea dragon, and they dived in retreat.

Poseidon and Zeus flew beside me, and we scanned the sea. The crewmen clung to the debris floating on the choppy surface. I could not see Helios or Menoetius or the general.

"Any sign of Helios?" Zeus asked.

"No," Poseidon said. "We should go."

The second half of the armada was arriving, and they were loading their ballistae.

"One more minute," I replied, still searching the waves for Helios.

"Althea," Zeus pressed. "We have to go."

Helios had fought to protect us, most of all Zeus. Turning away felt like a betrayal, but we soared back to the beach, where Bronte and Cleora were wet and bruised but ready to fly. The five of us took off, and we fled like a flock of sparrows from a bird of prey, sailing toward far-off Mount Olympus.

6

We soared northward through clouds of gloom. I checked for the sun continually to see if Helios had escaped and would join us, but it was only my siblings and me racing across the sky toward Mount Olympus. Wispy clouds wreathed the mountain's rugged peaks, brutal in their grandeur. I had never seen anything more awe inspiring.

Around midday, we landed in a barley field on the outskirts of an alpine village. The cooler mountain air was refreshing, but none of us was free from ash or soot, and we all stunk of smoke.

"I know we're close to Prometheus's stronghold," Zeus said, "but I could use a rest."

Bronte placed a hand over her heaving chest. "Me too."

I needed a reprieve as well. "Let's catch our breath," I said.

We ambled over to some oak trees near the barley field and collapsed in their shade.

"Now I understand why the biggest bounty is on Hera." Poseidon patted my back companionably. "You're terrifying, sister."

"Um, thank you?"

Zeus raised his head from where it rested between his arms. "I don't understand. I'm the Boy God of prophecy. Shouldn't I be worth the most coin?"

I spit on my finger and scrubbed at an ash mark on my arm. "It isn't a compliment."

"Someone who goes by 'Boy God' shouldn't tout any sort of importance," Bronte added, plucking a dandelion.

Zeus grumbled and rolled onto his stomach, facing away.

"I'm relieved to see Mount Olympus," I panted. "This mountain is something to behold, isn't it?"

Bronte twirled the dandelion in front of her nose. "The highest peak lies above the clouds and the path of stars, in a zone known as the aether, the bright upper air of the heavens. No man can survive up there, but many choose to live at its base. Speculation suggests that a doorway to the underworld lies in a cave on the mountain, and sometimes during the deepest undergloom of night, one can hear the rustlings of the dead."

"Eerie," Poseidon said, shuddering.

"The opposite, really. People live here to feel closer to their departed loved ones. I think that's hopeful." Bronte put the dandelion back. The stem grew into the ground as though she had never plucked it. "I'm intrigued by Mount Olympus. I thought my sisters and I might want to live here one day, after our godly duties are done."

Poseidon kicked a pine cone. "Why did the Titan warriors call us 'Upstart Gods'?"

"Cronus named us that," I replied. "He's not going to give us godly domains."

"We should choose our own domain," Zeus suggested, sitting up. "I'll be the god of thunderheads. What about you, Althea?"

"The goddess of naps," I said, yawning.

"I want to be the goddess of feasts," Bronte announced, patting her stomach. "I'm so hungry."

"In that case, I'll be the god of imbibing," Poseidon said. "I would give all the shells in the sea for a cask of wine right now."

"What about you, Cleora?" Zeus asked.

"I would be the goddess of hearth and home." She pressed a hand over her heart. "That's what my soul tells me."

Of course, Cleora would answer sincerely. As the oldest, she was the most dutiful. I had no sense what my real domain might be. My soul told me nothing.

Zeus nudged Cleora with his elbow. "Once I am the Lord of the Gods, I'll see that you're known as the goddess of hearth and home."

"*Virgin* goddess of hearth and home," Cleora corrected.

"Hestia, the virgin goddess," Zeus announced. "You shall not marry if you do not wish. Many gods will mourn your spinsterhood."

Cleora laughed warmly. I could have hugged Zeus. I only wished that throwing my arm cuff into the sea and calling upon Oceanus had brought Cleora aid. My arm felt naked without it.

"We should move along," I said. "The day will grow late if we tarry."

Cleora peered south, the direction we had come from. "I don't like the temperament of those clouds," she said.

Bronte sighed. "I hope Prometheus feeds us supper."

"And good wine," Poseidon said, lifting her to her feet.

The prospect of food and drink compelled us toward the village. Little huts were spread out, with chickens running about. Sheep grazed on grassy patches outside goat pens. A handful of people could be seen washing clothes in a muddy pond and feeding grain to the livestock.

Zeus strolled beside me. "Do you really think you're worth more coin than me?"

"I wish you would leave that alone. I don't want to discuss how much I'm worth to Cronus as a captive."

Zeus slipped his hand into mine. "You're worth more gold than any woman, goddess, or Titaness." Thinking he was teasing, I glanced at him sharply. He met my skepticism with unbridled sincerity and held my hand tighter. "I mean it, Althea. You're irreplaceable."

Heat wound up my throat. I squeezed his hand and let go.

Most of the villagers who saw us scurried into their huts and shut their doors. We carried weapons like any travelers or hoplites, and with more women than men in our group, we should not have been considered menacing. Perhaps they were running because my sisters and I were bearing arms, even though women weren't permitted to.

"Any guesses where Prometheus lives?" Bronte asked, eyeing the huts. A Titan would have a more notable abode.

A maiden holding a basket of laundry gaped at Zeus. He grinned back with more charm than anyone—man or god—should have been allowed. An older woman, most likely the maiden's mother, dragged her farther away.

"Would you direct us to Prometheus's stronghold, please?" Zeus asked.

The older woman walked faster, but the maiden pointed up the road at a wall partly obscured by trees.

"Divine day to you," Zeus called in farewell.

"A friendly smile won't always get you what you want," Bronte said.

"It's worked well for me so far." He grinned at another maiden before her father shut their door.

I frowned to myself. Someday Zeus's friendliness might do more damage than good.

We took the road littered with pine needles to the wall. The ashy clouds crept closer, dimming the verdant grove and lowering the temperature. A mother roe deer and her two fawns heard us and pranced off deeper into the woods. A foot trail through the trees ran parallel to the wall. We took it around and arrived at the gate. On the wooden door was a carving of a goddess bearing the sun on her shoulders. A bell rang within the stronghold, and then several guards appeared on the ramparts. I called out to them.

"Is this Prometheus's keep?" I asked.

"It is. State your name, woman."

"Althea Lambros."

"Never heard of you."

I lifted my chin higher. "Helios sent us. Two members of our party are here. Where are they?"

The guards appeared bored. They backed away from the ramparts, out of sight.

Bronte edged in front of me. "We're children of the Almighty!" she cried, and the guards reappeared. "This is Hera, and I'm Demeter. Prometheus should be expecting us."

The guards eyed us and then stepped out of sight again.

"You should have let me speak," Zeus said. "They aren't accustomed to hearing from women, especially armed ones."

"You grew up on an island inhabited by warrior women," Cleora reminded him. "I would think you would have more faith in armed maidens."

Zeus closed his mouth. As a child, the warriors of the cult of Aphrodite had been his guardians. He should have been more open minded.

Murky clouds hung over our heads, strangely not accompanied by wind. The heavy sky felt stagnant, as though the clouds had captured the air between them and the land.

The gate creaked opened, and five guards greeted us.

"We'll take you to the other members of your party after you relinquish your weapons," said the guard in front.

Zeus dropped his sword as fast as I did mine. Our siblings disarmed themselves, and we were permitted into the courtyard.

The stronghold was surrounded by forest, but within the walls, the land had been cleared so only a few trees remained. The main lodge, constructed from logs stacked on top of each other and mudded together with clay, was the most prominent structure. Several minor outbuildings were set around it. As I scanned for any sign of Theo, something struck me on the head. I shot Zeus a glare.

"What?" he asked, his brow furrowed.

Bronte picked it up. "It's hail."

The second she gave it a name, the hail drummed down faster, beating us with an icy onslaught. The hail that missed us ricocheted off the ground, as high as my chin.

The guards waved for us to follow them to the portico off the front of the main lodge. We sprinted after them as the hail pounded down heavier and faster, some bigger than my fist, tearing away pieces of rooftop and ringing the bell.

"This weather is unnatural," Cleora said.

My gut soured in agreement. Who was doing this?

The hail finally petered off, and we wandered out from beneath the overhang. Hail crunched under my feet. The storm had damaged shingles and left holes in the roof of sheds and lean-tos. Branches littered the ground, torn free from the few trees in the yard, and more broken branches hung limply from the trunks. I dared not imagine the damage to the village's barley field and other crops.

"We'd like to see the other members of our party now," Zeus said grimly.

The guards led us past the stables to a windowless cabin. Its roof was intact, unlike the shed beside it, which was in tatters. A guard knocked once on the door, and another answered. I pushed my way into the cabin, hardly realizing how much I was shaking until Theo crushed me in his arms.

"You're really here," I said, burying my face against his shoulder.

He squeezed me harder. "We were told the mansion was demolished."

"By quakes and fires, and then the royal armada came with General Atlas. He sent Pallas and a band of Titans after us. Helios directed us here."

Theo bundled me closer. Since I had arrived to find the Midnight Mansion in ruins, part of me had been prepared to learn that he had not survived. Until now, I hadn't realized how much losing him would have wrecked me. His shoulders rounded down, curving around me and tucking me even tighter against him. I had never felt anything more wonderful than the weight of his big body pressed around mine.

"Did you find your brother?" he asked.

"Yes. His name is Poseidon." I nuzzled his neck with my forehead. "I'm so glad to see you. Quakes, tempests, hail . . . The whole world has gone mad."

"The whole world, or our Titan ruler?"

"Cronus wants us to turn ourselves in."

"You cannot," Theo said strongly.

"I know."

In my periphery, I caught sight of Metis kneeling on the floor, head down, palms resting on her lower abdomen. "Is she all right?" I asked.

"Soon after Helios dropped us off, they put us here without letting us speak to Prometheus. Metis soon fell into a trance."

I stroked Theo's beard. "Why are they holding you prisoner?"

"We've been told we're 'guests.'"

I disagreed. The guards outside had not let anyone else enter, and the cabin only had one way in and out. This was a cell.

"Did you tell them who you are?" I inquired.

"No."

Either they didn't know Theo was Prometheus's son, or they knew and had imprisoned him regardless.

Zeus's voice came from the doorway. "Release my wife at once! She's with child. Should anything happen to her, I will fry you with lightning."

Metis was with child? But they had not gotten married that long ago.

"Dog," Bronte said, swatting Zeus. "You couldn't wait for the wedding night?"

Zeus replied from between clenched teeth. "Now is not the time to question my morals."

"True," she retorted. "You'll give me plenty of opportunities later."

"Both of you, *please*," Cleora said, begging for quiet.

Metis's chin snapped up. Her open eyes were milky in color, which occurred whenever she was having a vision. Her eyes faded back to their usual stormy blue gray and locked in on the people in the doorway. "Zeus," she said.

He pushed past the guards, lifted Metis to her feet, and embraced her lightly. "Come along," he said. "We'll see Prometheus now."

"That's not possible," a guard replied. "He's meeting with someone."

Zeus swept his arm out, indicating us all. "Who could be more important?"

"Goddess Rhea."

A collective beat of silence settled through the group.

"Our mother's here?" Poseidon asked.

Without waiting for a reply, he marched toward the main lodge. The rest of us hustled after him. One of the guards reached for Poseidon to try to stop him, but he threw open his wings, and the man was flung backward.

I tried not to pay any mind to my sisters, but I sensed their excitement. I felt only dread. Rhea may have birthed us, but that did not make her our mother.

At the front door to the lodge, Zeus and Poseidon began arguing with the guards to let us inside. Their vehemence escalated until Poseidon began shouting.

"Mother! Mother, we're here!"

Zeus joined in, and then so did Bronte and Cleora.

Over the yelling, Metis stepped up to Theo and me. "Both of you come along," she said. "I need to show you something."

Theo fell into step behind her. Curious, I did too. Due to the ruckus my siblings were putting on, no one noticed us cross to the stables. Metis paused at the open door. "In the vision I had today, I left you at this point. She's waiting inside for you, Althea."

"Who?" I asked, peering into the stables.

A magnificent griffin was being saddled by a stately woman with my exact deep-brown-red hair color and soft bone structure. I thought I was seeing myself in the future, and then she quirked her left eyebrow, which I was unable to do.

Rhea.

7

Theo entered the stables ahead of me and sank to one knee. "Goddess Rhea."

Her catlike eyes never left me. "Hello, Hera."

I did not feel the need to correct her. For the first time, the name "Hera" didn't sag off me like an oversize cloak. Coming from her, it fit.

"Goddess," I replied, entering and bowing my head. "We heard you were here. My siblings are eager to meet you."

"I will meet them later. I haven't long to speak with you."

Her low voice was a sensual purr. Everything about Rhea exuded polished femininity, and she possessed a regal poise that was heightened by the intellect shining from her active stare. She had an apprehension about her, seen in the tight lines around her mouth, but none of that detracted from her graceful beauty. She was intriguing, compelling, like a lioness on the prowl. It felt vain to say I took after her, but the resemblance was undeniable.

"Hera, I know where you can find your last missing brother," she said. "You must fetch him and bring him home. Cronus could not have defeated Uranus without his four brothers aiding him. The same monstrous Titans are still on his side. You second-generation Titans may not grow to our massive heights, but you have your own strengths—and your wings. Your brother will be needed in the battle ahead."

"Cronus didn't have all his brothers on his side," I said. "Oceanus refused to align with him. I have Poseidon, Zeus, Bronte, and Cleora. That's four too. Isn't that enough?"

"The story you know as *The Fall of Uranus* is an alteration of the actual events that transpired." Rhea's crimson lips tensed. "Cronus changed the story to suit his ego. The truth is that not only did he have the assistance of four of his brothers but his sisters helped him as well."

I exchanged a confused glance with Theo. "You and the other Titanesses helped?" I asked.

"I stood with my husband," Rhea answered. "I will not make that mistake again."

Unfortunately, this made sense. Cronus altered people's memories, so why not change history? "Why won't he admit that he had your help?" I asked.

"By claiming all the glory, he ensured that his power was absolute and his throne would go unchallenged. Now that you and your siblings are grown, it's time for that to change."

"I don't understand," I admitted. "Why ask *me* to find my brother? Zeus is the god of prophecy."

"Zeus is still a lot like his father," Rhea replied wearily. "With the right companion guiding him, he will grow into his strengths, but he's not yet ready for this responsibility. You see, your missing brother isn't in the mortal realm. He's in the underworld."

I was slow to comprehend her. "My brother is in the *underworld*? Why?"

"He was stationed there by Gaea and me, to fulfill a very important assignment."

Theo rose from his knee. "I will go in Althea's place."

"That's noble, Colonel Angelos, but as a demigod, you will perish should you linger in the underworld too long. Only a Titan can travel there and back without long-term repercussions."

My chest pumped hard. If my brother was there willingly, this didn't sound like a rescue mission. "Why not send a messenger to tell him to come back?"

"You *are* that messenger," Hera replied. "We've no more time to waste. Cronus cannot notice my absence for the length of time that the journey requires, or I would go myself. Hera, your strengths make you ideal for bringing your brother home."

"Goddess Rhea," Theo said, "forgive my boldness, but isn't this dangerous for anyone?"

Rhea's eyes glittered with centuries of wisdom. "Not all Titan strengths are visible, but those that are not obvious are no less important." She took up the reins and mounted her griffin. The beast shouldered her weight with ease. "Your family follows you, Hera. You are more than your wings and your fury."

Rhea rode out of the stables.

"Wait." I rushed after her. "My siblings wish to see you."

"And I them, but it's Gaea's will that our reunion be postponed until another time. Prometheus will tell you what you need to know and direct you to the gate." Rhea glanced at the sun and rubbed her neck as though it ached. "I must go. Your brother answers to the name 'Hades.' He will know you."

She snapped the reins, and her griffin threw out its immense wings and took off. They soared up the forested mountain face toward the dreary clouds.

"Althea!" Zeus's voice carried across the yard. He and our siblings hurried over in time to see Rhea disappear into the stormy abyss. "Was that Mother? Why did she leave? What did you say to her?"

I frowned at him. "Pardon?"

"It's no secret that you dislike her."

I waited for my sisters to defend me, but they did not. Unlike the two of them, who appeared merely disappointed, Zeus was mad.

"I didn't say anything to make her leave," I replied. "I swear."

Zeus relaxed and pulled back on his anger. My word was my honor. He knew I would not swear to anything that wasn't true.

"Why didn't Mother stay?" Poseidon asked quietly.

"Rhea's responsibilities have taken her elsewhere," said a new voice. A young man approached, walking with the support of a wooden staff. He was older than me but younger than Theo, and shorter than any of us. His legs bowed inward, and his two clubbed feet were braced with wooden splints shoved into his knee-high sandals. Despite his misshapen lower body, he carried himself with the pride of a peacock. He had a polished refinery about him that was majestic, including silky black tresses that framed his comely face. Each of his ten fingers was laden with gold rings, and his robes were well made and spotless. His confidence gave him an agelessness that was perplexing.

"Who are you?" Zeus asked.

The stranger cranked his jaw, weathering the inquiry with patience. "I'm Prometheus."

Theo's brows lowered in confusion. How could this be? His father appeared younger than Theo, and Prometheus had always been depicted as a mature man of bearish stature.

"You're Atlas and Menoetius's brother?" Zeus inquired. "But they're so, so—"

"Hulking. Our size difference often baffles people. Our mother, Clymene, is a second-generation Titan. Atlas and Menoetius resemble our father, Iapetus, whereas I take after our mother."

Bronte narrowed her eyes at him. "You cannot be Prometheus. The god of forethought is old."

"My Titan strength prevents me from maturing." Prometheus adjusted his necklace—a silver vial pendant. "Any sculpture or portrait you've seen of me depicts how I would appear if I aged."

Bronte scowled deeper. Her childhood idol was not the profound old philosopher she worshipped. Theo must have been having similar feelings. Prometheus had yet to even glance at his son.

"Demeter," Prometheus said. "You don't appear convinced that I am who I say I am."

"You're not what I expected," she confessed.

"Can anyone else here tell you that the seeds in your pocket will change your life, and the life of your future daughter?"

"Daughter?" Bronte questioned.

"You've already named her." Prometheus beckoned Bronte forward and spoke softly in her ear.

She jolted backward. "How did you know?"

"Fate is easy to see if you know where to seek it, for each soul tells a story."

"My mother, Stavra, used to say that," Bronte said.

Prometheus's eyes twinkled with untold secrets. "Stavra sounds very wise."

I wanted to know Bronte's future daughter's name, and I was somewhat jealous. Bronte hadn't even told me she wanted children.

Prometheus walked toward the lodge, his footing slow yet smooth. "Come along. My brother Epimetheus and I have a meal prepared for you."

The others perked up at the mention of food, and everyone left except Poseidon, who stayed back with Theo and me.

"Are you all right, Theo?" I asked gently. "Your father—"

"I'm fine." His tight jaw indicated otherwise, but I let it alone.

"Hera," Poseidon interjected. "You spoke with Mother?"

"She was sorry she couldn't stay."

Poseidon brushed that aside with a slight lip press. "What did she say to you?"

"She asked me to fetch our missing brother. Apparently, he's, um, in the underworld." I added a light laugh, as though such an idea was ridiculous—both that he was there and that Rhea expected me to go get him.

Poseidon's eyes expanded. "If our brother is there, then I'll go. You came and found me. I'd like to return the favor for one of our siblings."

"I offered to go in her place, but Rhea refused," Theo said. "She said this task is for Althea."

Poseidon clapped his hands together decidedly. "Then all three of us will go."

"Isn't safe for Theo," I countered. "Rhea said he could perish if we took too long."

"Then we won't take too long," Theo said. He grasped my shoulders, and his thumb traced my upper arm where my cuff once was. "When Pallas and his crew came, I didn't think of anything but your safety until I saw you again. I'm not repeating that torment."

The ordeal of finding the mansion in ruins, wondering if he was in the smoldering debris, had been almost unbearable. I never wanted to live through that again.

I squinted at him. "Are you using your persuasive voice on me?"

"I don't need to when I speak reason." The corners of Theo's eyes crinkled slightly from amusement. "Wherever you go, I go."

"Even to the underworld?"

"Especially to the underworld."

"We can finish this later," Poseidon said. Our other party members had reached the entrance to the lodge and were waiting for us.

Upon our arrival, Prometheus continued to ignore Theo and me, and then he gripped his vial pendant necklace and went in.

8

Prometheus's stronghold had an air of rustic elegance. High ceilings extended to the rafters in the great hall, held up by big, suspended beams. The wide central building was divided by furniture, but no walls sectioned the open area into rooms. The wings on the right and left had lower ceilings and corridors. I presumed that's where the bedchambers were located. An inviting fire flickered in an enormous river-stone hearth that was half the width of the wall opposite the entry. The wooden floors had been polished and softened with rugs. Tapestries draped from ceiling to halfway down the walls, each bearing Prometheus's crest, the symbol of a goddess carrying the weight of the sun on her shoulders. A long table had been set with candles down the center. In front of each of the twelve stools were plates piled high with thick beef and wild boar and chalices of nectar for our midday meal.

A blond man with tight curls waited there as slaves finished setting out platters of delicious-smelling dishes.

"Epimetheus," Prometheus said, gesturing at us with his staff. "Our kin have arrived."

Epimetheus's face lit up. His pointed features were impish, like a river nymph's. Unlike his brother, his legs were long and thin and straight. His arms were also gangly, and his middle was thick but not portly. He wore an abundance of fox fur: cape, boots, and even a hat, as though he were outside as the black frost of winter set in and slew the fresh green life of the fields instead of in a hearth-warmed lodge. He rushed right to me and embraced me in a light hug.

"Hera! I've heard so much about you." He beamed at me with an unfounded sense of familiarity that was mildly uncomfortable. "My brother and I are so honored to have you all."

"Don't crowd them, Epimetheus," Prometheus said, his tone affable.

"Of course, brother. It's not often that we get to visit with our nieces and nephews. Please, sit, so we may feast." Epimetheus beckoned everyone, including Theo, who stood awkwardly off to the side.

As we sat, Metis excused herself to rest, and a slave showed her to a bedchamber. Zeus tried to go with her, but she insisted he stay, so we all bid her farewell.

"For a gathering such as this, I thought it would be prudent to exhume several casks of nectar from the cellar." Epimetheus touched his pointer finger to the indent in his long chin and examined the full chalices and several waiting barrels. "Come to think of it, I should have the slaves bring up one more barrel."

While the others cut into their thick slabs of meat, I sipped from my chalice. The nectar tasted sweet—of lavender-laced honey. Epimetheus must have been used to Titans with a higher tolerance for spirits, because from my perspective, we had more than enough to get us through the day. Then I saw Poseidon drain his cup and down another, and I understood Epimetheus's concern. Poseidon would more than make up for the fact that Theo didn't drink nectar.

"Is there something wrong with your drink, Colonel Angelos?" Prometheus asked, his voice carrying across the open hall.

These were his father's first words to him. Theo stilled, obviously unnerved. "I've no tolerance for nectar."

"You've not had it before?"

"Once, when it was watered down. I prefer wine, truth be told. I was informed that nectar was unsafe for me."

"And who gave you that ill advice?" Prometheus asked, grasping his staff and showing no interest in his own food or drink.

Theo met his father's glower full-on. "I'm the only half Titan I know. I've had to learn my limits on my own."

"I think you mean demigod," Prometheus corrected. "That's what you're called."

His condescending tone set me on edge.

"I advised Theo to water down the nectar," I said. "None of us had experience with half Titans. We didn't wish him unintentional harm."

"Nectar won't harm a demigod, unless you're deterred by a headache the next day. Most mortals experience that after drinking a jug of wine." Prometheus laughed dryly. Only Epimetheus joined him.

Theo picked up his cup and drank deeply.

"You don't have to do this," I said.

He swallowed another gulp.

"Tell me, Zeus," Prometheus said, stoutly ignoring his son again. "Do you regret your attack against General Atlas?"

Zeus had shoved a piece of wild boar into his mouth. He chewed as fast as he could, but I answered before he could swallow.

"Why would we regret defending ourselves?"

"Cronus is displeased with his armada's failure to capture you. Since earthquakes and tempests weren't enough to flush you out, now—in retaliation for your attack—he has beset mankind with plagues. Livestock are dying from gadflies all over the world. In a week's time, most people will be without water. In a fortnight, crops will be dying or dead from locusts and hailstorms, and we've heard reports of outbreaks of lice. Cronus will cause mankind to suffer until you turn yourselves in."

I set down my spoon, my appetite gone.

"What do we do?" Zeus asked.

"You lead your allies into war, Zeus," said Prometheus.

Poseidon stopped eating from the full plate of beef he had put in front of himself. "Often the ruler doesn't lead the campaign," he said. "We need a general."

Prometheus snorted. "And you think that should be you?"

"No. Our general should be Hera."

I was glad I had swallowed my last bite, because I would have choked.

"She crippled the armada and attacked General Atlas," Poseidon went on. "For that alone, warriors and fighters will follow her."

Bronte spoke up. "She also attempted to save Helios."

"And she destroyed the Almighty's greatest trireme," Cleora added, her finger dancing in and out of a candle flame. Her plate was untouched, but she had finished her chalice of nectar, and Epimetheus was pouring her more.

Zeus fisted his spoon. "Does none of you think I can lead you into war?"

"It will be more difficult to protect you if you're at the front line," Theo replied. "A general must be with his troops."

"His or *her* troops," Bronte added.

Zeus gawked incredulously, his temper escalating. "Althea? Is this what you want?"

His use of my mortal name irked me. In this setting, it felt diminutive. "I don't know anything about leading an army," I said.

"There you have it," Prometheus announced, twirling one of his gold rings. "Someone is speaking sense."

"Althea has an instinct for leadership," Theo cut in. "A strength that no one else here has."

Zeus sat straighter in his chair. "No one, Colonel?"

"That I have witnessed," Theo hedged. "Did the oracles not send her to find Zeus on Crete? And did she not lead us all to divest Cronus of your Titan strengths?"

"But she won't be here to lead, will you, Hera?" Prometheus inquired.

Bronte swiveled toward me. "Where will you be?"

I had the attention of everyone now. Even Epimetheus, as he played host, refilling our cups, spied me from the corner of his eye. I kept my tone light. "Rhea tasked me with fetching our final brother."

"She asked only you to go?" Bronte questioned.

"Theo and Poseidon volunteered to accompany me."

"How lovely for them," Bronte said wryly. She drained her chalice of nectar all at once.

"When do you leave, Althea?" Cleora asked.

"If I go, I suppose it will be soon."

Bronte set her empty cup down with a hollow bang. "You won't fetch our brother? But Rhea asked you to go. There must be a good reason why she asked you and not us."

I shrank into my seat. "She said I was particularly suited for the task, though didn't explain why. However, she did say where I could find him. Our brother . . . well, he's in the underworld."

A hush fell over the table. Zeus dropped his chin to his chest so I could not read his expression. Bronte helped herself to Cleora's cup of nectar, and Cleora put on a false front of cheeriness, as though everything was fine. I half expected Prometheus to offer his unwanted opinion, but no one made an argument either way.

Epimetheus donned an overly bright grin. "What does everyone think of the veal? In hindsight, I would have added more rosemary."

No one had touched the veal, or much of any other food, for that matter. Our plates had gone cold.

Prometheus stood, leaning on his staff. "Zeus? Poseidon? Let's retire to my study. I've insight to offer you about the tribulations ahead."

"Only they are invited?" Theo asked, adding a pointed stare in my direction. His tone had an alluring lilt that easily rolled off his tongue.

Prometheus wore a hard glare. "Your opinion is noted, Colonel, but this is a closed meeting, and I don't appreciate your trying to persuade me with your demigod strength."

"Theo really should sit in," I said. "He's more versed in warfare than any of us."

"His experience is in fighting men, not gods." Prometheus touched his pendant briefly, and an emotion entered his eyes that was so deep and meaningful that it caught me unaware. I had seen this expression from Theo, before I got to know him better. He was as layered as epic music, and apparently, so was his father.

Zeus and Poseidon threw me silent pleas that said, *Try to understand*, and then they were gone with Prometheus.

Epimetheus began clearing the table with the slaves, his disposition cheerful. With his arms full of dishes, he beamed. "I'll be right back. Make yourselves comfortable by the fire."

Once we were alone, Bronte set her cup down on the table again, almost slamming it. "What did we do to deserve to be left out of their meeting?" she demanded. "We've saved our brothers time and time again. And Althea will do so again with our last missing brother."

"Separating right now may not be a good idea," I hedged.

"You would go if it was one of us," Cleora replied quietly, her fingers still manipulating the candle flame.

"Without question," I responded, "but it isn't you."

"The request came from our mother," Bronte said. "You cannot refuse."

"Rhea is not my mother," I countered firmly. "Stavra Lambros was my mother, and she's dead."

The naked hurt that crossed both their faces caused me to regret my bluntness immediately. I didn't mind that they had a kinship with Rhea, but I would not have one forced on me.

Theo spoke up, his tone gentler than mine. "Rhea would not have given up your brother's location and risked putting him in harm's way unless it was necessary."

"Consider going, Althea," Cleora said, blowing out the candle in front of her. "For our brother's sake."

Bronte grunted low in agreement. "And ours. Cronus and his allies are much more powerful than we are."

"And more ruthless," Cleora said. "These plagues . . ."

Theo sipped the full-strength nectar. "The battle for the throne has begun. We are at war."

Every point they made was right. Perhaps I didn't belong in the war room with my brothers. Perhaps my final, fated act to bring Zeus to power was to retrieve Hades and step aside.

Epimetheus came back with a tray of hot tea. "Would anyone like a warm drink to ease their bones? On second thought, I should have brought honey to sweeten it. I'll have a slave bring some."

"No, thank you, Epimetheus," Cleora said, rising from the table. "I'd like to lie down for a bit." She paused, her expression blank. "Where are we?"

Her question took me off guard. "We're at the base of Mount Olympus, remember?"

"Oh, yes."

Epimetheus set down the tray, adjusted his fur hat, and then looped his arm through hers. "Let me show you the way, cousin."

Cleora leaned into him, and they carefully ambled toward the door.

"I'm going too," Bronte muttered.

She caught up to them and took Cleora's other arm. The trio left the hall. Cleora was in good hands, but I couldn't shake my worry. Everyone was concerned about finding Hades. Where was the concern for restoring Cleora's mind? At a tactical level, it would behoove us to restore her before battle. I also wanted to see her well.

"You're fretting about Cleora," Theo stated.

"If Oceanus is aware of our circumstances, then why hasn't he offered her aid?"

"Maybe he isn't fully aware of how unreliable her memory is," Theo said. "I'll admit, sometimes she seems lucid, while others . . ."

I thought about telling him that I cast my arm cuff into the sea to engender Oceanus's sympathy, but now that act of faith felt ridiculous. "Perhaps Prometheus knows where to find Oceanus. He may not tell us, though."

"You should be in that meeting." Theo ran a hand over his face, scrubbing at his beard. I knew he was more upset about Prometheus's treatment of me than of him. I felt the opposite. I could strangle Prometheus for his coldness toward his son. "Zeus may be destined to reign as the Ruler of the Titans, but he has a lot to prove yet."

"Zeus is the one to lead," I insisted.

"Then why did he leave you out of that meeting? Any good leader knows he's only as strong as his strongest allies. Zeus feels threatened by you. Cronus feels the same about anyone who shows more propensity for power." Theo tucked a strand of hair behind my ear. "Did you really attack General Atlas?"

"He had Helios, and he was trying to hurt Styx and her sea dragon."

Theo chuckled. "Didn't we once attack a sea dragon?"

"That was different."

He rested his hand on my knee. "I'm going with you to the underworld. You heard Prometheus. I'm more god than man."

"I don't know . . ."

Theo took my face in his hands. "I've made up my mind."

I pressed my lips to his. They were always soft, unlike the rest of his body. His gentleness never ceased to delight me.

Epimetheus strolled back into the room, tucking his fur cape close around him.

"Are you cold, Epimetheus?" I asked.

"Why?"

"Your fur is so . . . warm looking."

"Oh, my temperature is fine. Don't you simply adore a good red fox's pelt? This color suits my skin and hair like no other."

I swallowed a laugh. "Why, yes. It's, uh, flattering."

Theo finished his cup of nectar and wobbled as he stood. I reached out and steadied him. I had never seen him this drunk before.

"Why don't you go lie down?" I suggested. "I can prepare for our journey while you sober up."

"I'm not drunk." He placed a fist to his chest and burped into his mouth.

"All right," I replied amiably. "Epimetheus, where is your armory? We should stock up."

Epimetheus wore a pout of confusion. "Why would I want weapons?"

"Not you and I, myself and the colonel."

"Oh, of course," he said. "This way."

He led us outside to one of the lean-tos with a damaged roof. Inside it, sharpened spears lined one wall and javelins the other. In the center was a pile of swords and a heap of shields. Bows and arrows, as well as crossbows and bolts, were stacked neatly in the far corners. Our own weapons were there as well. Theo leaned over to pick up his sword and nearly toppled to the side.

"Steady," I said, bracing him up.

"Will he be all right?" Epimetheus asked.

"He'll be fine. Maybe give us a moment?"

"A moment for . . . Oh, I see. I'll take my leave. You know how to find the lodge? Oh, never mind. We came from there. All right, then. Enjoy picking out weapons." The god of afterthought strolled away, studying the dour sky as though it were the most beautiful day.

"Do you think he's always like this?" Theo asked. "So . . . happy?"

"I'm guessing so." I turned over a crate and urged him to sit on it.

"I'm not drunk," he repeated, sitting heavily.

"I didn't say you were." I stepped between his knees and pushed his hair out of his amber eyes. He wrapped his arms around my waist and rested his cheek against my breast. Touching him always infused my heart with smoky sweetness and desire. I used to enjoy the weight of different men on top of me. Now I never thought of anyone other than Theo. I longed only for his touch, and that needn't lead to humping. Though I was certain there would be some of that soon, what I anticipated most came afterward. He would wrap both arms around me and fall asleep, his limbs dead weight, pinning me to bedsheets that smelled of him, the two of us surrounded by his soft breathing, the aftershocks of our passion tremoring down my legs.

"I love you," he said.

My tongue bound itself to the bottom of my mouth, heavy and thick. He was drunk, but that didn't diminish his sincerity.

He sighed and relaxed. I pulled him closer, not ready to release him. What I felt for Theo was more than I'd felt for any other man, but was it love? How could he know with certainty? We felt affection for one another, but love?

Theo regarded me with such trust, and faith in us. How could I disappoint him?

He rubbed my back. "You don't have to say anything."

"I . . ."

Theo rose and nuzzled his soft beard against my cheek. I tilted my head against his chin, the beginnings of tears in my eyes. No man had ever been more patient than he was with me. He could have been embarrassed or angry that he had made himself vulnerable only for me not to reciprocate. Instead, he kissed my forehead and let go.

"I'm sorry," I said.

We sat in a long silence, hearing our own hearts beat. When I looked at him again, his expression was downcast, but not with disappointment.

"You needn't be sorry," he said, his voice downy soft.

He really does love me.

My head dipped to the side, as though I had been struck in the temple. The ground seemed to buckle, and the world twisted. All the times he had told me he loved me lanced through me like a hot blade.

He rested his hand over mine, and his voice filled with concern. "Althea—?"

The bell at the gate rang several times, each one louder and faster than the last. On the ramparts, a guard shouted, "Titans!"

9

Zeus and Poseidon barreled out of the lodge as Theo and I reached the courtyard. More guards lined up along the ramparts. Prometheus strode steadily to the ramparts' ladder and climbed to the top. One by one, we joined him.

The gate faced west, toward the sunset. I shielded my eyes from the low-hanging sun breaking through the clouds and saw the approaching party: two finely dressed women riding horses, with their guard of three behind them. Both women were blonde and thin and stately, identical in every way except one—the one on the left was heavy with child.

"Does anyone recognize them?" I asked.

"I do," Zeus answered. "The one in the white is Asteria, and the one wearing the evergreen gown is Leto. They're Lelantos's twin sisters."

Lelantos had attacked us with Pallas, Perses, and Menoetius. Asteria, Leto, and their brother, Lelantos, were Coeus's children. Asteria, the one with child, was wed to Perses, brother to Pallas. My mind spun with what their arrival could mean. Were they bringing a message from our enemies? Perhaps a threat, or another petition for us to turn ourselves in?

They stopped in the trees, and Leto called out to us. "We come from Eleusis, in search of the Upstart Gods."

Zeus straightened. "What do you want from them?"

"We wish to join them," Leto replied. "Rhea told us they would be here."

The goddesses were travel worn and dusty. Asteria rested one hand on her big belly and the other on her lower back. Riding on horseback from Eleusis would have taken two days, a long time for someone this heavy with child.

"Guards, open the gate," Prometheus commanded.

"We don't know if they can be trusted," I replied.

He arched a brow. "This is my keep. I've issued my order."

"This could be a trick," I said to Zeus.

"It could," he said, observing Leto. "Or they could be telling the truth."

I supposed it was possible that the goddesses had turned on their brother, and Asteria had also turned on her husband, Perses. After all, Styx had fought against her husband, but my nerves still simmered as we descended the ladder. The gate opened, and the twins rode into the courtyard. Prometheus helped Asteria dismount. She slid out of her saddle with her back bowed and then clutched her belly with both hands. Zeus helped Leto down from her horse. She had not taken her eyes off him since they entered.

"Hera," Asteria breathed. She waddled over to me, took my hands in hers, and kissed the tops of them. "Rhea told us so much about you."

"Rhea has a bad habit of discussing me with strangers. When did you last speak with her?"

"She visited us a fortnight ago and invited us to join your coalition."

"My what?" I asked.

"Your coalition," she repeated, as though that explained everything. "She's been petitioning all the Titanesses to join her in standing with you against the Almighty."

A hand rested on the small of my back. I had not realized I had rocked back on my heels until Theo pushed me forward onto flat feet again.

"Althea has no coalition," Zeus said. "She stands with me."

"Then why wasn't she in our meeting?" Poseidon posed.

For once, Zeus had the good sense to shut his mouth. I dipped my chin at Poseidon in thanks. I hadn't thought he cared whether I was included.

"Cousins!" Epimetheus came out of the lodge with his arms open, his blond curls bouncing. He bounded up to Leto and kissed her on the cheek, then placed his palms on Asteria's belly. "You must be exhausted. Come in, come in! I'll have the slaves open another barrel of nectar and bake up a batch of ambrosia. We can have a proper feast to celebrate the union of this many Titans."

Epimetheus ushered Asteria and Poseidon inside. Theo and I hung back with Zeus and waited as Leto ordered her guard to care for their horses. The second they left for the stables, she buried her face in her hands and began sobbing. Zeus threw me a panicked look.

I stepped forward to comfort her. "Leto, what—?"

"My father disowned us." She hiccupped on tears. "He wanted us to be more like Lelantos, and follow Cronus, but the Almighty didn't treat our brother the way he treated us."

"What do you mean?" I asked.

Leto uncovered her face, showing her puzzlement. "You don't know?" Before I could respond, her eyes lit up. "Oh, forgive me. I forgot that Rhea said you were raised among mortals."

This was a statement, not an accusation. "I was."

Leto's vibrant green eyes glowed with fervor. "Then you know that Cronus helps himself to any maiden he desires. His 'honor maidens,' he calls them." She wrinkled her nose. "It's the same for the Titanesses, except that each of us is required to visit him before we're given to a husband."

"Visit how?" I asked, my stomach souring.

"He tests our Titan strengths before he assigns us a domain. He claims the only way to do that is to take our womanhood, but he doesn't touch the Titans as he does the Titanesses." Leto sniffled, and my gut churned harder.

"Your parents allow this?" Theo asked.

"No one will stand up to the God of Gods. Our father was going to send me to Cronus, so Asteria and I ran away from home. Then the earthquakes and tempests started. We had a cart of belongings, but a hailstorm destroyed it." Leto covered her teary face again. "Cronus is punishing me."

Zeus took my place beside her. "You're in the path of his rampage, but you aren't to blame."

"My father spotted us as we were leaving," she cried. "He said we would never be welcome home."

"You're welcome here," Zeus said, pulling her into his arms. His hands were a little too close to her backside for my comfort, but Leto leaned into him.

Behind them, the sunset stained the stormy horizon scarlet. A shiver coursed through me. A blood-red sunset was an omen. Everything was about to change.

I drank a lot of nectar at supper. After the fifth or sixth cup, I lost count. Nectar gave me a burst of vigor, as if I could fly around the world fifty times.

Now, as I danced in front of the fire, I thought back over the hours I had spent with my kin. What had begun as a solemn meal had turned into a joyful family reunion. We gorged ourselves on the rich food and dizzying drink. After we had eaten until we were bursting, Epimetheus began telling stories around the hearth while we drank chestnut and black mulberry tea. He had no mind for common details, and often apologized for things he thought of after the fact, but when it came to telling stories, he spoke with the most captivating, enjoyably immersive imagery. He told of Uranus and Gaea's first meeting, when the sky god had rested his forehead against the earth goddess's, and they had intertwined in a union that shot aftershocks through the universe, birthed the sun, and bloomed the stars. While the rest of us listened, Poseidon and Asteria spoke off to the side, deep in discussion, where they stayed until the stories ended and the music began.

Prometheus brought in two lyres, and he and Cleora played duets while we danced and laughed. Asteria sat among us and rubbed her pregnant belly lovingly. During a song about the heavens, she clapped her hands three times, and the ceiling of the lodge transformed into a midnight sky studded with twinkling stars. The hall felt cozy, set apart from the world. No one mentioned what was happening outside Prometheus's stronghold.

Cleora slowed the music and played Stavra's favorite lullaby, the one Theo sang to me on sleepless nights. Bronte harmonized with him. Her voice was rich and compelling, but Theo put his soul into his singing. When it was over, Prometheus turned away, clutching his vial pendant, his eyes glossy with tears.

Poseidon dipped his finger in and out of his water cup. Occasionally, the reflection in the water changed. It was a while before I discerned that the image was of a horse galloping across a sea. He caught me staring and winked.

Metis never joined us, and Zeus and Leto were the first to retire. Asteria gave a great yawn and left for her bedchamber, rubbing her belly as she waddled away. The rest of us sat around the fire sipping the dredges of our tea. I stared into the crackling fire and tried not to think about the next time I would get to have a night such as this with my family.

"Poseidon, what were you and Asteria talking about earlier?" Bronte asked.

"She's worried about her people," he replied glumly. "The crops in Eleusis are dying of drought. They have food stores, but they were depending on the autumn harvest."

"Cronus?" Theo asked.

Cleora flinched.

"Asteria thinks so," Poseidon answered.

Theo traced his thumb over the sensitive spot behind my ear. "I'm off to bed," he said.

"I'll be there soon," I replied.

As he left, Metis wandered in. Epimetheus immediately got up to offer her food and drink, but Metis refused it all. "A woman heavy with child arrived?" she asked.

"Yes," Epimetheus replied. "Asteria."

"She will deliver on the night of the next full moon. Her daughter's name will be Hecate." Metis said this vacantly, as though something compelled her and she could not contain herself. Her focus tightened on us. "Have you seen my husband?"

"I assumed he was with you," I replied.

Metis strode to me with a heavy-footed walk and squeezed my shoulder. "Be careful. You will be missed."

She wandered out before I realized she was probably referring to my trip to the underworld. Had she foreseen it? How much of what was to come had she envisioned? Metis was truly an asset we took for granted. My heart ached for her. Zeus should not neglect her this way.

I got up to find him. Bronte pointedly looked away from me, but her attitude was the least of my worries. I wrapped a wool blanket around me and went outside. Night had fallen on the mountainside, bringing with it a crispness. My breaths stained the air with silver puffs.

"Zeus?" I called.

A guard pointed at the stables.

I walked across the yard and in through the open door. A lamp was lit in the corner, casting a glow over a couple entangled in the shadows. Leto was pressed against the wall with her skirt up and her legs wrapped around Zeus. I froze, then pivoted on my heels. I was almost out when I stopped, grabbed the door, and slammed it shut.

Leto and Zeus jumped apart. She yanked down her skirt, and he wrestled up his trousers.

"Your bride was asking about you, brother," I said.

"Bride?" Leto asked, her brow furrowing.

"Zeus's wife, Metis," I replied. "Have you met the goddess of wisdom? She's with child."

Leto's mouth hung open, and then she slapped Zeus across the face. His head pitched to the side and his cheek was instantly red. Leto smoothed her skirt and strode out.

I picked up a handful of hay and threw it at Zeus. The pieces rained down around him, leaving bits stuck in his hair and clothes. "You fool!"

"She kissed me first!"

"She's not married! You have to control your passions, Zeus."

"The way you control your temper?"

"I have good reason to be mad at you. Metis deserves better."

He brushed hay off his shoulders. "Let my wife speak for herself."

"She has plenty of wise things to say, which you would know if you spent any time with her."

His attention sharpened. "What prophecy did she foresee now?"

I was tempted to tell him that she had seen his brutal, gruesome death by sunrise, but I held my tongue. "She spoke of my decision to bring our brother back from the underworld."

"You aren't going, are you?" His eyes widened at my silence. "You cannot. You're not equipped for this, Althea."

"Don't use my mortal name against me."

"I'm concerned." Zeus stepped in closer. "What will I do without you?"

"I saw what you do when I'm not around."

His lips curled. "Jealous?"

"Delusional?"

His warm chuckle almost made me forget he was a terrible husband. "Althea, we both know I need you."

His sincerity was convincing, but it hardly made up for his behavior. "Where was this sentiment when you left me out of your meeting?"

"I was doing you a favor. Prometheus wouldn't have allowed Theo to attend, and I didn't want you to have to choose between us."

Zeus was portraying himself as too benevolent, but it wasn't worth the argument. "What did Prometheus tell you?"

"He reiterated what we already know."

"Which is?"

"We cannot succeed unless all of Cronus's children stand against him." Zeus skimmed his fingers down my jaw. "Stay here, Althea. Let Poseidon go to the underworld."

I thought of Metis's goodbye and bit my lower lip. Was venturing through the underworld my fate? Or was I to stand with Zeus as the oracles told me?

"Please, Althea." Zeus stepped closer, his chest nearly touching mine. "I know I'm difficult at times, but I'd be lost without you."

His desperation was undeniable. Lately, I wanted to strangle him, but right now, I needed to reassure him. I wrapped my arms around his broad shoulders. "When did you get muscles?"

"You just noticed?"

"Don't be arrogant."

"So . . . don't be myself. Duly noted."

I laughed. "You're horrible."

"The worst." He rested his chin on top of my head. "You're the only person who understands the weight of the prophecy, and what I must do. I don't know what I'd do without you, Althea."

Sighing, I eased further into his arms. "It's impossible to stay mad at you."

"I know."

I scoffed, and his chest shook with silent chuckles.

A silver light shone into the stables, growing brighter and brighter. We stepped outside in time to see Selene's winged steed land in the courtyard. The goddess of the moon dismounted and threw back the hood of her cloak, revealing her grief-stricken face.

General Atlas captured Helios.

"Oh, no," I said. "I'd hoped he'd gotten away."

Cronus has him.

"What is it?" Zeus asked.

"Cronus has Helios," I explained. "What does this mean, Selene?"

Cronus will force Helios to continue moving the sun across the sky, but he's under heavy guard and badly injured. The sun will not shine brightly again until he's free.

I remembered the blood-red sunset, and my chest sank.

"We'll get him back," Zeus said.

Selene narrowed her eyes. *He will do nothing, as usual. To think Helios sacrificed himself for this child.*

"What did she say?" Zeus asked.

"Uh . . ."

"Althea, tell me."

"She doesn't think Helios should have sacrificed himself for you."

Zeus recoiled. "Pardon, cousin? Helios and I are kin too."

Again, Selene spoke to me. *My brother is a thousand times the Titan Zeus will ever be.*

"Selene," I said. "I know you're upset, but please don't say anything you don't mean."

I mean every word. We're at war, and he's sport-humping every woman he meets.

"What is she saying?" Zeus pressed.

Selene stepped right up to him and sneered. I didn't hear what she said, but his expression changed to anger. Overhead, thunderclouds gathered and boomed.

"Be careful," Zeus said. "I will be your ruler one day."

I don't care about the prophecy. Selene scoffed. *Once a coward, always a coward.*

"What did she say now?" he demanded.

"I'm not repeating that," I replied.

"Fine." Zeus stormed toward the lodge. Thunder clapped, louder than before, then the clouds dissipated the second he went inside.

"Selene, I'm sorry about Helios. We tried to free him."

I heard what you did, and I appreciate your efforts.

"Any word from Eos?" I asked.

The plagues and earthquakes aren't affecting the east. Selene's lips turned downward. *My father made an agreement with Cronus. He will provide food from his crop yields to feed the Titans, and in exchange, he's permitted to stay neutral in the war.*

Clever bastard. Cronus and his followers would eat, and everyone else would starve.

Be wary of Zeus, Althea. He thinks too much of himself and puts his needs first. That's not a leader one can trust.

Zeus was selfish, but he was also young and inexperienced and had a big responsibility to the entire world. Could he do better? Yes. But none of his flaws was unforgivable. "What did you say to him?"

The truth. He spent his whole life in hiding, and he's still hiding. He depends on others to protect him, not considering the burden of their sacrifices. Selene glanced up at the night sky. *I must go. Your mother told me you're headed to the underworld?*

"She did?"

You're fortunate that you can get to your brother. If I could go to the underworld to get Helios, I would. The goddess of the moon embraced me. *I will not be able to see you while you're there. Be safe, Hera.*

"You as well."

Selene mounted up and drew down her hood. As her winged horse charged toward the waning moon, I trudged back to the lodge. Prometheus opened the front door as I reached it. His compassionate expression caught me off guard.

"Zeus told me about Helios," he said. "These are uncertain times, indeed. Come along to my study, Hera. It's time that we talk."

10

Prometheus's study was a small yet comfortable chamber. The walls were covered with colorful maps that Bronte would have loved to peruse. I wandered from one to the next while Prometheus stoked the fire in the little hearth.

"You've made your decision to go," he said.

"Did you foresee that I would agree?"

He donned a charming smile, a first from him. "You could have changed the projection of what I've seen. Agency is more powerful than any Titan strength."

"You mean I control my own fate?"

"Yes and no. Quite often, in running from fate, we end up right where we were always meant to be." He sat in the chair by the fire and laid his staff across his lap. "Rhea asked me to direct you to the entrance to the underworld. The nearest passage isn't far from here. In fact, after Uranus was dethroned, Rhea dragged him down to Tartarus through that very same passage."

My brows shot up. "Rhea locked Uranus in Tartarus?"

"Cronus thought it was unwise to leave his new throne unattended, so he assigned Rhea to bind their father in bitter chains and deliver him to his eternal prison." Prometheus tilted his head to the side in consideration. "Rhea thought Cronus would serve the world well, but this is no Golden Age, as he would have future generations believe. She feels partly responsible for assisting his rise to power, rallying her sisters to fight for him against their father. The Titanesses followed her into battle and held off Gaea while Cronus and their brothers unmanned Uranus. Gaea has since forgiven Rhea, but Rhea has never forgiven herself. Your mother hopes that bringing her children into power will give her redemption. She will do all she can to see that you succeed."

"Such as deserting us on islands or leaving us to be raised by mortals?"

"At least you had your sisters. Your brothers were alone." Prometheus tilted his head to the ceiling and let out a heavy breath. "Your mother saved you from your father. It was very difficult to give up her children, even for a goddess as strong as her."

I shifted from one foot to the other. This version of Rhea made me uncomfortable. It defied everything I thought about her abandonment of us.

"You should pack," Prometheus said. "We leave immediately for the passage."

"Tonight?"

"The passage can only be accessed at the final hour of night. The slaves are readying supplies."

"All right," I said, giving up on the idea of sleep tonight. "I'll let Poseidon and Theo know to get ready."

Prometheus reached for his necklace. "Theo is only a demigod."

"Why don't you like your son?" I asked bluntly, without ire. "He's done nothing to you."

"Dislike him?" Prometheus shook his head. "You don't understand."

"*You* don't understand. Theo waited his whole life to meet you, and you treated him like a stray mutt wandering down the road."

Prometheus picked up his staff and slammed it down across his lap. "I don't wish to see my son harmed."

I stepped back in surprise. "All right, then I'll tell him he cannot come."

"His destiny is to go." Prometheus fiddled with the vial on his necklace again, rolling it between his thumb and pointer finger. His eyes shone wet with tears. "I have seen Theo's future. He will risk everything for your cause."

"*My* cause?"

"I do not disdain my son," he asserted. "I kept my distance because I saw what was to come. Before Theo was even born, when his mother was with child, I foresaw that I would have to sacrifice him for the good of the world."

"No one is sacrificing anyone," I countered. "If fate can be changed through agency, I will change this. Theo will live through the war. This will be just one part of his story."

Prometheus eyed me closely, scrutinizing. "You love my son."

My mouth bobbed open and shut.

"He loves you," Prometheus continued. "This was his destiny, to stand equal with Hera, the goddess of fury."

My pulse hammered doubly hard. I had not been given a domain, but fury was certainly not what I imagined I would be known for. I would rather it be something like Aphrodite's, the goddess of love. Still, it was ridiculous of me to presume that I could choose. I hadn't been a Titaness very long, but I had learned that happiness was not something a goddess was supposed to dream of for herself, only for others.

"I will protect your son," I promised.

He pinched the skin at his throat, fingering a small mole. "I'll meet you at the stables in an hour."

I wandered toward the bedchamber I shared with Theo in the opposite wing of the lodge, my thoughts on what Prometheus had said. I had immediately dismissed any possibility that Theo would be a casualty in this war, but how could I fight fate? How would I know that in trying to defy destiny, I was not doing precisely what destiny desired of me?

My sisters were in the main hall, and they had been joined by Asteria again. As I approached, Bronte passed Asteria the pouch of seeds she had recovered from the mansion's garden.

"I infused these barley and wheat seeds with my Titan strength," Bronte said. "They're indestructible to any scourge and will grow faster than usual seeds. Your people will not starve."

Asteria bowed her head in thanks and passed the pouch to one of her guards. "Take these to Eleusis straightaway. Make sure my people know they come from the goddess Demeter, and may they always welcome her into our village as her home."

Bronte blushed, then spotted me and lost her glow. She got up to leave, but Cleora put a hand on her shoulder and held her there.

"Althea," Cleora said. "We were wondering where you'd gotten to."

"Were we?" Bronte muttered.

"I thought you had gone to bed, Asteria," I said.

"Leto came in upset, and woke me." Asteria put her hands on her swollen belly. "Then this one started kicking. Want to feel?"

I tentatively touched her round stomach. A small movement tapped against my palm, like bird wings beating against a cage. I had never considered motherhood, but to create a life was a beauty unlike any other of life's joys. The fluttering came stronger, melting my heart. "I think Hecate will keep you on your feet."

Asteria's eyes went wide. "How did you know what I'm going to name her?"

"Metis mentioned you were having a baby girl."

"What name have I chosen for *my* future daughter?" Bronte asked, her chin set stubbornly.

The sweet connection between Asteria and me was over. I lowered my hand from her swollen womb. "I don't know," I said.

"You can tell her, Cleora," Bronte said.

"Cleora knows the name?" I asked, hurt that Bronte had left me out.

"Bronte told me this afternoon," Cleora replied. "She wants to name her Persephone."

"Pretty," I murmured.

"I'm going to check on Leto," Asteria said, yet she stayed. "Hestia, Demeter, and Hera? I know you still prefer your mortal names, but all this talk about babies got me thinking about what an honor it is to name a new life. I would guess your mother put as much thought into the names she gave you as I have with my daughter's. Good night, goddesses."

Each of us bid her a quiet good night, and then Bronte pushed to her feet.

"I'm going to bed too."

"Prometheus is taking me to the passage tonight," I said.

Bronte absorbed this news. "Then good night and good luck."

I grabbed her and hugged her briefly. I could not stand her coolness, not when I was leaving and didn't know when I would see them again. She gave me a quick peck on the cheek and hurried off.

"You two." Cleora sighed and looped her arm through mine. "I'll miss you."

"I'll miss you too."

We headed toward our bedchambers, arm in arm. As we approached the doorway of the west wing, Poseidon appeared in the shadows. Cleora stiffened and shoved me behind her. Before I could figure out what was going on, she leaped at him and had him by the throat.

"I knew you would find us eventually."

Poseidon tried to speak, but she choked him harder.

"Cleora," I said. "That's Poseidon, our brother. Remember?"

"Oh, I remember everything. This is a trick. This is what Father does. He meddles with minds."

Poseidon began choking audibly, though he was not fighting back. In fact, he was utterly incapacitated. He began to convulse, and his face drained of color. A charred, stomach-turning smell wafted off him.

"Cleora, stop," I said. "You're hurting him."

"No more than he hurt me." She dug her fingers deeper into his neck. Poseidon gagged harder. His eyes rolled into the back of his head. A light began to brighten in Cleora's hand.

She was draining his soul.

I placed my hands on hers. Her skin was hot. "Let him go, Cleora. He's our brother, and I know we all recently met, but you love him. You would go to the underworld for him, just as I will go for our other brother."

Cleora's brow creased a little.

"Look at him," I begged. "He's Poseidon."

Cleora stared into his face and saw her handiwork—the pastiness of Poseidon's skin. Recognition dawned, and she gasped and let go. Poseidon shuffled back, his hands over his throat. She had left handprints but nothing more, though the smell emanating off of him was foul.

Cleora backed away and saw him, really saw him. "Dear brother, forgive me." She pressed her fingertips to her lips, and her fingers let off blue sparks. She swiftly held her hands away from herself.

"What's that?" Poseidon croaked.

"Your soul," I whispered.

Cleora let out a groan.

"Give it to me," I said. She shook her head, so I spoke firmer. "Cleora, I will take it from you." I cupped her hands between mine and consolidated the blue light into a sphere. It writhed and wriggled, even more than the plant's soul had, and it was warmer, almost too hot to hold. The light pulled me toward Poseidon as though it knew that was where it belonged. I passed it to him, and the brightness of his soul sank into his open hand and joined him once more. A little bit of sparkling dust, like blue cinders, clung to my palms. I brushed it off on my skirt.

Cleora wept gently. Poseidon stepped forward to comfort her, but she shied away, and he put his hands up in surrender.

"It's because you resemble him," I said, which only added a pained scowl to his distress. "I'm sorry."

He shook off my apology, his head swaying. "Prometheus told me we're going. Take your time. I'll delay as long as possible."

"Thank you."

He left, his strides swift, and Cleora folded her arms in front of her, gripping her elbows.

"Did you know you could do that?" I asked quietly, both terrified and in awe of what she had done.

"No." She held her hands out, as though they had betrayed her. "I don't know what to do."

"What do you mean?"

"How do I . . . how do I forget what he did?"

My jaw clenched. "Forget what who did?"

She answered, her words interrupted by little sobs. "I remember bits and pieces. It took a while to put them together. Those first days were a blur, but now I know. I know what he did."

I hugged her hard. I desperately wanted to ask her more, but after speaking with Leto, I could guess what Cleora was referring to. Cronus felt he had a right to every woman. Goddess. Titaness. Daughter. It didn't matter.

Cleora's eyes overflowed with tears. "Althea?"

"Yes?"

"Where . . . where are we?"

I pulled her in close again. "You're in a safe place. I have to leave tonight, and I need you to remember something very important. Can you do that?"

"Althea," she said with mock sternness. "I'm your older sister. I remember everything you say."

"No one can take anything from you that you don't give them."

"All right."

"No 'all right.' You're my older sister, and I need you. I need you to remember that no matter what happened before, or what's to come, you're mine. I will never forsake you."

Cleora straightened her shoulders. "I'll always be here for you, Althea."

"I know." We hugged so hard, it probably hurt her as much as it did me.

Then another set of arms encircled us.

"You two cannot go hugging each other without me," Bronte said. "It's a rule."

We clung to one another for I don't know how long. I sensed from Bronte's quick, emotional breathing that she had seen and heard at least part of what happened.

"I need to get ready to go," I said.

Bronte drew Cleora away from me. "Let's go to bed. Say goodbye to Althea."

"See you later," Cleora said, kissing my temple.

I waited until they were gone to release the pressure in my chest with a low moan. Placing both hands on the long dining table, I bit my lower lip to suppress a furious scream. Whatever must be done, whatever was needed from me, I would do it. I would see Cronus torn from his perch on high and thrust into Tartarus for all eternity.

A little voice in my head asked, *Even if you have to give up Theo?*

I had no immediate answer, and that bothered me more than I cared to consider.

I walked to our bedchamber, threw open the door, took a step inside, and stood with the light of the corridor behind me. Something kept me from entering, as if doing so might be what fate wanted, and I desired nothing to do with fate unless it would benefit Theo and my family.

Theo rolled over in bed and peered at me from across the unlit chamber. "Althea?"

I undressed in the light, dropping my chiton and underclothes, leaving only my nakedness. With the door open behind me, it felt daring. I had to do something fate wouldn't have predicted, an action that felt spontaneous, even to me.

His eyes roamed the length of me, then he got out of bed, also naked, and crossed into the light from the corridor. I waited as his need for me grew until the stirring in my belly could not be contained. Closing the door, I cast us into velvet shadows. He walked closer, noticeably savoring each step as he would a strong glass of wine.

"Are you all right?" he asked.

I felt his need sizzling in the air, but he would not touch me until he knew I was steady.

"I only want you," I said.

He stilled, waiting, even now, after I offered myself to him. He waited for me to close the distance. That power, that choice, was a gift.

I kissed him gently. He kept his hands down and let me kiss him. I must have been a little drunk still, because time disappeared until his hands encircled my waist and backed me against the wall. "I only want you as well," he said.

It began slowly, but we finished with the speed of gods. He picked me up and thrusted, and time vanished again until pleasure burst from my core. Stars filled my vision, lighting up his face. His name peeled off my lips like a wish, and he drove into me harder. My voice was the impetus he needed to finish, quivering and sealing me between himself and the wall. My legs clung to his waist. My back was jammed against stone. I thought only of him, his presence that orbited me. My very own moon. If this was fate, then perhaps I should never fight it.

Theo set me down. I leaned against the wall and pretended I hadn't flown around the sun and come back to earth.

"Prometheus wants to leave tonight." I pushed his damp hair back from his face. "Stay here, Theo." I longed for his persuasive voice, for a Titan strength that could force him to do my bidding. Amazingly, he had never used his gift on me, not even when he thought he knew best. He always gave me my agency. Always.

"My place is with you, Althea."

"You *need* to stay here."

He touched his lips to my cheek in the barest of kisses. "I have my own reasons for going."

I knew his reasons. They were valid, as valid as my own. They included his mother and his duty to his homeland, but also his duty to me. Despite his reservations, he believed in Zeus because I did. Theo understood that the future of the world relied on us, and Zeus and I were inexplicably entwined. I wasn't certain I would have been as understanding had Theo been tied to someone else.

He strolled away into the evening dimness. I slumped against the wall and swallowed the scream I had been holding in. I listened as he dressed, and then he brought me my clothes. And there, in the night, in the safest place I had ever felt in my life, I thought about uttering three words I swore I would never say to any man, and unfortunately—very unfortunately—I would mean them.

A knock came at the door, followed by Poseidon's voice. "Prometheus is ready."

"We'll be right there," Theo called back.

I dressed, and then the two of us faced each other in the shadows. I secretly hoped he would kiss me one more time, but we needed to go. As I reached to open the door, he pulled me into his arms, and his lips landed on mine.

Theo always knew what I needed. I would give up a lot, even the very stars, to stay like this forever.

11

The journey on horseback was steep but shorter than I anticipated. We climbed into cooler mountain air for maybe an hour before Prometheus waved for us to halt.

"We'll travel the rest of the way on foot," he said. "Hurry along. We must reach the passage before dawn."

He dismounted onto his clubbed feet. Theo was there, ready with his staff. Prometheus thanked him, and we took a narrow path through the forest. A cold north wind blew. The night was alive with the voices of owls, crickets, and frogs. Bronte could have identified every sound, and all the shrubs and trees, which would have delighted Cleora. I missed my sisters already.

Poseidon, Theo, and I each carried a satchel packed with water, nuts, and dried fruit, as well as our weapons. Poseidon glanced at a patch of sky between the treetops. The handprints on his neck hadn't faded, but he seemed well otherwise.

"What are you doing?" I asked.

"Viewing the stars, before they're gone."

My mouth went dry. In the underworld, I wouldn't have access to the heavens—or my main weapon. I gripped the hilt of my sword, hoping it would be enough.

Despite his misshapen legs, Prometheus set an ambitious pace up the mountain. The silence between him and Theo was awkward, more so the longer it lasted. I thought of ending the quiet, but Poseidon did it first.

"Colonel Angelos, when did you join the First House's guard?" he asked.

"I started as a deckhand on a trireme as a boy and worked my way up through the ranks."

"That's young," Poseidon noted.

"My mother, Lois, and I were captured from Kasos by slave traders and brought to Thessaly. We were sold to the Aeon Palace. My size and strength drew the attention of a higher officer, and I was transferred to work in the armada."

"How is your mother?" Prometheus asked.

"She's no longer a slave," Theo replied. "No thanks to you."

Prometheus released a pent-up sigh. "When I first met Lois, I foresaw her future would be difficult, but had I not pursued her, you would not be, and you bring her more happiness than anything else. Had I warned Lois what her life would become, she still would have chosen all of it to have you."

Theo fell silent. Now I was uncomfortable for a different reason. They should have had this conversation in private.

"Lois wasn't aware she was with child when we parted ways," Prometheus continued. "As you know, most women do not survive giving birth to a demigod. I asked my mother, Clymene, to make certain that you both lived. She defied my father to be with Lois when she birthed you. For the first three years of your life, while you were still living on Kasos, your grandmother defied her husband to visit you often. Lois made even bigger sacrifices so you could fulfill your destiny as a warrior for the gods."

Theo did not reply. I wondered if he remembered Clymene. He had never mentioned a grandmother to me, but his expression brightened, so he must have recalled something.

Prometheus stopped and banged his staff against the ground. "We're here."

Behind him was the mouth of a cave, half-hidden by a wild fig tree and monkshood, also known as wolfsbane. The purplish-blue flower had extremely poisonous roots that could be applied to arrowheads for hunting.

Poseidon stepped up to the entrance and listened. "I hear rushing water."

"All of you, listen closely. The mines where Hades works are outside Tartarus. Once you're through the gates to the underworld, it's a trek to get there. Tartarus descends as far below the underworld as the sky rises above the earth. You must conserve your strength." Prometheus took off his necklace and offered it to Theo. "This is the same elixir your mother took to survive childbirth. In the vial is spring water from Oceanus's private fountain. I fortified it with one drop of the oldest aged nectar ever distilled. The second you step through the gates into the undergloom, your body will begin to decay. You must wait until your last breath to take the elixir. Time moves slower down there, so once you do, whether or not you have arrived at the mines, turn back, or you will perish."

Theo put on the necklace. "Thank you."

I withheld a groan of frustration. I could no more persuade Theo not to come along than I could convince Zeus to be faithful to his wife.

Poseidon stepped through the wolfsbane, up to his shins in the violet flowers, and peered into the cave. "There's a steep drop-off."

"This pit will take you into the land of evening," Prometheus explained. "Follow the sound of water, and you'll find a lake fed by three rivers. Cross the middle river to the gates and answer the gatekeeper's questions honestly. You must go now, before sunrise, and I must return to the keep."

"We will *all* see you soon," I said.

He leaned against his staff heavily and strode off into the starry woodland.

I joined Poseidon and Theo at the entrance to the cave. A few steps inside was the opening to a black pit. Far below, water surged. Theo found a large basket tied to the wall. He tugged on the rope and released it. The basket swung back and forth until Poseidon pulled it over to us on the ledge. Both the basket and the ropes appeared solid enough to hold our weight, but it was only big enough to carry us one at a time.

"Titanesses first," Poseidon said.

I was nervous as I stepped in and the pulley creaked. Once I was suspended over the pit, I made the mistake of looking down.

"Oh, gods," I said. "Can't I fly instead?"

"You heard Prometheus," Poseidon replied. "Conserve your strength."

Theo placed his hand over mine. "You move the basket by pulling on the right side of the rope. When you reach the bottom, give it a tug and we'll reel it up again. If anything happens, I'll immediately pull you up from here."

Poseidon lit a torch and handed it to me. I set it in a holder in the corner of the basket and then pulled on the rope, lowering myself. Soon, I could no longer see Theo or Poseidon. The night was replaced by utter darkness and a bone-deep chill.

The drop seemed endless. My only point of reference was the sound of the rivers getting closer. I continued, hand over hand, seeing nothing beyond the glow of the torch.

Finally, the bottom of the basket hit something hard and the rope would go no more. I climbed out into a field of wildflowers. I had thought nothing could grow in the underworld, but these flowers were thriving. They reminded me of wolfsbane, except their blooms were pale gray. I assumed it was nightshade, a very poisonous flower. Yanking on the rope, I waited, and then the basket began its ascent. I had to leave the torch with it, providing me with no light.

The basket disappeared above, and a nothingness crept in around me. I stood in total obscurity, my pulse hammering in the quiet.

A wind swept past my ankles, slithering along the floor of the field in an unnatural way. Another gust tugged at my hair, and I heard a deep-throated woman's laugh.

"H-hello?" I stuttered.

A rustle came from behind me. I reeled around and drew my sword.

"Fool," snarled the guttural voice. "Your weapons have no power over me."

"Who are you?"

"I am the night."

Nyx. The goddess of the night dwelled in the underworld with her brother, Thanatos, and sister, Hypnos. They were the awful gods, predecessors to Cronus and his siblings, as old as time itself.

A gust whipped at me, tossing my hair and ruffling my chiton.

"Gaea bid that I come," I said. "You cannot harm me or my party."

"Your party? But you are alone."

I *was* alone.

She laughed again, in my face, with a gust so strong it stole my breath away. I gasped, but nothing entered my throat. The wind continued to batter me, simultaneously pummeling and suffocating, whisking the air away from my mouth.

I dropped to the ground, clutching at my throat. The gusts assaulted me from all directions. I was asphyxiating, and trapped by the very thing I needed.

Reaching a hand up, I called for the stars. No tingling came to my fingers. The heavens were too far away from my grasp.

My eyes closed as an unfathomable sleep fell over me. I slumped over and lay down in the silky nightshades. My arms fell loose beside me, limp and useless, and my sword slid from my grip.

A different voice whispered in my ear, her voice barely audible over the wind, "You are the stars."

Stavra?

I tried to call for her, but no air lingered in my lungs.

Stavra spoke again. "Remember your wings."

My wings.

Drawing upon my last thread of strength, I threw open my wings and wrapped them around me, creating a cocoon from the wind. I gasped in the immediate stillness.

"You don't belong here, godling," Nyx hissed. "Go back to the mortal realm, where your strength is sufficient."

A bright flame of fury lit inside me. Within the circle of my wings, my skin began to glow orange as though my entire being were smoldering with embers. I threw open my wings, and my light radiated outward, melting the flowers at my feet. Nyx's smoky figure recoiled with a hiss, and she retreated into the protection of the ill-lit meadow.

I lowered my wings in the dying winds. My body shone in pulses, slower and slower until the glow faded and the nothingness surrounded me again. High above, torchlight marked the descent of the basket. I tucked my wings away and picked up my sword. The basket hit the ground and Theo hopped out.

"What happened?" he asked. "I thought I saw . . . You were glowing."

"Nyx paid me a visit. It wasn't a warm welcome."

Theo examined the withered flowers at our feet and then tugged on the rope to send the basket back up. Again, we fell into utter murkiness.

His arms came around me from behind. "You're very warm," he said. "Almost feverish."

"I feel fine."

He pressed his chin into the nook of my shoulder. I almost told him I had heard Stavra's voice, but my mind had been very foggy. I could have imagined the whole thing.

Poseidon lowered himself to the bed of dead flowers. After a brief assessment of our surroundings, he got out of the basket. "I've been in the underworld for but a moment, and I'm ready to leave." His lisp was more prominent, and he sounded anxious. He bent over one of the live flowers and plucked it. "This is intriguing." He shoved the bloom in his mouth and chewed.

"That's poisonous!" I cried.

He plucked another bloom. "This? This is asphodel."

"Oh. I thought it was nightshade."

"Asphodel flowers are edible, though bland. The Telchines eat them sometimes." Poseidon picked a bunch more and crammed them into his satchel. "Our supplies may not last to the mines and back. Grab some now. I doubt we'll find them again."

Theo and I also stuffed our satchels full, and then Poseidon picked up the torch and led the way across the field toward the rushing sound of the rivers. I searched the abyss around us for Nyx, but the goddess of the night stayed away.

We walked so long that the noise of the three rivers confused me. Poseidon stopped and tilted his head to listen, and then he turned around and retraced our steps.

"Where are you going?" I asked. "That's the way we came."

"I hear the rivers from this direction now."

"Are you certain?"

"I trust my ear when it comes to water."

"But how is that possible?" I asked.

"Time doesn't function like we're used to here," Theo replied. "Direction might be the same."

In the mortal realm, four pillars held up the sky. North, south, east, and west were also alternate names for the gods that dwelled at those corners—Coeus, Crius, Hyperion, and Iapetus. But in the underworld, where the gods were outsiders and foreigners, our ways of navigating did not apply.

We tracked the sound of the rivers back the way we came. Occasionally, I heard the flowers rustle nearby, but I never saw anything.

The sky began to lighten in the distance, so slightly it might have been a false dawn. But no, the land of evening materialized into view under a cathedral of churning thunderheads. Lightning flashed in their moody obscurity, but even the lightning was spiritless, like everything else in this monochromatic landscape.

"I don't understand," Theo said. "It's a whole world down here with its own sky and no obvious light source. No sun or stars. Nothing but drab, muted heavens."

"Gaea crafted it cleverly," I replied. "My mother, Stavra, told us a story about how Gaea wanted a proper home for the dead, so she patterned the underworld after the mortal realm. This way, the souls that come down to the undergloom don't feel lost and abandoned. They feel at home."

"Home," Poseidon said, shuddering. "I would have to be dead to think this was home."

He extinguished the torch, and we walked under the brazen sky to a rise that overlooked a great valley. At the base was a midnight lake with three rivers flowing into it. They originated in the mountainous distance where the stormy sky never quit shifting and stirring. Under the muted light of the tempest sky roamed the dead. Some of them appeared out of nowhere and stumbled forward toward the rivers. The crowd congregated at the middle river and crossed a bridge to the other side. There they gathered in front of freestanding black metal gates. Hundreds of souls roamed toward the gates and waited to gain entrance to their final resting place.

Our brother was on the other side of those gates.

"Ready?" I asked.

"No," Poseidon countered, and then sighed. "Lead the way."

12

The valley smelled of rot and decay. I presumed the stench came from the dead, but the closer we got to the riverbank, the more certain I was that the slow-moving water was what reeked of death.

A woman appeared beside me. Her eyes were wide open, her mouth shut and arms stiff at her sides. She blinked once and floated forward, her feet hovering over the ground.

Another soul, a man, materialized directly in front of Poseidon. He jumped back, clutching his chest.

"Where are they coming from?" he asked.

"I think they're the recently deceased," Theo replied.

More souls appeared ahead of us, and Poseidon jolted again.

"Let's cross the river before death's cloud corrodes my heart," he said.

The dead roamed steadily onward, as though heeding the sweet voices of muses. None of them paid us any mind as we weaved between them on our way to the bridge. Nothing grew along the muddy riverbank. Two skiffs were tied to the closest bridge's piling, both in questionable repair.

"We'll take the bridge," Poseidon said. "Those skiffs are a death trap, and I don't want a single drop of river water on me."

We shuffled into the line to cross the bridge with the recently departed. I bumped into one, and it felt like brushing past draperies, eerily devoid of the intimate warmth of flesh. Unlike my glowing soul, theirs were like everything else in the underworld—drained of the vivacity of life.

The second our feet touched the first creaky plank of the bridge, every soul around us went still. Ever so slowly, the dead in front turned to face us. Though their expressions were vacant, their collective attention felt personal.

Screeching sounded above us, and then three blacked-winged monsters darted across the sky. The goddesses of vengeance flew right at us, their inky robes whipping around them. Long leather scourges dangled from their fists and trailed behind them like wicked tails.

"Who in the deep sea is that?" Poseidon asked.

"The Erinyes," I said. "Go!"

We took off running across the bridge toward the gates. The dead did not acknowledge our panic. They were like columns in our path that we had to elbow our way around. Poseidon pushed a soul so hard he fell into the water. A splash sounded, and the dead around us raised their heads and let out a great, unified bellow. They were like the wolf packs that roamed the peaks of Mount Othrys. I covered my ears as I dodged them.

The howling stopped, and then all at once, the dead began to flee with us. I adjusted my speed to match the stampede's and fell behind Poseidon and Theo, who were faster. Overhead, the Erinyes dived at me. One of their barbed scourges snaked down, hissing through the air like an asp, and wrapped around my arm. The Erinys tugged and lifted me off my feet.

I rose higher and higher. I gripped the scourge around my forearm with both hands and threw open my wings. The Erinys sneered at me. I waited until we made eye contact, and then I took off for the ever gloomy clouds.

She screeched and fought me, trying to break free. I held the scourge tighter.

Higher up, the winds shifted. Gusts tore through the thunderheads in battling vortices. The Erinys let go of the scourge. I unwound it from my forearm and let it fall. One of the other Erinyes caught it before it landed in the river.

As I soared toward the gates to the underworld, an imperceptible barrier took form, much like the one the Telchines had over the center of their island. I met the blurry wall and pitched straight up it.

The Erinyes pursued me, shrieking and whipping their scourges. I took off for the thunderheads again, dodging lightning bolts. Before I reached the clouds, I noticed a second gate across the rivers. Gold and polished, it shimmered even in the deplorable light. Not a soul was lined up in front of these gates. Beyond their golden wall was light, real light. That must have been Elysium, the final resting place for the souls of heroes. Elysium was where Stavra belonged.

In the misty clouds, I lost sight of the Erinyes, but I could hear their robes flapping behind me. One of them darted at me and raked the side of my face with her claws. Another grabbed me while the other two tore at my clothes and hair. One of them sank her fangs into my shoulder while another kicked me in the stomach.

My wings faltered under their weight, and we went spiraling toward the lake. I kicked one off, and she landed in a meadow of asphodels. Then I cast off another, and she landed on the opposite shore, by the gates. Before I hit the inky surface of the lake, I thrust my wings and flipped over so the last Erinyes connected with the depthless surface, and then I shoved hard and broke her hold on me. She fell into the water, and I flew higher into the sunless sky.

Poseidon and Theo waited for me in front of the gates. They were easy to spot, as they were the only two beings with color to their skin. The dead had resumed their lumbering pace.

I landed beside them, and Theo checked my injuries. They were all shallow and not worth fussing over.

"The Erinyes remember you," he remarked.

"Our dislike is mutual."

Poseidon waved us closer to the gates. "I cannot believe I'm saying this, but I'd really like to pass through the gates now."

We circumvented the dead and maneuvered our way to the front of the line.

A gatekeeper stood in front of the double-doored gates. A soul approached him, stopping on a stone marker carved with an eye—the symbol of fate—and the gatekeeper waved her through the left door. He did this again and again. No one passed through the gates without his direction, and no one went through the right door. Oddly, I couldn't hear either the dead or the gatekeeper conversing.

As we arrived at the front of the line, the gatekeeper's milky eyes met mine and his voice filled my head.

You have strength like your mother's, and fury like your father's resides in your heart.

He spoke as Selene did, directly from his mind to mine.

Approach.

I stood on the stone marker. I could see that the landscape was different through each door. On the right was a pathway toward mountains in the distance, and on the left was a desolate land with fallow trees and cracked dirt.

Why have you come, goddess?

"My brother Hades works in the mines outside of Tartarus. Rhea asked me to bring him back to the mortal realm."

I have not seen Rhea since she and her sisters delivered Uranus to the pits. His colorless eyes drilled into me. *One door leads to plains as dark as Erebus, and the other leads to the pits of Tartarus. Only the progeny of Gaea and Uranus are permitted to enter. For me to let you in, you must state your name and heritage.*

Behind me, Theo clasped the vial around his neck. He and his father had made amends, of a sort. I wasn't being asked to do the same. All I had to do was admit my lineage.

"I'm Hera, daughter of Cronus and Rhea, Titaness and goddess of the First House."

The gatekeeper bowed and extended his arm to the right, to the door leading to the roadway to Tartarus.

Do not wander, Hera.

I walked backward through the gate so I could keep an eye on Theo and Poseidon. As I passed through the threshold, a curtain of gloom dropped, and a bout of dizziness pulled me to my knees. I reopened my eyes and saw the gatekeeper summon Theo forward. The gatekeeper pointed to the other gate. Theo furrowed his brow, and then the gate-keeper's arm stopped . . . shook . . . and gradually pivoted and pointed to this door.

Theo stepped forward and disappeared. Another wave of dizziness hit me as the light flashed again. I held my head in my hands as a noise came from beside me. Theo was on his back, unmoving.

"Theo?" I leaned over him. "Theo? Theo!"

He crushed me against him, his chest bouncing from quiet chuckles.

"It's not funny!" I said. "What happened with the gatekeeper?"

"Oh, that? Nothing."

Poseidon stepped through the gate and weaved a bit before sitting hard on the ground, clearly light-headed. "How did you do that, Theo?" he asked.

"Do what?" he replied.

"The gatekeeper was going to send you through the left gate, but he changed his mind."

Theo shrugged. "I said I belong with Hera."

I was slightly taken aback. This was the first time I recalled him using my goddess name.

"The gatekeeper was vexed after you left," Poseidon said.

"Theo's Titan strength is that he can persuade someone to do something they might not otherwise do," I explained.

Poseidon arched a brow. "Really?"

"Your nose is itchy," Theo said in a smooth, direct tone, maintaining eye contact with Poseidon. "Scratch it."

Poseidon scratched his nose, and then immediately dropped his hand and his jaw. "How did you . . . ?"

"I don't use my Titan strength often, but when I do, it's effective."

"Impressive." Poseidon stood and brushed himself off. "I would use your strength to get whatever I wanted. Free wine mostly, and barrels and barrels of nectar."

"Theo doesn't use his Titan strength selfishly," I replied. "Only for the benefit of others."

Poseidon scratched his chin, unconvinced. "Does it work on everyone?"

"The stronger the will of the individual, the less likely they will heed me," Theo answered. "Battling someone's will leaves me with a week-long headache, and the effect is not guaranteed to work."

"I didn't know that," I said.

He pursed his lips, his eyes sparkling. "Why do you think I rarely try my persuasive voice on you and your siblings? Gods are notoriously rebellious."

"But I scratched my nose," Poseidon reminded him.

"Some gods are weaker than others."

Poseidon guffawed.

Theo flexed his left hand and grimaced.

"What is it?" I asked.

"Nothing."

He tucked his hand away, but not until after I caught sight of his fingertips. I grabbed his hand and lifted it. The ends were bluish purple and turning a gangrenous gray. He gritted his teeth as I checked his other hand. It appeared normal, for now, but the decay had begun.

"We haven't been here long," I said in disbelief. "Maybe you should go back and wait—"

He set off down the roadway. After several steps, he paused. "Are you coming?"

Poseidon hesitated. "Hera, is he using his persuasive voice? I cannot tell."

"He isn't," I replied.

"So I *do* want to go to the pits of Tartarus."

"We're just going on a walk to visit our brother," I said, steering him to face the path. "Nothing to worry about."

"Do you think that's how Theo stays so calm?" Poseidon asked in a low tone. "Do you think he uses his persuasive voice on himself, and that's why he's keen to go?"

I hadn't considered whether Theo could convince himself to do something he wouldn't otherwise do, but that could explain why he always kept his word, why he was steadfast and loyal to those he loved, and why sometimes, like now, he was too stubborn.

Poseidon rolled his head. "All right. Let's get this over with."

We trudged after Theo. I almost would have preferred that Theo had used his persuasive voice on us. At least then we wouldn't dread this so much.

Our small party traveled the narrow road toward the grim, jagged mountains, which I could not help but notice were the same color as Theo's fingertips.

13

The path to the mountains led us through a swampy area overgrown with haggard trees. Their branches hung lifelessly over the sludge like dangling, broken limbs. Our path was dry, but we were surrounded by a soupy bog. Even though we had not seen another soul on the trail in hours, I got the sense that we were being watched.

Theo tried to keep his hands where I couldn't see them, but I was acutely aware that the fingers on his left hand had turned gray and his palm was bluish purple. His right hand, the sword hand, gripped his hilt, despite that those fingers were also dusky. The tips were white as if frostbitten by the undergloom's full blight.

After a time, I couldn't say how long, the bog dried, and we walked on hardened ground. A range of spiky mountains leered at the sky like a sea dragon's open maw. The trail took us right to the base of the mountains and then descended into their belly through an enormous tunnel.

"Tartarus lies at the lowest point of the underworld," I said. "This must be the entrance."

Poseidon grumbled as he readied the torch. "Our brother couldn't have lived on a white sandy beach, near a tavern, with endless ale and shellfish?"

Theo hissed.

"What is it?" I asked.

"The metal."

I touched the metal on his leather vest. It was so cold, it burned. I pulled off every piece of his clothing that had metal, leaving him in his underclothes, and gasped. Everywhere the metal had touched skin had turned bluish purple.

Our fingertips touched. His were ice. "I'm all right."

"No, Theo, you aren't." My throat sealed shut. "I should never have let you come."

"Let me? You couldn't have stopped me."

We both knew he would not turn back. He would travel for as long as warm blood flowed through him.

Poseidon gave a low moan, drawing our attention. He gaped in horror at his hands. His skin was covered in angry, pustulous red boils.

"Did you touch the torch?" I asked him.

"No."

"Then how . . . ?"

"It's the undergloom," Theo answered.

He took the torch while I bandaged Poseidon's hands. I wasn't decaying, though I suspected that I would soon suffer the effects of the underworld too.

I took the torch and the lead. The air warmed as we entered the tunnel and descended into the recesses of the mountains. The experience was the opposite of going underground in the mortal realm, where depth often brought a chill. Here, heat radiated from the stone walls and ground. As I wiped the sweat from my brow, I tripped forward and caught myself.

"Careful of that step down," I warned the others.

The roadway was covered with lips and indentations. At one point, the torchlight cast a glow over several dips and rises that appeared to be the indentations of toes. I spun around with the torchlight and confirmed that we were standing in a huge footprint. The big toe was longer than I was tall.

We left that footprint and stepped down into another the same size, though it was difficult to tell how far apart they were in the dimness.

"Something very big left these," Poseidon said.

"See this?" Theo ran his hand across the tunnel wall. Deep slashes, starting about the height of our heads, ran up the wall and disappeared toward the ceiling.

Poseidon examined them closer. "A wildcat attacked a member of the Telchines once. The man sustained similar markings."

My senses jumped. Long before Uranus was dethroned by Cronus, he had trapped his first children in Tartarus—the Gigantes, the three Cyclopes and their three brothers, the hundred-handed monsters more commonly known as the Hecatoncheires. Human blood was ambrosial drink to them.

The footprints continued. We stepped in and out of them, silently dropping deeper into the bowels of the underworld. Hot and sticky heat pulsed around us in waves. My back was drenched in sweat. We drained our water supply, and I ate all my nuts and dried berries, but I was still famished.

The tunnel broadened so the torchlight no longer reached the walls. After a time, the footprints petered off and disappeared. My mind concocted a story of Rhea marching Cronus down to Tartarus in chains, and when he resisted, she and the other Titanesses hauled him off his feet and carried him kicking and yelling the rest of the way. I was deep in thought when I stubbed my toe.

Behind me, Poseidon cursed vehemently.

"What?" I asked.

"I stubbed my toe," he replied.

I lowered the torch closer to the ground and shivered. Gravestones covered the area as far as the light shone. Theo and I bent down to inspect them. Each was marked with an eye, the symbol of fate, but no name.

"I don't understand," I said. "Does the underworld have its own dead?"

"The Telchines believe the fate of a soul belongs to the underworld once it departs the body," Poseidon replied. "Maybe there's a greater end than death."

Death was the end to mortality. Could a soul perish too?

We roamed through the gravestones silently, stopping at a fork in the path. The cave split into two narrower tunnels. The air emanating from both was stale and hot.

"Which way?" Poseidon asked.

A roar came from the right tunnel, and then a clinking, like chains dragging across the ground. The echo faded. My forehead was still slick with sweat.

"We should go the other way," Theo said. "Hopefully, the left tunnel leads to the mine."

We walked into the dizzying heat. New boils pockmarked the sides of Poseidon's face and neck. They must have been painful and itchy. He scratched at a really large one on his cheek, and it popped, leaking amber pus. He didn't touch them again.

Theo limped along. The toes on both his sandaled feet had turned gray. I slung his arm over my shoulder, and he let me take on some of his weight.

"Do not fall," he mumbled to himself. "Do not stop. Keep going."

He was using his persuasive voice on himself.

Tears stung my eyes as I imagined the pain he must have been in. I gradually supported more of his weight to try to lessen his discomfort, but I wasn't certain he noticed.

We came upon another tunnel, and at its end was a light. Theo and I staggered to a stop. It had been so long since we had seen any light but our own that it dazed us. The light was moving—toward us. I couldn't understand why the dead would require a torch. What monstrous shades dwelled down here?

We shuffled into a nook to hide. I dropped the torch and stomped out the fire, casting us into a void. Theo leaned heavier against me. Poseidon panted softly beside us.

The torch bobbed nearer. Two harpies were lugging a handcart. They had women's heads, but their bodies were birdlike and covered in glossy blue-black feathers. Their big round eyes were depthless, like a bird of prey's, and they hopped along in a harness attached to the cart. In the back, stacked in a row, were four souls. Unmoving, eyes shut, their color was as pale as a shade's. I recognized a face among them and inhaled sharply—Jacinta, the kitchen slave who perished during the earthquakes.

Theo's weight suddenly felt heavier than a world. What would happen if he died here in the underworld? Would his mortal form *and* his soul die?

Poseidon panted beside me. Could a god perish in the underworld?

I wasn't certain I really wanted to know. All I wanted was to find Hades and get out of here.

We traversed the tunnel the harpies had come from. Many of the boils on Poseidon's arm had burst, but we were out of bandages. Theo limped worse than before and was very quiet. His skin was ashen up to his elbows on both arms, and the bluish-purple patches from the metal had spread, creeping nearer to his heart. How could I force him to keep going? But then again, how could we stop? The longer he spent in the underworld, the worse his condition would be.

"When this is all over, we should revisit Crete," he rasped.

Crete was where we first danced and kissed. The cult of Aphrodite dwelled there, isolated from the rest of the world. I thought my sisters and I would end up living there with them one day. Our fierce warrior friend Euboea had a strong dislike for men, but she and the cult had come to adore Theo.

"I wonder if Euboea will muzzle you again," I said.

He chuckled and leaned heavier against me. My Titan strength provided me the fortitude to withstand his weight, but extreme fatigue was setting in. The underworld was affecting us differently: my pains were a brittleness in my bones, like a log turning to ash in a fire.

The tunnel opened to overlook another set of mountains. A depraved storm writhed over its craggy, deep-crimson peaks, the dismal clouds roaring with thunder. I thought briefly that we had gone in a circle and were back outside near the bog, but the base of these mountains was lined with bars—prison cells. I had seen the pits of Tartarus once in a vision. Uranus and other monsters lay submerged beneath the mountains, trapped far below the mortal realm, where they could neither harass nor molest humankind.

A bronze fence with a tall gate enclosed the prison. Parallel to the fence was a road that led to lights on a lower hillside outside of Tartarus proper. That had to be the mines.

We ambled in that direction under the shadow of the sky-high fence. Following the light like a beacon, we saw a great fortress constructed in the ridge, a network of tunnels disappearing into the hillside around it. Scattered before them both was a bustling camp. The dead wandered out of the tunnels with handcarts of soil, dumped them, and carried the empty carts back in. More harpies wielded whips, striking at any worker that paused. These dead moved slower than the others we had encountered.

We sneaked to a pile of rocks outside camp and hunched down behind them. The head taskmaster probably dwelled in the stone fortress. Harpies guarded the entrance, as well as the openings to the mine. Theo was struggling to sit up, and Poseidon wasn't doing much better.

"Why don't you two stay here?" I said. "I'll investigate."

I expected a protest, but they both settled in for a much-earned rest. I smoothed Theo's hair back from his eyes and ran my fingers across his scruffy jaw.

"Be careful," he said.

"You too."

"Come back with our brother," Poseidon panted.

I crept out from behind the pile and darted from rock to rock, closer and closer to the fortress.

A loud screeching sounded overhead. Harpies had been perched up the hillside, and I had not seen them. Four of them swooped down on me. I thought about opening my wings and taking them on a journey, but in doing so, they might spot Theo and Poseidon, so I put my hands in the air. They landed, and the biggest one screeched in my face. Her sharp talons snatched at my sword, and then another harpy wearing a chest plate over her feathered breast put her beak in my face.

"Who are you?" she squawked.

"I'm here for someone. I was told my brother Hades is here."

The harpies quit screeching and hopped around agitatedly.

Their spokesperson sniffed at me. "You're a goddess."

"She looks like Rhea," one of the underlings replied.

The harpies' enormous, murky eyes sized me up. None of them had glanced in the direction of Theo and Poseidon yet.

Their spokesperson grabbed my arm with her talons. "Come," she said.

They led me toward the fortress. The dozen or so front steps were carved from the stone hillside and in ideal repair, as were the pillars and smooth façade. The styling was older than what was currently being built in the mortal realm, but the classic, grand architecture was unexpectedly wonderful in this awful place.

The interior was no less impressive. We stepped into a heat wave that nearly melted my eyelashes. I blinked to clear my dry eyes as the harpies marched me across the sweltering throne room in the cavernous hall. Torch sconces were placed every few paces between stone pillars, all leading to an imposing throne carved into the opposite wall. It was the loftiest throne I had ever seen, extending three stories high to a ceiling of stalactites. The armrests and base of the narrow seat were inscribed with an intricate array of rectangular runes that I didn't recognize and could not interpret, but their design was dignified and the detail of the workmanship remarkable. The throne's high back resembled an immense set of harpy wings.

Sitting off to the side at a table playing a board game by himself was a man—no, a god. The game used white and black oval marble pieces on a checkered stone board. He glanced away from his game and froze. His eyes widened so gradually it was like witnessing the dawn turn to daytime.

"Mother?" he asked.

"Your sister, master," replied a harpy.

He stood, slowly unfolding his lanky frame to its full height. I surmised that he was older than me by a year or two. Thinly built with trimmed onyx hair at the back and longer fringe at the front that hung in his light-green eyes, he was alluring in the way one catches their breath upon spotting a wolf in the woods. His olive-toned skin was deeply tan, and he was clean-shaven. Loose robes draped open about his rangy body, exposing his bare abdomen. Across his chest were six tattoos, all sets of wings black as night.

"Hades?" I asked.

"You got that right, and you must be Hera."

"I was told you're here on an errand for Rhea."

He tilted his head slightly. "Mother knows I have work here to finish."

"You're needed in the mortal realm."

"So I've been told." Hades's soft-spoken voice was almost drowned out by the harpies tramping out of the hall. "How are the Upstart Gods fairing against Father?"

"We're outnumbered, overpowered, and inexperienced. We need your aid."

Hades wandered to the throne. His svelte body practically glided, like a shade in a graveyard. "Isn't this throne a masterpiece?"

"It is . . . ?" I sounded as baffled as I felt. What was this place, and why was he here?

"The dead toiled over every detail while crafting it. The underworld was patterned after the mortal realm so closely that they miss having a ruler. They want a Titan to claim the undergloom as their domain, but putting a god on a throne always leads to bad things."

"Is that why you won't come back home? You won't leave your . . . people?"

"This has been my home for many years," Hades said, gripping the arm of the throne. "Why would I leave? Do you see Cronus here? Do you see anyone trying to find me and throw me in a pit? No. Down here, I'm removed from the mortal realm and the competition for power. I have no place in your world."

"What if you did?" I asked, wiping at my sweaty brow. "Once we dethrone Cronus, Zeus will lead. He won't turn his back on his brothers and sisters."

Hades arched a slim brow. "Do you know what I like most about the dead? They have no ambitions. They have no artifice. They have only one desire."

"And that is?"

"To love."

"Love?"

"Yes, they serve the gods because they love them. At one time, they hoped Mother might be their ruler, but she's tied to Cronus. A female leader is what these souls truly seek. They long for the comfort and caring that a mother has for her children, like Gaea, who made this world for their souls to find rest."

I wiped perspiration out of my eyes. How was Hades not sweating?

He ran his fingertips across the unique rune carvings, his long nails beautifully shaped, like the talons of a wondrous beast. "One of my Titan strengths allows me to heal. I'm not susceptible to the decay of death. My soul is impervious." He scanned me from top to bottom. "You're hardly touched by the undergloom."

"I hurt, but it's manageable."

"Your will is strong. You won't let the underworld claim you. You know your place is not here, and I know mine isn't."

"Yet you won't come home?"

"I would for a ruler. No male god could rule the Titans without one of them always trying to overthrow the other. They will always battle for power. But a goddess? I could support her."

I shifted on my feet. "Rhea spoke with you about the coalition she's gathering in my name. I think she means for me to be more than Zeus's defender."

"I've heard about no coalition." Hades sounded intrigued. "I'm not surprised, though. We're newly acquainted, yet I would wager you're more suited for the role of ruler than our youngest brother."

"You don't even know Zeus."

"I know he isn't here. Rhea asked you to come because you would not fall prey to this place. The decay comes from despair. Achieving happiness here has taught me that peace isn't found outside of us. Peace is internal. We carry it, we emulate it, we offer it. Those who recognize that can find contentment anywhere."

How could he have found happiness surrounded by death? Was it a choice? Could my sisters and I be content anywhere?

I felt the weight of my responsibility then, to Hades and Zeus and my sisters, and to Theo and Poseidon waiting outside. "You can be happy anywhere?" I asked Hades. "Then surely you can find peace in the mortal realm too. Come stand with us."

Hades perched on the edge of the throne and traced the long nail of his pointer finger up and down his thumb thoughtfully. "You believe in this Zeus?"

"I believe we are destined to win."

Hades's vivid green eyes were startling in this monochromatic setting. I understood his hesitance. Our little brother was not flawless, but he would rule, and no matter our reservations, our duty was to dethrone Cronus and save humankind. It wasn't ultimately about us. We were gods, and gods served.

Or maybe that was mainly the role of goddesses . . .

The harpy with the breastplate reentered with two of her crew carrying Theo and Poseidon over their feathery shoulders. They flung them to the ground, and they both stayed down.

"Master," the harpy hissed, "we found these intruders outside camp."

Hades blinked quickly at Poseidon. "Brother?"

Poseidon extended his arm. Hades lifted him to his feet, and they embraced.

"Wait, what?" I asked. "You two know each other?"

"We lived with the Telchines as little children," Poseidon said. "Mother came for Hades a few years ago and brought him here, I suppose."

"The Telchines gave me these tattoos," Hades said. "Each one represents one of Mother's children."

Poseidon patted his shoulder. "It's good to see you again, Hades."

"You've been in better condition," Hades remarked and then regarded Theo. "Who is this?"

"Hera's, uh, guard," Poseidon replied. "Colonel Theo Angelos."

Theo was much more than my guard, but the moment to correct Poseidon passed. Hades touched a sickly patch on Theo's chest, and his expression grew somber.

"His will is strong," Hades said. "He's come farther into the underworld than any mortal I've known."

"He's a demigod," Poseidon explained.

"Regardless, he mustn't stay much longer," Hades replied. "I have one last thing to do, and then we can go."

I helped lift Theo to his feet, and he teetered until he rested against me. "What must be done?" I asked.

"Mother asked me to oversee the mines and coordinate with the Cyclopes. We've been working on crafting indestructible weapons to wield against Cronus."

Hades walked through the pillars to a balcony on the long side of the hall. We hobbled to his side of the vista and viewed the pit of the mines. The dead plodded in and out of tunnels, disappearing below and returning tired and haggard.

"Adamant is the rarest substance in the universe," Hades said. "The cost of one *daktylos*, or a finger's worth, requires one hundred souls."

"Souls?" I asked, stroking Theo's arm. I wanted to leave, but the function of the mines took on a whole new meaning now that I understood they were harvesting adamant.

"What is more indestructible than a soul?" Hades asked vacantly. "As a boy, I didn't make the association that for every scrap of adamant, a hundred souls disappeared. Then one day, my nursemaid went missing. She was Forgotten."

Adamant wasn't a precious metal, or a substance at all. Adamant was *made of souls*.

"What does 'Forgotten' mean?" Poseidon asked, his lisp pronounced.

Hades rested heavily against the banister. "The dead can expire. When they do, there's nowhere else to go. They become unaccounted for, and the dead here no longer remember them. They lie in unmarked graves that no one visits, except me. The dead are good at following, but they are not good at remembering. Their story has been written, and they have reached their end. They act on impulse, thinking no further than their next move. The memory of their time since arriving in the underworld is fleeting. They are compelled by instinct, with no aspirations to achieve or grow. They just *are*, and when they cease to be . . . they are Forgotten."

"Why mine at all?" I asked. "The adamant isn't worth the cost of a single soul."

Hades pushed off from the balcony. "Tell that to mankind, which depends on us to attain the proper weapons to defeat Cronus."

"Listen to him," Theo rasped. "We cannot win without proper arms." He clutched my hand with astonishing strength and then let go to grasp the vial on his necklace. He couldn't drink the contents until he had taken his last breath. He had time yet, but I loathed to see him suffer.

"Come," Hades said. "Let me show you."

14

Hades led us to the gates of Tartarus. The iron gates were almost as tall as the crimson mountain peaks behind it, their delicate bronze construction strangely magnificent in this abysmal place. Outside the entry, we encountered more huge footprints and claw marks in the ground.

"Who left these marks?" I asked.

"Our grandfather, Uranus," Hades answered. "I've been told he put up a struggle until the very end of his freedom."

"I thought those might have been made by one of the monsters trapped down here," Poseidon remarked.

Hades lightly touched his elbow. "Not everyone who looks like a monster is a monster."

At the gate, Hades gave a quick knock. Nothing happened. He sighed and knocked harder. Still no answer. Hades murmured under his breath and then called out, "Gyes! Cottus! Obriareus! Open the gate!"

The ground began to quake. The vibrations grew closer and louder as three of the biggest monsters I had ever seen emerged from the shadows. Each one had fifty heads and a hundred hands. Chains encircled their ankles, the clanging of which could hardly be heard over their thunderous footfalls. The Hecatoncheires stopped at the gate and pulled it open. I gaped up at them, no protective barrier between us, and my hands turned clammy. Then I saw they were at the end of their chains and could venture no farther.

"Thank you." Hades sighed. "We've come to see your Cyclops brothers."

"They're working," said one of the Hecatoncheires.

"I'm well aware of that, Obriareus," Hades replied, his tone impatient. "Quit wasting our time and let us in. You made a bargain with my mother, did you not?"

Obriareus's shoulders fell. "Sorry, Hades. Come in. Come in."

Hades strolled in confidently. Poseidon was more cautious. I assisted Theo inside, and 150 heads loomed over us, each one grinning.

"Rhea!" one of the Hecatoncheires boomed.

A big hand scooped me up and lifted me into the air, and I was stunned speechless in front of so many grinning heads.

"Put her down!" Hades said. He flew up beside me, his big wings heathered and feathery, like an owl's. "That's not Rhea. That's my little sister Hera."

"Hera?" said one of the Hecatoncheires as he held me.

"Yes, Gyes."

Gyes sniffed me so hard my hair flew around my face. I caught my breath, and he bowed. "Hello, goddess Hera." Gyes was huge and hideous, but his countless eyes were no longer frightening.

"Hello," I replied. "Would you please put me down?"

"Of course, little bird." Gyes set me on the ground.

Poseidon had taken over propping up Theo.

Hades landed beside me. "They're mostly harmless," he said. "They like you."

"Little bird is pretty," said Cottus, the last of the Hecatoncheires.

My cheeks reddened.

"You cannot go around picking up goddesses," Hades scolded, his voice full of exasperation. "You're fortunate Hera didn't poke one of your eyes out."

"Sorry, Hades," Obriareus replied.

"No harm done," I said. "This is Poseidon, another of Rhea's children."

Obriareus squinted his many eyes at Poseidon. "He reminds me of Cronus. We don't like Cronus."

His brothers growled in agreement.

Poseidon lifted his chin and set it stubbornly. "Some of us here are monsters, and *I* am not one of them."

"None of us is particularly fond of our father," Hades inserted smoothly. "Now, will the three of you escort us to the forge, or shall we go ourselves?"

"We will take you." Cottus's voice was higher and softer than his brothers', a stark contrast to his mangled face and permanent sneer. "After you, little bird."

I went to Theo, and he slung his arm over my shoulder. "I believe you have admirers," he said.

"They don't know me very well yet. They'll change their minds."

He chuckled, as I had hoped he would.

The Hecatoncheires meandered, allowing us to keep up with them. They were so wide they couldn't walk side by side down the trail. The three of them began to whistle a tune as we headed toward the crimson mountains. With fifty heads each, they were their own choir. The harmony of their whistling was a delightful surprise, the melody bright, jaunty, and upbeat, an unexpected choice for three monsters enchained in the deepest, darkest pits of the underworld. Theo, a talented vocalist in his own right, wore the barest of smiles.

Hades gave me a side-glance that said, *Told you so.* Maybe it was true. Anyone could find happiness, anywhere, if they sought it. Like a story, happiness was a matter of perspective.

The prison cells at the base of the mountains had bars taller than Gyes, Cottus, and Obriareus. The first cell we passed appeared empty.

The bars were set so far apart, I could have walked right in. I was not tempted.

"Each bar is made from sorcery-infused adamant," Hades said. "The adamant itself is taken from the spine of the earth that stretches down into the underworld and holds the realms together."

I tried to calculate how many souls it had taken to craft each adamant bar and shuddered.

"As the Mother of All Gods, Gaea *is* the earth," Theo rasped. "Why would she take souls in exchange for adamant?"

Hades gave Theo his full attention. He knew how much strength it cost him to speak. "Gaea sacrifices pieces of her own soul for the harvest of the adamant. To maintain balance and not create upheaval in the world, she must replace what she has granted."

"So the Forgotten you spoke about become part of her?" I asked.

"Yes," Hades replied. "In the same way their bodies decompose into the earth. The cost is high, but it should be, to craft a weapon for a god."

"Then they're heroes," Theo concluded.

Hades paused to touch one of the prison bars. "That they are."

"Gyes," I said. "Are your chains made of adamant too?"

"They're metal. Easily breakable for us."

"Then why stay here?"

Gyes shrugged his enormous shoulders. "We're not wanted in the mortal realm. This is our home."

"We do miss the sunrises and sunsets," Cottus said.

"And the moon and the stars," Obriareus added.

I frowned. This dreadful place was the most they hoped to have for a home. The Hecatoncheires were daunting in size and somewhat unsightly, but was their appearance enough to condemn them to the underworld for all eternity?

Something enormous hissed from within the cell we had paused in front of, and then whatever was inside rammed into the bars and snarled. We backpedaled in a hurry, but not before I caught a glimpse of a black serpentine monster with spiny sapphire wings.

Gyes, the closest to the cell, banged his fists against the door. "Get back, Typhon!"

The creature hissed, spewing its sweltering, rancid breath over us.

"Typhon, I said back!" Gyes hit the bars harder, rattling the foundation of the mountains.

The vile beast expelled another putrid breath and slunk away, snarling. I couldn't decide whether I was more intimidated by Typhon or Gyes. The Hecatoncheires were gentle with us, but they were still formidable.

"Do not touch the bars," Gyes warned.

Hades bent forward at the waist and clutched his knees. I thought he was collecting himself, but he shook with laughter. "Gyes, you scared Hera and Poseidon."

"Did not," I countered.

"Speak for yourself," Poseidon said. Still, his lisp was more pronounced. "What . . . what was that thing?"

"Typhon is the meanest monster Mother Gaea has ever created," Gyes replied.

Obriareus pointed at the next cell. "His female mate, Echidna, is in that prison. She's even nastier."

Hades smirked. "Isn't that how it goes?"

I should have been offended, but I was preoccupied with Theo. Retreating from the cell had depleted the last of his vigor. I supported his full weight now.

"Theo?" I asked. "How can I help?"

He crumpled forward into my arms. Exhausted myself, I laid him on the ground. He pushed shallow, shuddering breaths out of his blue lips. The faded patches on his chest had spread to his heart, which was now bluish purple. Soon it would also be as white as hoarfrost.

"Theo?" I asked. "Can you hear me?"

"Let him rest." Hades touched the patch of color over Theo's heart. "It's a testament to his fortitude that he lasted this long without losing consciousness."

I wanted to ask if he would ever wake up, but I knew the answer. We had to get him out of this poisonous pit of death and back to the mortal realm.

"I'll carry him," Hades said. "You help our brother."

Poseidon's lips were cracked and bleeding, and boils covered the entirety of him, even inside his nose and ears. More alarming were the stretches of skin peeling off his chest and legs. One patch on his knee had split down to the bone.

"I will carry them both," Gyes said. The monster picked up Theo with such care that my eyes misted. "I'll take good care of him, little bird."

Poseidon climbed onto Gyes's other outstretched hand and sat in his palm. As we passed the next cell, another beast growled from inside.

"Echidna," Hades stated matter-of-factly.

Perhaps if I lived in the underworld, I would be desensitized to its monsters too. As it was, the skin on my arms was puckered with gooseflesh, even in the heat, and my pulse sped up when the growling changed to snarling and gnashing teeth, as though Echidna was intent on gnawing herself free.

Finally, we left the shadow of the mountains and came upon a ravine. Obriareus picked me up, carried me over it with one giant step, and put me down. Hades allowed Cottus to do the same with him. The drop-offs occurred more frequently until we were traversing a stone path with sheer ravines on either side. Far below, at the end of the path, a roaring fire flickered, punctuated ever so often by flying sparks. A river ran through the base of the canyon, its foreboding, blood-dark waters moving slowly.

The Hecatoncheires' chains reached their end near the top of the ravine.

"We'll wait here," Gyes said. "Little bird, I will take care of your demigod."

"Let me know if he worsens or wakes," I said. Theo's breaths were fainter. I didn't like letting him out of my sight, but the Hecatoncheires were big enough and loud enough that I could probably see and hear them from below.

Poseidon got down. Hades and I propped him up, and we descended toward the lights.

The deeper into the pit we headed, the more excruciating the intense heat became. My bones felt on fire. Hades hadn't broken a sweat, but Poseidon was dripping and panting. The rank scent of sulfur around us was unbearable. I wouldn't try to wash it out of my clothes. I would burn them. Hopefully, I could rinse the stench out of my hair.

Ahead, by the river, a clanging noise preceded every flash of sparks near the fire, which outlined three hulking giants. Bald and muscular, with brawny shoulders and chiseled chests and backs, they were an impressive sight. Unlike the Hecatoncheires, their faces were not deformed. In fact, they were somewhat comely. Despite their toned, hulking bodies and regal facial bone structure, each had a single large eye in the center of the face that blended seamlessly into their noses and foreheads.

I couldn't believe I thought the Cyclopes were handsome. Clearly, I had been in the underworld too long.

The Cyclopes took turns swinging their tools against an anvil, sending a cascade of red embers into the air. One held a hammer, another a chisel, and the third stoked the fire in the forge. They wore chains around their ankles like the Hecatoncheires, only shorter. I doubted the length allowed them to climb out of the canyon. The one tending to the fire noticed us, and his face lit up.

Good stars. The heat really was going to my head.

"Brothers," he said, signaling to the other two Cyclopes.

They cooled their tools off by dipping the glowing red ends into the river and then set them down and stalked over to us. About as tall as the

Hecatoncheires, they were at least ten times our size. The Cyclops who had first spotted us sank to one knee and bowed his head.

"Master Hades," he said.

His brothers followed suit, kneeling before us.

"Arges, do stand up," Hades replied amiably. "You all mustn't bow every time we meet."

Arges stood, and then his eye locked on Poseidon and me. "Your kin have come for you at last?"

"So it seems. Meet my sister Hera and brother Poseidon."

Arges sank to his knee again. "Master Poseidon and Mistress Hera. My brothers Halimedes and Steropes"—he pointed, indicating which was which, and each one gave us a polite bow—"and I have waited for this day for a long, long time."

I didn't understand what that meant, or how much time his explanation would take, and my attention darted to Theo and the Hecatoncheires above. The Cyclopes caught sight of them and waved up at their monstrous brothers, who waved back.

"Have you finished?" Hades asked, rubbing his hands together eagerly.

"Only just," Arges answered. "We were waiting on that last shipment of adamant."

"Yes, yes, yes. I made certain they delivered it to you immediately. Now, show me." Hades sounded excited, even giddy.

Steropes went into the forge and came out carrying six packages. "Master Hades, if you don't mind, we'll give Hera hers now." He handed me a small but heavy package. "Titanesses first."

"Are you certain?" I asked.

"Please open it," Hades said, bouncing on the balls of his feet. "I've been waiting for this occasion for *years*."

Poseidon had found a stump of firewood to sit on. He was trying to appear interested, but he was exhausted. "Maybe we can open these in the mortal realm," I suggested.

"Open it," Hades pressed.

Halimedes murmured to his brothers. "Do you think we got the size right?"

"Shh," Steropes replied. "We followed her instructions exactly."

"Whose instructions?" I asked.

"Rhea's," Arges said, his voice reverent.

I had no idea how the Cyclopes had managed to tie the packages closed with their huge fingers, so I took care untying the string. The parchment wrapping fell to the side, revealing an expertly crafted iron glove.

Hades gasped. "Is that . . . ?"

"Solid adamant," Arges answered. "Only the best for Rhea's children."

"Hera, see if it fits," Halimedes urged.

"Yes, try it on," Steropes added.

The glove was suited for my left hand, the opposite of my sword hand. I slid it on, and the adamant vibrated, as though it had a heartbeat, and then it molded to my fingers, knuckles, palm, and wrist.

I flexed my fingers, and the joints in the glove moved in sync with my hand.

"How did you get the size of her hand right?" Hades asked.

"We took a cast of Rhea's," Halimedes replied. "She assured us it would fit."

"We call it 'Star Catcher,'" Arges said. "But you may name it whatever you wish, Hera."

I held up my hand and imagined summoning stars into my palm. The Cyclopes beamed at me. It must have taken them a very long time to build this glove, not to mention the amount of adamant it took to craft it.

"How many souls' worth of adamant did this require?" I asked quietly.

"Hera," Hades scolded. "Those souls did not sacrifice themselves so you could disrespect the Cyclopes."

"There's no disrespect," Arges replied. "Rhea mentioned that Hera might respond this way, so she asked us to inform you that not a soul was taken that did not volunteer. They gave of themselves to Gaea, who will remember their names always. She remembers and loves all of her children."

I flexed my gloved hand into a fist. "I'm sorry I sounded ungrateful. It's magnificent. I've never seen anything like it."

"It was complex," Arges answered. "We spent more time on your glove than on any other specialty item."

"Arges is being humble," Hades said. "Adamant is a complicated material to work with. It takes immense practice and skill to manipulate over a forge. Once it's heated, it cannot be left unattended. The smith must toil nonstop while concentrating on the god or goddess for whom they are creating the item. The Cyclopes built altars for each of us to aid their focus on us as individuals." Hades pointed out an area of worship on the far side of the forge. My altar stood out right away. It had images of a woman dancing painted upon it, many of my favorite foods, and a spear and shield—my favorite weapons. I felt the care and love and thoughtfulness of the altar, and in the fine quality of the glove.

"Try to call a star," Steropes suggested.

"We're too far away from the heavens," I replied. "I tried nearer the surface and failed."

Arges arched his brow, which made him appear even more intelligent. "You didn't attempt it while wearing our glove."

"Try it," Poseidon rasped.

He hadn't spoken in a while, and he sounded awful, so I couldn't deny his request. Reaching up, I shut my eyes and searched deep inside myself for that light that flapped around inside my rib cage. I caught hold of it and breathed in through my mouth, out through my nose.

"Bring me the stars," I said.

The glove warmed, not unpleasantly, and emitted an empowering hum. Then it glowed golden, and my wings opened. My skin emitted a soft light, as it had done during Nyx's attack. I heard a bit of a gasp, I didn't know who from, and then a great wind sped my way. I opened my eyes and saw a star shooting over the mountains of Tartarus, leaving a glittery trail in its wake.

Above us, the Hecatoncheires gawked as the star flew over their many heads, down the ravine, and into the palm of my hand.

The star vibrated against my humming glove, and the Cyclopes shielded their eyes from the sudden brightness. The star didn't sting my eyes, nor Poseidon's, but Hades squinted.

"I had forgotten how perfect stars are," Halimedes said.

The Cyclopes kneeled before me and bowed their heads.

"Our goddess," Arges said.

From up the rise, the Hecatoncheires clapped with a hundred hands each. I shot Hades a perplexed glance.

"They worship most of the gods and goddesses they meet," he replied. "You get accustomed to it."

Arges lifted his head. "Hera, with the adamant glove on, your grip is powerful enough not only to summon a star into the darkest places in the universe but to crush it in your grasp."

I closed my fist around the star. It shrank, intensifying in luminosity. I squeezed harder until the star crumbled to embers that flowed out of my hand like sand. I dusted off the last of the cinders into the forge, and the glow of my skin faded.

"May I *please* open my package now?" Hades asked.

I wanted to test out my glove again, but Steropes handed Hades another wrapped package. The other four parcels were probably for our siblings. Hades pulled off the parchment and held up a warrior's helmet that covered his cheeks but had openings for the eyes, nose, and mouth. It had a feathered owl plume on top, and it, too, was solid adamant.

Hades slid the helmet on and disappeared.

Poseidon straightened in alarm. "Hades? Where did you go?" After no reply, Poseidon turned on Arges. "What did you do to him?"

"I'm right here," Hades replied, sniggering.

"Where?" I asked.

Someone plucked a hair off my head. My hand flew to my scalp in astonishment. Hades laughed again.

"It's a helm of invisibility," Arges explained.

"It's brilliant!" Hades took off the helmet and reappeared, grinning.

"You needn't remove the helm of invisibility to reappear," Arges said. "It will obey your thoughts and will."

Hades put the helmet back on. He disappeared, then almost immediately reappeared, still wearing the helmet. "You've outdone yourselves, friends."

All three Cyclopes reddened.

Steropes handed a package to Poseidon. So far, it was the largest. "Master Poseidon, this may help you feel better."

Poseidon's hands were a mess of boils and peeling skin. He could hardly hold the package. I helped him peel away the parchment to reveal a long-handled trident. Poseidon stood, bracing himself with it, and tapped the ground. The earth rumbled. He straightened and slammed the trident against the ground. The ground trembled louder, quaking beneath our feet. A few rocks were loosened by the vibration, and they tumbled down the canyon wall and splashed into the river.

"I call it 'World Shaker,'" Arges said. "When you strike the sea with it, the waves will froth and stand mountain high."

Poseidon walked to the river's edge and dipped the three-pronged tip of the trident in the water. The river began to flow faster until rapids formed and then horses materialized on the whitecaps and charged down the river. He lifted the end of the trident out of the water, and the river went back to flowing lazily along. Poseidon released a heavy breath of satisfaction. He was stronger when he held the trident. Maybe that was the adamant. Since putting on my glove, I felt less worn down, and less hot, tired, and thirsty.

"Little bird?" Gyes called from above, his voice booming from fifty heads. "Your demigod needs you."

I threw open my wings and flew to them. Gyes had rested his hand on the ground, palm up, so I could see Theo. The bluish-purple patch around his heart had shrunk and turned gray.

Hades landed behind me and tucked away his owl wings.

"What's the quickest way back to the main gate?" I asked him.

"The river will take us. I'll carry Theo. You help Poseidon."

Gyes draped Theo across Hades's arms.

"Thank you," I said to the Hecatoncheires. I gripped their chains in my gloved hand and broke them apart one at a time. "Now whether you stay or go, it's *your* choice. You will always have a home where I am."

Gyes patted my head with one finger, and Cottus gave me a silly, twisted grin that might have terrified someone else, but I found it endearing.

"Fly swiftly, little bird," Obriareus replied.

Hades and I flew back down to Poseidon, who waited at the river's edge in a skiff, prepared to depart. Hades laid Theo down at the bottom of the vessel, and then I got in. Poseidon sat at the stern, with Hades at the bow to balance the weight. Arges passed me the final three parcels, tied together, and I slung them over my back.

"We could never repay you," I said. "Be well."

Arges bowed his head. "Mistress Hera, I think we will meet again. Go quickly. Your demigod is fading."

Poseidon placed the three-pronged end of his trident in the water. The river lifted beneath us, horses rising within the whitecaps, and charged us downriver. As we sailed past Tartarus's stormy crimson mountains, I held Theo tightly and tried not to think about losing him forever to the undergloom.

15

Theo's soul was disappearing. I didn't know what that meant, only that I could sense him fading.

I was going to lose him.

Every time I hadn't touched him, every time I had pretended I was strong enough on my own, every time I had stayed silent when he declared his love, now burned deep. I forced down my tears. If any part of him was conscious, I couldn't let him believe I had given up hope.

Why was it taking so long to reach the gates? The skiff soared down the river faster than if I had grabbed Theo and tried to fly back, but it still wasn't swift enough.

I patted his cheek. "Theo?"

No response.

I tried again with a firmer voice. "Theo."

"Hmm?" he replied dimly.

"You need to wake up. Try to stay awake."

"Althea," he rasped. "Even as a girl, you were fierce."

"Fierce as in scary?" I was trying to keep him awake by asking questions, but I had never heard what he thought of me when we first met. I had been a child. It was on the night my mother, Stavra, had died.

"I knew straight away . . ." Theo panted, stopping for a breath. "Nothing could stop you. Don't—don't let this stop you."

"Don't talk like that."

Poseidon propelled us faster, the wind in our faces and the fetid water speckling us. Hades winced but said nothing. The gates were still somewhere out of sight ahead. A prayer to Gaea slipped past my lips.

"Please," I said.

Theo's eyes rolled back into his head. I took off his vial necklace and tested the flip top. I was ready, but it had to be done on his last breath.

"Theo Angelos, you cannot leave me. You said you would be by my side. Did you mean it?" He nodded, so slightly that I thought it might have been caused by the movement of the skiff. I shook him again. "Tell me you'll be by my side."

"Aren't I?" He licked his dry lips. "From the instant I first saw you grown up, I didn't want to live without you."

I scanned the horizon, my eyes misty. "You won't have to live without me, so stay by my side or I'll kill you myself."

Hades called out over the wind, "You two have an odd relationship."

We sailed through the bog. The eerie trees stretched out over the water, their branches like the Erinyes' emaciated fingers. Poseidon had to slow down to navigate around them, and we still hit roots hidden right below the surface that jolted us hard. I was bent so far over Theo, holding him firmly against the bench, that I smacked my head against the side of the skiff. The burst of pain was nothing. Nothing could hurt me more than Theo's gasping.

All those years of swearing I would never fall in love now laughed at me. Theo lived in my dreams. The future I envisioned with my sisters included him.

"Althea," he said. "Find joy."

A guttural moan pushed past my lips. "Don't."

"This is my fate."

"Unless you're going to tell me you're about to take your last breath, reserve your strength and shut up."

He chuckled once, quietly. I would give anything to keep this man at my side. I didn't care if I was known as Althea or Hera. I only cared that Theo Angelos was known as mine.

We emerged from the bog. Up ahead were the gate, two other rivers, and the lake. Between us, almost invisible to the eye, was the opaque barrier to the land of evening.

Hades shouted directions to Poseidon. "Keep onward!"

"Are you certain we can get through the barrier?" I asked.

"The barrier only keeps in the dead." Hades glanced at the vial in my hand. "I presume that is for your demigod."

"It's nectar laced with spring water from Oceanus's private well."

"How is Oceanus? I haven't seen him in some time. He invited me to Fort Admiral for a visit, but I've been busy in the mines."

I whipped my head around. "Do you know how to get to Oceanus's fort?"

"Al-the-a." Theo gripped at his chest where the whiteness had spread over his heart. His mouth bobbed open and closed wordlessly.

"Theo, it has to be your last breath. Squeeze my hand when you're ready, and don't you forget. All right?"

He nodded weakly, only this time it *was* from the rocking skiff.

I flipped open the vial and held it over his lips. A breath tremored there, then another, and another. The barrier was up ahead. As I tried to calculate how far we had to go, Theo stopped breathing.

"Theo? Theo Angelos!"

He did not respond. I tipped back his head and poured the contents of the vial down his throat. The barrier loomed closer.

"Theo?" I patted his cheek. "Wake up."

He still did not move.

"He's gone," Hades said.

"No," I countered.

"He's one of the dead now. He cannot leave the underworld."

"No!" I shook Theo. "You said you would stay by my side. You said."

Hades waved for Poseidon to slow the skiff, then shifted to sit beside me.

"The barrier will not allow us to bring Theo beyond this point," Hades said, his voice quiet. "I'm sorry, but we must leave him."

"I'm not leaving him," I growled. "Give the tonic more time."

"I know the dead," Hades said, even softer. "I'm sorry."

A voice called out to me from nearby.

"Althea!"

Stavra waved at me from the riverbank. My mother bestowed on me one of her stunning smiles, and then her sweet voice whispered to me again.

"My shooting star, remember that a woman's wings are her love."

Hades squinted at Stavra. "Is that . . . ?"

My voice sharpened. "That's my mother."

"In a matter of speaking, she *is* your mother."

On the riverbank, Stavra's soul had disappeared, but Theo was still here, and I was still her shooting star.

I stood in the center of the skiff and raised my gloved hand to the ever-drab sky. "Bring me the stars."

My glove hummed, and in no time, three stars soared across the meadow of asphodel toward us. The first one crashed into the barrier low, skimming the water, and shattered into little flames. The second struck the same location and burned a hole half the size of the skiff through the invisible wall. Sparks and flames showered down. The third star flew at that opening, burst through, and soared into the palm of my glove.

"Poseidon, go as fast as you can," I ordered.

He propelled us even faster, equally eager to get out of here.

"We cannot take the dead from the underworld!" Hades cried. "Please, Hera. You could disrupt the balance of the entire universe."

"Theo isn't dead," I snapped, positioning myself at the bow. "Poseidon, go!"

He guided us in a sprint toward the barrier. The skiff was too large to fit through the hole, but Hades braced Theo against the bench, and right before we slammed into the barrier, I hurled the third star. A wider hole exploded open, but it was still too small for the skiff. We hit the barrier. I cringed, expecting to crash and be flung into the water, yet we pushed through to the other side.

Hades opened his eyes, and Poseidon lifted his trident from the water.

"Althea?" Theo rasped.

I kneeled at his side. "I knew you wouldn't leave me."

Theo saw the smoke and flames from the burning barrier. "Was that you?"

"I got worried."

"He's alive," Hades said, "but his decayed flesh won't heal. We must take him to Oceanus. He's the greatest healer in the world."

"How do we get there?" I asked.

"The lake." Hades signaled for Poseidon to go that direction. As we passed the gates to the underworld, Hades sat forward and gripped the bow of the skiff. "Something's wrong."

Both sides of the river were full of the dead. The fields were so packed with souls that when new ones appeared, they knocked into others.

Hades's scowl deepened. "Too many souls are waiting to enter through the gate."

"What does it mean?" I asked, gripping Theo's decayed hand. It was cold and stiff and oddly solid compared with Poseidon's missing patches of flesh.

"It means souls are dying at a higher rate than usual, and the gate-keeper is overwhelmed. This happens during times of war or drought or pestilence."

I glanced sideways at Poseidon. "When we left the mortal realm, Cronus was plaguing humankind," I said. "He's trying to coerce us into turning ourselves in."

Hades curled his lip. "These souls will wander until they find rest in the underworld. The life of mortals and the fate of their souls is not for a god—*any* god—to abuse for his advantage."

We passed under the bridge and came out the other side.

"Are you saying these people weren't supposed to die yet?" Poseidon asked.

Hades answered, his voice hot with venom. "I'm saying every life has a beginning, middle, and end, and it's not the place of anyone—not even a god—to interfere."

The dead appeared lost, even lonely, as they huddled along the riverbank, waiting for the bridge to clear.

"Is there anything we can do to help them?" I asked.

Hades raked his nails across his scalp, messing up his hair. "We either turn ourselves in, or we stop Cronus." He seemed indifferent as to which, but it wasn't only our decision. All six of us had to agree on how to move forward.

We continued upriver and into the lake. Hades motioned for Poseidon to stop, and then they both inspected the dusky water.

"Where's the gate?" I asked, stroking Theo's cold hand.

"Under us," Hades replied.

Poseidon began to undress.

Hades raised a brow. "What are you doing?"

"I'm getting ready to swim."

"Or you could use that magnificent trident you were given and part the waters. That's how Oceanus comes and goes."

"Oh," Poseidon replied sheepishly. He dipped the pronged end of his trident into the lake. The water began to swirl, sending us in circles.

Hades gripped the side of the skiff. "Can't you do this another way?"

145

"This was your suggestion," Poseidon replied.

"This was not what I had in mind." Hades gagged and covered his mouth.

The lake whirled us around as we sank lower and lower below the waterline until we were surrounded by a wall of water. The parcels with the other adamant gifts stayed secure to my back.

I pointed at an opening at the bottom of the lake. "There."

The hull of the skiff hit the ground with a jolt, and we skidded to a stop. Poseidon held back the swirling water while I hopped out. Hades draped Theo over his shoulder, and I led the way down the slippery rock stairway into the dripping wet tunnel. A trickle of water flowed at our feet, running toward a light, and another set of stairs, at the other end.

Poseidon descended into the tunnel behind us and held the water a few steps behind him. In the center of the tunnel, the only light was straight ahead. Poseidon's grip on his trident changed, and his arm shook, the wall of water creeping in closer after us. We hurried faster toward the dingy glow. The slick stairs were wide and steep. I ascended them first and exited the tunnel into a cavern. My brothers caught up to me, and Poseidon let go. Water rushed into the hole behind us.

The melodic sound of waves crashing against a seashore drew me to the opening of the cavern. I stepped outside onto a black-sand beach with a night sky and huge stony waves crashing against the shore. Peculiar rock pilings, also black, jutted out of the water along the rugged coastline. I could not place where we were or what time it was. Given the colorless view and lack of sunlight, I might have thought we hadn't left the underworld, except for the cold and the swift winds. The howling gusts smelled invitingly of seawater.

Down the coastline, high on a ridge above a grassy knoll, stood a rugged stronghold.

We had found Fort Admiral.

16

A downpour began from the ceiling of dreary clouds. The heavy sheets of rain drenched us in seconds. Even the packages from the Cyclopes were soaked. I could hardly see the fort ahead, except for its ever-burning lanterns.

Hades was shaking so badly from the cold, I thought he might drop Theo. Poseidon's trident doubled as a staff, but his endurance was lagging. The clumps of flesh hanging from his legs and arms were heartbreaking. As he stumbled along, I felt guilty that I wasn't equally injured.

Overhead, half-shielded by the blinding deluge, an enormous bird of prey swooped in and out of the tempest. I noticed flashes of white and gold, and then it was gone.

Torches outlined the main entryway of the fort. Poseidon came to a halt and wheezed. Hades had his hands full with Theo, so I hoisted our brother over my shoulder.

"Put me down," Poseidon slurred. "I can walk."

"You cannot."

"I can."

"Cannot," I repeated. "Are we having our first argument? That's sweet. Quit squirming or I will put you down and leave you behind."

"How does Theo tolerate you?"

I rubbed Poseidon's back, where I had not seen any wounds. "You're my brother. I would carry you to the ends of the earth. Family doesn't leave family behind."

He laid an unsteady hand on the back of my neck. "Mother sees all of us clearly, but most of all you. She said you understand that to fail requires a tremendous amount of effort. Failure is not the natural state for mankind or the gods."

"No, it isn't."

"That's why I will follow you anywhere. You will never lead me into defeat."

I was undeserving of such praise, but I patted his back, encouraging him to rest. My knees shook under his weight, and my lower back screamed at me to put him down. I pushed onward, certain that the effort would pay off.

At the gate of the fort, I called up to the ramparts. "Notify your master that Hera, Hades, and Poseidon have arrived."

The gate opened, revealing three figures on the other side.

Poseidon groaned. "This is humiliating."

"Oh, stop your harping. By now you should know that anything that gets done around here is accomplished by Titanesses."

"But we never get credit for any of it," a voice replied.

Cleora.

A burst of happiness washed over me. She and Bronte greeted us at the gate with Styx. Through the mist, with rain falling in my eyes, my sisters seemed different.

"Welcome back," Bronte said, her voice brimming with relief. "Took you long enough."

"They're here right on time," Cleora countered warmly. "Good morning."

"Morning?" I asked.

"It's very early in the day," Bronte replied.

We entered the fort, and I set Poseidon back on his feet. Archers that I hadn't seen from the outside lined the ramparts. Cleora assessed Poseidon's and Theo's conditions and beckoned for us to follow her.

"This way," she said.

"I'll stay here," Styx replied. "I'm glad you made it, Hera. Zeus will be overjoyed to see you. He's missed you."

With all these pretty goddesses around, I wasn't so certain.

The courtyard housed a small village. The low-roofed, rectangular huts were constructed of sections of cut sod layered into walls. This method of building wasn't used in Thessaly, the islands, or its surrounding lands. I didn't know how far away from home we were, but it felt like a long distance.

"When did you get here?" I asked my sisters. "How long have you been here? Did everyone come?"

"Metis stayed with Epimetheus, but everyone else is here," Bronte replied, and then examined Hades from head to toe. "You must be our brother from the underworld."

"How could you tell?" he asked.

"You smell of sulfur," Cleora answered.

Hades smoothed down his wet robes. "You two must be Demeter and Hestia. Or should I use your mortal names?"

"No," Bronte—Demeter—said. "We go by our Titaness names these days."

"These days . . . ?" I trailed off. "Did Prometheus or Metis predict our arrival?"

"Both. We've been waiting for you a long time," replied Bronte—*Demeter*, eventually I would get that right. "We have much to tell you."

"It can wait until after they're healed," Cleora—Hestia—said. "Oceanus is expecting you."

In the torchlight posted outside the main stronghold, I could better assess my sisters. Both were thinner and had scars on their arms and legs. They wore full armor that was dented. A lot had changed in a short time, and one change I was hoping for.

"Hestia, are you feeling better?" I asked.

"Yes. Oceanus healed me soon after we arrived."

She and Demeter exchanged sideways glances. I was beginning to sense they were withholding something. I had missed so much already. The underworld had no day and night, but it could not have been more than a day since I left, at most.

We entered the main entranceway into a receiving hall. The interior was well lit but plain. The temperature inside was much warmer, and it was quieter without the patter of rain. They led us down a corridor to the wide-open doors of a bathhouse. Dangling his feet in a steaming pool of water beside a tiled fountain sat a man with a long, gray-streaked beard and light-blue eyes. A red scar ran across the length of his bare chest, and another on his back mirrored the first, as though something had slashed him straight through.

"Oceanus," Hestia said as we entered. "We've brought the sick."

He beckoned us to a pair of cots beside the pool. "Let them in. We'll join you in a little while."

Those of us who had come from the underworld entered, while my sisters left. Hades laid Theo down on one cot, and Poseidon sat on the second. Oceanus collected a cup of water from the fountain and brought it to Theo. He poured two, maybe three, sips down his throat and then offered the cup to Poseidon, who drank the rest.

Oceanus took the cup back. "That should do it."

"That's it?" I asked.

"We don't waste the waters from the river of my name," Oceanus replied.

The River Oceanus ran underground, between the underworld and the mortal realm, and circulated the whole earth. As the primordial god of such a font, only Oceanus and his wife could access the waters, and their mysterious yet effective medicinal properties. One small vial had revived Theo. A couple mouthfuls were certain to restore him to health.

Poseidon's boils and sores vanished before our eyes. The biggest wound on his knee took longer, but it eventually closed and left not a trace.

"Remarkable," I murmured.

"The ever-living waters heal gods rapidly. Colonel Angelos will take a little longer." Oceanus added more water to the cup and gave it to me. "Have some, goddaughter."

"Goddaughter?" I asked.

"Your mother asked me to care for you, so drink up."

"But I feel all right."

Oceanus lightly gripped my upper arm where my cuff had been. A soothing, tepid trickle flowed into the bones there and eased the achiness I had been carrying. The sensation disappeared when he removed his touch.

"Hera, you carry your pain with meekness, but the effects of the underworld linger. You must heal and rest before battle."

I wanted to ask what he had done to my arm—and if he could please do it to my lower back, which ached after carrying Poseidon—but I asked a more pressing question: "What battle?"

"Drink first," Oceanus replied, "then we will meet the others."

"Good," Hades said. "I have questions about what has been happening in the mortal realm for the gates of the underworld to be jammed with souls."

Poseidon got to his feet. "I'm ready to go."

"Change out of those wet clothes first," Oceanus said, indicating a folding room divider in the corner.

My brothers took turns behind the changing divider while I sipped the ever-living waters. The taste was sweet and refreshing. The aching in my bones went away so they no longer felt brittle. I thought about pouring more down Theo's throat while Oceanus wasn't paying attention, but if he said Theo didn't need more, I believed him. As it was, Theo slept peacefully, and the decay that had rotted at him was fading.

Poseidon came out from behind the divider carrying his sandals. He sat to put them on, and I saw a mark on his heel.

"I have a scar like that too," I said. "As do our sisters."

Hades took off his sandal and showed us the bottom of his foot. "It seems we all do."

The scar, from being pricked by Cronus's sickle, was evidence of his divesting us of our Titan strengths, draining them and taking them into himself.

Hades changed and strolled out. I almost didn't recognize him with so much clothing on. Then it was my turn. The chiton and cloak waiting for me were clean and warm. My set of clothes included my helmet. I put it on as I reemerged.

"You two go ahead," Oceanus said. "Hera and I will give Colonel Angelos a little longer to rouse. Hades, you know the way to the war room."

Hades patted him on the shoulder. "It's good to see you again, Uncle."

"And you," Oceanus replied.

Poseidon picked up the packages from the Cyclopes and paused at the doorway. "Hera, are you good without us?"

I pretended I was comfortable alone with our uncle, but when they left, I did feel somewhat disoriented. I perched on the edge of the cot and held Theo's hand.

"Your mother told me much about you," Oceanus said.

"Rhea talks about me too freely."

"I was referring to Stavra," he replied, and my chin jerked up. "I helped her protect you and your sisters from Cronus, in particular you, her shooting star. Stavra asked me to be your godfather."

"I thought that was Rhea," I replied.

"You're very blessed to have two mothers who believe in you."

"Which one am I like?" I asked, my throat tightening. "Am I the mortal woman or the Titaness?"

"Why must you be one or the other? Your mortal half makes you more of a goddess, not less." Oceanus threaded his fingers together. "Bring your histories together, like a marriage."

"Marriage," I scoffed.

"True marriage is an equal partnership. A love that binds forever."

Thinking of Theo, my face flushed.

"The colonel makes a fine partner for you. He does not hold you back, nor does he direct you in what to do. He supports your choices. For any man or god, that is respect, love, and most of all, trust. He, as well as your mothers, has shown you how you deserve to be treated by everyone, including yourself."

I rubbed a palm over my heart. "I miss Stavra. She knew me better than anyone."

"Your value is not in how others treat you but in how you treat yourself. We must believe in ourselves first or there is nothing anyone can say, Titan or mortal, that we will believe." Oceanus pointed at my glove. "That adamant strengthens what is already there. Whether you knew it or not, you have always been a goddess, a Titaness—a leader. Your family and friends follow you. Your mothers understood that your true strength is in making heroes, Hera."

"What?" I asked, equally confused and astonished.

"Think of everything your family has done for you."

"For me? No, they do it for Zeus and the prophecy. I'm here to help him rise."

"If you're told a lie often enough, you begin to believe it's true. Your belief in that prophecy makes it real to yourself and others. They follow you and whoever you serve." Oceanus touched the scar across his chest. "My brother Cronus gave me this for not following him. All my brothers turned on me and made me an outcast and their enemy.

My whole family came to live here alone, and then Rhea found me. She wept over her first child, Hestia, and her future children. She knew you would all suffer at her husband's hand. Together, with the aid of our mother, Gaea, we devised a plan. We knew a prophecy that mimicked the tale Cronus perpetuated, about a youngest son overthrowing his father, would haunt him. The strongest stories are built upon truth."

"I don't understand," I said. "The oracles told me Zeus would overthrow Cronus. I heard the prophecy directly from them."

"Zeus believes the prophecy because others do, but no matter how many times you hear a lie, it still doesn't make it true." Oceanus took my lioness arm cuff out of his pocket. "The oracles repeated what Gaea told them to say."

"Are you saying the prophecy is a lie?"

Oceanus put the cuff back where it belonged, on my arm. "In order to dethrone Cronus, it was a necessary diversion from the truth."

"That's the same as a lie."

"Not if it comes true."

The lingering sweetness of the living waters soured in my mouth. Without the prophecy, we had no guarantee of winning. What was I even doing here? Why had I risked Theo's life and gone to the underworld? My belly pitched and curdled. How could I have done all this— risked *everything*—when it was not our fate to unseat Cronus? When he was just as likely to prevail as we were?

Theo moaned and opened his eyes. "I feel like I'm dying."

"Not anymore." I put on a happy face as I helped him sit up, and then I gently pressed my lips to his, savoring their softness. "You cannot ever die on me. All right?"

"I'll do my best." He scanned his hands for signs of decay and found none. "It appears I've been healed."

"Oceanus saved you."

Theo bowed his head to the Titan of the sea. "I'm in your debt."

"I did it for my goddaughter," Oceanus replied. "Hera cares a great deal for you, Colonel. You're fortunate to have her."

"Yes, I am." Theo touched my glove. "This is new."

"It's adamant. It helps me summon stars. They're never too far away now."

He threaded his fingers through my gloved hand. "Hera, goddess and star summoner."

Oceanus strode to the doorway. "Colonel Angelos, are you well enough to walk unassisted?"

Theo lowered his feet to the ground and stood. "I can manage."

"The effects of the underworld are gone, but they will be reversed should you ever go back. You would not survive another journey to Tartarus. Your soul would perish there. Do you understand what that means?" Oceanus asked. Theo and I winced. It meant he would be Forgotten. "Good. Change quickly, and then we will go."

I helped Theo behind the folding screen to dress. He didn't need my assistance, but I wanted to check him over and see that all the rot was gone. No part of him was left unhealed.

"You're really feeling better?" I asked.

"Yes." He slid his hand up the side of my face and kissed me. "All of me still works like before."

"I noticed." I kissed him back, and then heard Oceanus clear his throat.

Theo finished dressing in the leathers and armor set out for him. Along with his clean clothes were a sword and a shield, both of which were engraved with Prometheus's crest of a goddess bearing up the weight of the sun.

"Come," Oceanus said. "They're waiting."

Theo fell into step beside me without any indication of lingering weakness. My relief was so great, I had nearly forgotten what Oceanus said about the prophecy.

A lie. The whole thing was a lie . . .

"Where are we going?" Theo asked.

"The war room," I replied.

"What happened while we were gone?"

"We're about to find out."

Oceanus directed us down the torchlit stone corridors to a double set of doors at the far end. Upon our approach, two armed guards opened them and invited us into a large gathering hall with a huge hearth and a long rectangular table in the center. Seated around the table were many familiar faces, including my sisters, Poseidon, Hades, Styx, and the stunning blonde twin goddesses, Leto and Asteria. Helios, Eos, and Selene were markedly absent. Among them were others I didn't recognize, including two young girls about eight years old. One was sitting with Asteria, and the other was with a muscular man on the far side of the room at the head of the table. The well-built man, who must have been in his twenties, had bushy black hair, a beard, and remarkably bright-blue eyes like Oceanus. I thought he might have been Oceanus's son, but then he put on a silly grin, and my feet stuttered to a halt.

"Zeus?" I breathed.

"Hera!" He rushed over and scooped me up in a lung-cracking hug. "They told me you'd arrived. You're as beautiful as ever."

"You've . . . changed." Nothing about him was boyish anymore. This was the man I had seen in my vision all those years ago. That vision couldn't have been concocted like the prophecy, could it? My imagination was good but not that good.

"I have someone for you to meet." Zeus waved to the little girl beside him. She came forward and stared up at me solemnly. "This is my daughter, Athena."

"Your . . . who?"

"We haven't told her yet," Hestia said, rising from her chair.

"Told me what?"

"They explained it to me, right before you joined us," Poseidon said, rubbing at his face. "We were in the underworld maybe . . . what, a day? As Prometheus warned us, time moves slower down there, much slower than the mortal realm."

"How long were we gone according to the mortal realm?" I asked.

"A little over nine years," Zeus replied, patting the girl on the head.

I could not comprehend what I was seeing or hearing. "You're a *father*?"

"Athena is my little warrior," he said proudly. The girl carried a modified short sword at her side and a bow slung across her back. Everyone in the room wore battle attire.

"Years," I breathed. "Nine years."

Theo pulled out a chair for me. I sank down into it with my body feeling far, far away. Though he seemed to take the news of the time lapse in stride, I knew him well enough to know that he would put aside his emotions to deal with the present, which—considering this monumental gathering of second-generation and first-generation Titans—was of great importance.

"Where is Helios?" Theo asked.

"Still captive," Hestia replied.

"And the plagues?"

"Worse than ever," Demeter murmured. "Cronus has starved most people out of their villages. They've fled to the main cities and banded together for safety and food. Most everyone in Thessaly has gone to Othrys, but they're no longer accepting refugees. People are turned away and left to starve."

Hades rolled his hands into fists. "That explains why the gates to the underworld are inundated with the dead."

I dropped my chin to my chest, light-headed from all this news.

"Give yourself time, Hera," Hestia said, her tone brimming with compassion. "This is a lot all at once."

They pitied me, but their collective stares also told me they were impatient to discuss the reason for this meeting. I had no doubt it wasn't to welcome us back. I straightened in my chair and gave my attention to Zeus. "What else did we miss?"

He formed a steeple with his hands and pressed them to his lips. "We've been at Fort Admiral almost seven years. Soon after you left, General Atlas laid siege to Prometheus's keep. Demeter kept us supplied with food for nearly two years, but when the general dried up our water supply, we were forced to seek shelter elsewhere. Metis, Prometheus, and Epimetheus fought the general by anticipating his strategy so we could escape. We made it to a ship where Styx met us, and then with directions from Rhea, we sailed here. We, the Upstart Gods, have coordinated our attacks against the Early Gods from Fort Admiral ever since."

"Early and Upstart?" Hades asked.

"That's what we call the two sides," Zeus explained. "The Early Gods are closing in on us each day. We were sending messengers back and forth with our allies, but even that's not safe anymore. Recently, all communication has stopped."

"Communication with who?" Theo asked.

"Mother's liege. Until nine moons ago, they kept us apprised of events outside these walls, but without word, and with Helios captured and Metis and Prometheus gone, we are left mostly blind."

"What about Selene and Eos?" I asked.

"Hyperion forbade them to assist us. He's still supplying food to the Early Gods in exchange for immunity, so he will not let his children stand with us, especially after what happened to Helios."

"With the lack of sunlight, the world has shriveled," Demeter said. "They hold Helios in chains and force him to ride his daily journey across the sky while blindfolded."

"All right," Hades said, surveying everyone at the table. "So what's the plan? How do we set things right again?"

Zeus tilted his head a fraction. "Rhea said Hera would bring the solution."

"What?" Hades, Poseidon, and I all said at the same time.

"Where is Rhea?" Theo asked. "When did you last see her?"

"Not for a few years." Zeus squeezed his eyebrows together. "Hecate here has a gift for seeing, like Metis and Prometheus."

Asteria stroked her daughter's midnight hair. "Go ahead, dearest," Asteria said. "You can tell them."

The girl buried her face against her mother's shoulder. Hecate's father, Perses, was one of the Titans who held Helios captive.

"She's shy," Asteria replied. "You tell them what she saw, Zeus."

He cranked his jaw from side to side, as though fighting the words. "Hecate had a dream. She saw Cronus discover that Rhea was gathering allies against him."

"And?" Hades pressed.

Hecate lifted her head from her mother's shoulder. Her voice was small and bleak. "Cronus took Rhea captive and punished her."

Poseidon turned on Zeus. "What did he do to our mother?"

Zeus's lips pulled back in disgust. "He did the same thing to her that he did to all of his children, except me."

The tiny scar on the bottom of my foot suddenly itched. Poseidon realized at the same time and swore under his breath, but it was Hades who said it aloud.

"That bastard turned our mother mortal."

17

The war room grew quiet as everyone arrived at the same realization: Rhea had been divested of her Titan strengths. She would not be able to help us now. I may not have agreed with Rhea's lofty expectations of me, but at least she had been someone influential on our side.

"Cronus is despicable," Poseidon spat. "Rhea is the mother of his children."

"He hates us, his children," Hades replied flatly. "Why not her as well?"

"I'm surprised he hasn't cast her down into the pits of Tartarus like he threatened to do to us," Hestia said.

But Poseidon, Hades, and I were not surprised.

"Rhea is well liked in the underworld," I explained. "She's known there for delivering Uranus to Tartarus."

"Tethys went with her," Oceanus said, his demeanor solemn. "That was a long time ago."

"Where is your wife?" I asked.

"I haven't seen her since she left to meet up with Aphrodite and exchange information about the Early Gods. The goddess of love had gone to the Telchines for protection from Cronus. The tribe betrayed her. A messenger told us that Aphrodite and Tethys were set upon by

Perses and his crew. They captured Tethys, but Aphrodite got away. My wife is being held with Rhea and Helios."

The despair in the war room was absolute. They had been waiting for my arrival, but my only solution to end the suffering of our imprisoned family members, and all humankind, was to spare as many of us as possible by turning ourselves in.

Theo nudged me under the table. "The packages."

"The . . . ? Oh." Rhea had coordinated with the Cyclopes to provide us methods of defense. "Rhea arranged for these to be made for us," I said to the group. "Hades was living in the underworld on an assignment from her to oversee their construction." I handed the packages to Demeter, Hestia, and Zeus. "I don't know if this is the answer you've been waiting for, but these were made especially for you."

Demeter opened her package. Inside was a bow. She stood up to use it, her excitement concealed behind a mask of wonder. She pulled back on the string and paused. Setting it down, she checked the parchment. "The arrows are missing."

"Let me see," Hestia said. She, too, searched the package. "She's right. Could the Cyclopes have forgotten them?"

Hades tapped a long fingernail to the end of his nose. "I don't imagine Arges has ever forgotten anything."

I wouldn't think so either. The Cyclopes had been meticulous in their craftsmanship.

"This explains why Rhea told me to hold on to these for a future day." Oceanus took some arrows out of a box on top of the hearth. "They're adamant. The Telchines gave them to Rhea as a gift."

Demeter armed her bow with one of the silver shafts, aimed at a chair across the room, and let it fly. The arrow sank into the wood with a satisfying thump. She went to fetch it, but Hades halted her.

"Try calling it back," he said.

Demeter reached out for the arrow. "Like this?"

He released an amiable sigh. "Put some effort into it."

She concentrated harder, and the arrow flew back into her hand. She immediately armed the bow and shot the arrow again. She focused on it, and it returned to her.

Zeus began to open his package, but Hades gave him a scowl that said, *Titanesses first.* Hestia unwrapped hers, and the parchment fell away to reveal a labrys—a double-headed axe. The poll was pointed instead of flat and resembled a stinger.

Picking it up, she seemed bewildered. "This is my weapon?"

"A weapon says a lot about its wielder," Hades replied. "Poseidon has a trident, I have a helm of invisibility, and Hera has a glove that summons stars. Your axe says you're not afraid to get close to your enemy."

"You've never been one to shy away from a fire," I added.

Hestia swung the labrys at Poseidon. He lifted his trident in time to block her blow.

"Good arm," he breathed.

She readjusted her grip, lowering her weapon. "This will do."

Zeus decided that was the end of her turn and opened his gift.

Something shifted in the corner of my eye. Theo looked sharply to the same place as well. Reading each other's alarm, we immediately rose to our feet and drew our weapons.

"What is it?" Asteria asked, hugging her daughter close.

Hecate clung to her mother.

"Someone's here," I said. "Bar the doors."

The guards began to shut the doors, but they wouldn't close. Something on the other side shoved against them. Hades slipped on his helmet and disappeared. We heard footsteps and rustling, and then two invisible people were on the table, wrestling. I caught an elbow to the chin and backed away. Hades reappeared with his arms locked around an unseen person's neck.

"Lelantos," Asteria snapped. "Show yourself."

Her brother struggled. Hades choked him, and then he appeared.

"Spy," Zeus growled.

Poseidon lowered his trident to Lelantos's throat. "Are you alone?"

"Doubtful," Zeus said. He had opened his package. Inside was a quiver of thunder and lightning bolts. They probably functioned the same way as Demeter's arrows, returning to him on demand. He held a lightning bolt to Lelantos's throat. "Hades, can you hold him?"

"Gladly," he replied.

Zeus gestured at my sisters, who stepped forward. Asteria drew both Athena and Hecate against her, pressing one ear each to her shoulder and covering the others with her hands.

Leto leaned over her brother. "I'm sorry it's come to this, brother. Answer their questions and it will be less painful."

She and Asteria marched the girls out of the chamber, and the guards shut the door behind them. Given the speed of these interactions, I presumed they had a plan in case the fort was invaded and were following their training.

Demeter and Hestia leaned over Lelantos. Hestia put her hands on the sides of his face. Lelantos arched against Hades, who held his weight. Hestia's hands glowed. She passed the soul that she sucked out of Lelantos to me, placing it in my glove, and then Demeter put her hands on his arms and revived him, pushing life back into him as she would a plant.

He gasped awake.

"Where are the others?" Zeus asked.

Lelantos clenched his jaw.

Hestia and Demeter repeated the process of removing his soul and resuscitating him. Hestia brought Lelantos to the edge of consciousness, and Demeter revived him. A god couldn't die, so the point of this wasn't to kill him. It was torture.

"This isn't right," I murmured.

"This is war," Poseidon replied.

Zeus stood over Lelantos and threw out his white feathery wings, which made him appear twice as large and very intimidating. "Don't make us hurt you, cousin."

Lelantos spit at Zeus's sandaled feet. "I don't listen to traitors."

Zeus lowered his wings, his stance stiff. Hestia drained away more of Lelantos's soul, pushing him toward unconsciousness, and Demeter reawakened him. They repeated this gruesome torment a fourth time, the light of his soul growing bigger in my gloved hand, and he still would not answer Zeus's questions.

I stepped forward. "Where's Rhea?"

"Locked away," Lelantos rasped.

Finally, an answer.

"And Tethys?" I asked.

"With Rhea."

"Where?"

"The Aeon Palace."

"Who else is there?"

"Who isn't? Crius, Iapetus, and Coeus all stand with the Almighty." Lelantos glanced at Oceanus's scarred chest. "That's what Cronus does to those who don't stand with him. Those of you who stand against him . . . ?" His icy tone made it clear that our consequences would be far worse. "You're fools."

Zeus lowered the thunderbolt to his throat. It flashed, the lightning sizzling. "You're the fool for standing against fate."

I pushed his arm down and resumed my questioning. "How did you find us, Lelantos? Where are the others?"

"You're too late," he sneered. "They're all here."

Everyone tensed. Then we heard it—screaming.

"The children," Zeus said, storming for the door.

Poseidon blocked him. "You mustn't rush out there. You don't know who else is here."

"Zeus, we need a plan," Theo said.

Lelantos laughed coarsely. "Here's your plan: Turn over Hera. Give her to us, and we will leave you alone."

"Why Hera?" Demeter demanded.

"Those are our orders from the Almighty."

The screaming outside escalated.

"I'll go with them," I said.

"Hera, no," Zeus replied.

Lelantos laughed another sinister chuckle.

"Enough of this." Hestia sucked at his soul until he passed out, then handed me the golden orb, the total collection of which vibrated hotly in my gloved hand.

Demeter turned her back to Lelantos. "We must go. We cannot stay here."

Hades released Lelantos, leaving him prostrate on the table. Styx opened a passageway into a tunnel at the far side of the room by the hearth. Another scream came from the corridor, directly outside the door, followed by a male voice.

"Come out or we will deliver your daughters to Cronus!"

I recognized Pallas's voice. The god of battle and warcraft did not bluff.

Zeus's chest pumped hard. He wanted to protect the girls, but whether the prophecy was true or not, others believed in it—in him. More importantly, he believed he was destined to rule as the Ruler of the Titans, and if I agreed with him, people would follow us.

"Hera," Demeter said. In that one word, I heard a plea. We could not let any girl be taken to Cronus the way our mother and Cleora had. This time, we could do something about it.

"Cover me?" I asked.

Demeter sang her reply: "Al-ways."

Theo positioned himself beside the door, out of sight. I opened the door inward. Pallas held Athena on the other side. The little girl held herself with the grace of a goddess and the confidence of a Titaness.

"A man once held me like that when I was a girl," I said.

"Oh?" Pallas replied.

"He's dead now."

Pallas chuckled. "You don't even have a weapon."

"No, but I do." Hades voice came from between us, and then he struck Pallas in the nose. The god let go of Athena, and the girl ran to her father.

Demeter shot an arrow into Pallas's chest. "I never got to do that to the man who hurt my sister."

Athena took the shield from Theo, walked over to Pallas, and slammed it down on his throat. He drooped to the floor, moaning, and Athena passed the shield back to Theo. I almost told her she might regret her ruthlessness one day, but I doubted she would.

Zeus grabbed his daughter and drew her into the chamber. Arrows zipped at us from down the corridor, accompanied by shouts from Menoetius and Perses. Perses had found his wife, Asteria, and their daughter, Hecate. They held Leto captive, as well, at the far end of the corridor.

We shut ourselves back in the war room.

"Asteria?" Zeus asked.

"Her husband has her, their daughter, and Leto."

"I will hold them back." Oceanus picked up the huge table and set it in front of the door. Then he grew to his first-generation Titan height, double his original size, and leaned his shoulder against it. "Go."

"Father, be careful," Styx said.

We took turns going into the tunnel.

Menoetius knocked the door down. The bull-like god charged at Oceanus, slamming him into the wall.

"Hera, come on!" Theo cried.

A surge of anger boiled up inside me. I lifted the soul in my hand and threw it at Menoetius. It struck him in the chest and propelled him out the door. I ran back for Oceanus, hefting him to his feet. He had shrunk back to his normal size.

"What are you doing?" he asked. "Go."

"I won't leave my godfather behind."

We hobbled into the long tunnel. The ground inclined downward until we exited to the black-sand shore below the fort. A trireme was moored at a dock in a narrow inlet nearby. Everyone ahead of us was climbing aboard. Poseidon stood at the stern and extended his trident over the colorless ocean, preparing to disembark. The others raised the bow stones and tied them up astern.

Thunderheads stirred, and the ground rumbled. Oceanus paused and peered up the cliff face. The First House's army filled the ramparts of Fort Admiral and was lined up in formation outside its gate. A hulking liege man shod in golden armor led the troops. General Atlas was accompanied by an even more imposing figure.

My heart froze.

Cronus.

My father wore shiny black armor that complemented his outstretched wings. In his right hand, he held his sickle, except it was different than I recalled. The smooth, curved blade was now double sided, with ragged edges.

The beach beneath our feet shook harder.

"Hurry," Oceanus cried, pushing me onward.

I sprinted up the gangplank and leaped aboard the black-tarred ship. Oceanus raised a wave taller than the trireme and hurled it at the cliff from the open sea. The wave crashed over the liege men and knocked them aside. Most were dragged over the cliff in the receding waters and swept out to sea. General Atlas and Cronus withstood the attack as though they were immovable towers of adamant.

Hades rubbed at the tattoos on his chest. "Is that . . . ?"

"Yes," Poseidon said, the veins beating a visible pulse beneath his skin.

"How did he find us?" Demeter breathed.

Hestia's fingers trembled as she set her shoulders. "He can throw himself to the crows."

"Hera!" Cronus bellowed. "End this now! Come to me."

"Don't respond," Theo said. "No matter what you do, we're headed toward the shameless butchery of war. Poseidon, we must go."

"No," Zeus snapped. "He cannot threaten my family—my daughter—without consequences."

He opened his wings and launched into the sky.

"Zeus, don't!" I yelled, but my plea was swallowed up by the wind.

Zeus tossed a thunderbolt like a spear at Cronus. General Atlas reached out in front of his ruler and caught it in his fist. He raised the thunderbolt over his head and grinned viciously. Zeus hurtled another thunderbolt at them, and again, the general caught it.

With both thunderbolts in hand, Atlas leaped down from the cliff and landed on the beach in front of Oceanus. The god of the sea summoned another wave, but before it could collide with the shore, the general struck him straight through the chest with both thunderbolts.

"No!" Styx cried, and ran for her father on the beach.

Cronus tossed his sickle at Zeus. It whirled through the sky faster than lightning. This was not the sickle that pricked my heel as an infant. Its handle struck Zeus in the chest, and he plunged toward the sea.

I threw open my wings and took off. The sickle returned to its master, whirling like a star cut from a sword. Above the jumping whitecaps, I caught Zeus and brought him to the deck of the ship.

Atlas loomed over Oceanus, pressing the thunderbolts further into his chest, until they poked out the other side. They would not kill him, but they could weaken him forever. Styx had almost reached them. She needed help.

I spread my wings again. High on the cliff, my father waited, patient in his brutality. My fury grew as wide as my wingspan.

"Hera." Theo pressed his lower lip down until it reached his chin. "But that sickle . . ."

"I'll be careful."

"I know you will."

I took off for the beach. Styx arrived before me. She slammed Atlas into the cliff wall, picked up Oceanus, and dived into the depthless sea with him.

Cronus rose into the sky on wings black as night and cast his sickle at me like a flash of lightning. I extended my gloved hand to catch it, but I misjudged its rotation, and the handle struck my chest too, throwing me back into the dawn sky. Hestia and Demeter flew up, caught me, and lowered me to the deck of the trireme, gasping and coughing.

"Styx?" I scratched out.

"Gone with Oceanus," Demeter replied.

"They will be all right," Zeus added.

I begged the stars for that to be true.

Poseidon raised his trident, and a mighty wave lifted the ship. Born on the backs of water horses, we sped away from shore, out to the drenching ways of the sea.

Hades and Hestia took off into the sky, and the two of them monitored the thunderheads for any sign of pursuit. For good measure, Demeter shot her unerring arrows back at shore, but they pinged off Atlas's and Cronus's armor and came zooming back to her.

I took my stand at the stern and gave the battle cry of fifty soldiers. I wanted my father to hear me, to know that this was far from over.

A flash of lightning illuminated the gleam of Cronus's sickle. The Almighty did not pursue us, a choice that left a pit in my stomach deeper than Tartarus as we sailed away into a storm of flashing brume over uneasy waters.

18

Daytime diminished to a hazy twilight as a veil draped over the sun, muting its effulgence. The eclipse was one of the most depressing sights I had ever seen. I tried not to think of poor Helios, trapped in chains, destined to soar over the earth, day in and day out for all eternity, with no relief. And I was furious that Cronus hadn't sustained a single scratch in battle. Under the light of the blinded sun, victory felt further away than ever.

We voyaged to the only safe place we could—Crete, in the southern isles. We had been on the water for several days. All the while, a storm had pursued us, conjured by Zeus and his terrible mood. Morale was low as we approached the shoreline of the secluded isle of Zeus's birth. Ida Mountain was a comfort in the distance. We rowed to shore in smaller boats and trekked up the surf onto warm sand. Demeter dragged a rig ashore with Poseidon.

"I detest the sea," she said.

"'Detest' is a strong word," Poseidon replied.

"You're right . . . I *hate* the sea."

Theo and I hauled our own boat ashore, and then he pulled me against him for a kiss. "We made it back to Crete," he murmured against my lips.

"So we did."

I tangled my fingers in the hair at the nape of his neck. Demeter made a disgusted choking noise. Hestia elbowed her in the side, and then I caught Zeus monitoring Theo and me. I didn't know why his stern expression bothered me, but I let go of Theo and finished hauling our boat up the beach.

Euboea and her warriors greeted us. She embraced me with arms that were strong from wrestling, reeling in fishing nets, and throwing spears. She was older, with attractive wrinkles around her eyes and mouth, and several streaks of white hair. I had missed nine years in the mortal realm, and Euboea's aging forced me to accept that it was time I was sorry to have missed.

"I heard you were gone to the underworld," Euboea said.

"I came back recently, and then Cronus discovered us at Fort Admiral."

"How?"

"We don't know."

The seasoned warrior glowered at the eclipse. "Nothing escapes the eye of the sun. Let's go."

We followed the path through the forest. The all-female tribe was reticent to take in males, but after a brief explanation from Zeus that Poseidon and Hades were our brothers, they were welcomed, and the women immediately recognized Theo from the time we had spent here before.

Warriors milled about, doing their work. The cult appeared unscathed by the horrors of the outside world.

"You're thriving," Demeter noted.

"Crete has been practically untouched by the plagues," Euboea replied. "A gift from Rhea. She had the Telchines cast a protective enchantment over the isle after she delivered Zeus on Mount Othrys. Her forethought has protected us from many outside storms." Euboea directed us to tents, and no one gave any complaint. "We'll celebrate your arrival tonight."

"You needn't do that," Demeter said.

"Let them do whatever they'd like," Hades countered. His eyes roamed over warrior after warrior. The underworld didn't have many women that weren't dead.

"It's not only for you," Euboea explained. "We have another honored guest. The festivities commence at sundown. Get lots of sleep. You remember how we like to celebrate."

I remembered copious amounts of wine spiked with opium, and women dancing around a fire. Good clean revelry.

"We'll be ready," I said.

Theo and I were given our own tent. He helped me out of my armor, uncovering the bruises across my chest.

"Cronus's sickle has been changed," I said.

"Enhanced, you mean. The Telchines have chosen a side, it would seem."

"That's my assumption as well."

I lay down, and Theo was immediately at my side with his arms around me. He hummed a lullaby, easing me into a blissful daze between wakefulness and sleep. For the first time in I could not say how long, I fell asleep and did not worry about what I might dream.

Drums began the celebration, waking me to a drowsy haze. I didn't recall drifting off. My exhaustion had been utterly complete. Theo's arms were still around me. I turned over, facing him, and planted a wet kiss on his nose. He groaned groggily.

"Ready to dance?" I asked.

"You've seen me dance, yet you're still asking?"

"You don't have to be good at dancing to enjoy it." I kissed his right cheek and then his left. "Remember how I let you hold my hips as you swayed against me?"

He did so again, nuzzling his bearded chin against my neck. "I don't need to dance to do that anymore."

Before long, his weight was on top of me, and he was about to fill me up.

A shuffle sounded at the door, and then Zeus's voice. "Hera? We're getting started."

Theo rested his forehead near my ear. "Maybe if we're quiet, he'll go away."

"I'm never quiet with you." I kissed him and ran my hand down his chest. He groaned when I reached as far as I could touch.

"Hera?" Zeus said louder. "We need to speak."

I drew Theo's earlobe into my mouth with my teeth. "I *need* something."

"It sounds serious," Theo said, swaying against me.

"Everything is serious."

Neither of us wanted to stop. We moved against each other, our bodies acting and reacting, but then Theo rolled off me.

"Curse your restraint," I said.

"Don't misunderstand me," he replied, pulling on his underclothes. "I'd like to finish this later."

"Finally, something good to anticipate."

I rose and slipped into my chiton. Before I could finish the tie, Theo slid in front of me, took my breast in his hand, and lowered his lips to my nipple. I moaned. He took that as encouragement to kiss my other breast. Zeus still waited outside, the falling sun casting his shadow against the tent. Theo leaned back too soon, and I kissed his lips, which were warm from my skin. We must have been wearing silly expressions as we stepped out of the tent, because Zeus scowled.

"Colonel Angelos," he said.

"Your Excellency," Theo replied, bowing. "Until later, Hera."

I returned his smoldering stare with my own, and Theo strode away as though he owned the world.

Zeus scoffed. "Until later," he said, mimicking Theo's deep voice, and then batted his eyelashes in a poor imitation of me. "You two are sickening."

"You may be a fully grown man now, but you don't act like one."

"You left me outside the tent while you finished whatever you two were doing in there." Zeus's nose creased in disgust.

"Since when are you a prude?" I asked.

"Since I became a father."

Now I scoffed. "Right. You've suddenly lost all urge in your loins."

Zeus noticed my strap was askew and adjusted it. His voice dipped huskily. "You've never been with a full god. It's bound to be a better experience."

"What a tempting offer," I drawled. "But I'm plenty satisfied."

Zeus laughed roughly, lacking humor and warmth. "I told you this day would come."

"What day?"

"The day you would give yourself to a man. I'm surprised by you, Hera. You've lost your head over a silly little liege man."

"Theo is anything but silly," I countered. "And my feelings for him are none of your concern."

Zeus set his chin obstinately. "You cannot marry him."

"Says who?"

"You'd need Cronus's permission to wed, and since we're divided against him, your ruler would be the next male leader, which is me."

I gaped. "Are you saying you'd deny me marriage to Theo?"

"You yourself said you would never marry," Zeus retorted. "You should expect me to honor your wishes and spare you an eternity of grief."

"My affection for Theo has nothing to do with marriage. It's a commitment of love, a distinct difference that you should understand, considering that you disrespect the bonds of your own, and frequently."

Zeus's eyes flashed with temper. "You're too good for him, Hera. He'll always be beneath you."

"Not always. In fact, before you interrupted, I was very happily beneath him."

His face reddened. "What happened to you? Before you left, you never spoke that way."

"What's happened to *you*? You've forgotten your place, brother. I stand at your side because I wish to be here, not because you own me. Do not abuse my loyalty."

"Are you threatening me?"

"I have no need to threaten you," I countered. "We know who our allies seek for leadership. We know who they really follow."

Zeus's shoulders snapped straight, and his eyes flashed warningly. I shouldn't have said that, but he had insulted Theo, and me, and threatened to take away our choice as to what we did with our future. I couldn't abide that from anyone, particularly not the brother I had given so much to in service.

"Are you conspiring against me?" Zeus demanded.

"What?"

"You met with Oceanus alone, and you had time with Poseidon and Hades in the underworld. You aren't planning to turn on me, are you?" This was not spoken as a plea but a guttural warning. He sounded so much like Cronus, I lost the heart to argue.

"No, Zeus," I answered softly. "I have not and will not turn on you."

He searched my countenance and, finding no deception, relaxed. "My apologies. Your change of heart toward Theo made me wonder if your other allegiances had changed."

That was a tremendous leap, and I couldn't understand the association, but we were on the cusp of the biggest battle of our lives. I understood his unease and insecurity, at least. I spoke as comfortingly as I could. "We will defeat Cronus. You and me, together."

Zeus's blue eyes rose to mine, but they remained hard. "*I* will defeat him. You will follow my orders."

The drumming picked up across the clearing. Our siblings were already drinking and dancing around the bonfire. Theo stood off to the side, conversing with Euboea. Though I didn't feel like celebrating, Zeus wouldn't hear anything I said right now, so I left him to stew in his pride and strode to join my siblings.

Demeter and Hestia twirled with our other brothers. Hades had gone back to wearing scant clothing, his chest bare, and Poseidon was drinking heavily. I knew he enjoyed imbibing, but the amount of wine he had consumed without tipping over was impressive. I tried a sip of Hestia's wine, but the opium in it was too strong. I wanted my wits about me this evening. A disquieting sense of doom hung in the air as the moon rose, something dismal and cloying that only I seemed to sense. Everyone else was deep into their cups, enjoying the brief respite from the rest of the world.

Demeter hooked her arm around my neck. "I was thinking," she said, her words slurred. "You, Hestia, and I should live here. This could be our forever home."

"I've had the same thought."

"You have?" She squeezed me harder around the neck. "It came down to Crete or Mount Olympus. I do love the forests and the mountain air, but I think this island is best. Zeus is partial to Mount Olympus. I have a feeling you're going to have to keep far away from him."

"What? Why?"

She pointed at him staring at me from across the clearing. "I haven't seen him ogle a female like that in nine years—not since you left."

"Oh, please. He's married, and he has a child."

"When have those things interfered with love?" She pinched my bottom playfully and sashayed away to dance with Poseidon, who of everyone here had the most grace and balance. Besides me, of course.

The drums beat, and the warrior women whirled around us. The warmth of their bodies was heady in the firelight, and despite the agitation that I couldn't shake, I swayed along with them to the rhythm.

Zeus joined us, a wine cup in his hand. I had to admit that despite our squabble, it was lovely to have all of us siblings together.

Hades sipped his wine, his attention solidly on the women around him. "Zeus, how did you get so lucky to grow up here? To think I was in the underworld."

"And I was with a tribe of cranky old men," Poseidon added, his lisp more pronounced than usual.

Zeus hardly paid attention to the other women. His gaze wandered over to me again and again. "I was here until Hera came for me," he said.

"In that, you're not alone." Poseidon looped his arm over his brother's shoulders, slurring every other word. "Hera came for me too."

"And me." Hades raised his cup to the moon. "To Hera."

My brothers joined the toast. "To Hera."

I laughed, but my humor was cut short when a woman rode out of the forest on the back of a griffin. The Cretan warriors immediately silenced their drums and dropped to their knees. Hades's and Poseidon's jaws dropped.

Zeus blinked at the woman and spoke under his breath. "Aphrodite."

19

The goddess of love wore a crown of crimson roses, an odd accessory to go with her full body armor. Her voluptuous shape included a generous bosom and rounded hips and thighs. Her blemish-free skin was naturally deep brown. The intricate detail of the roses engraved into her breastplate intrigued me, but more so her velo, a gold mask that resembled the one I had worn most of my mortal life. It had been Stavra's. The cult had adopted it in her name as a show of respect for helping them escape the world of men.

Aphrodite removed her velo, revealing a straight set of ivory teeth. Her plump lips had been stained petal pink, and long, sooty lashes framed her brown eyes. "Upstart Gods," she said, her voice musical. "You've arrived."

Aphrodite was stunning beyond belief, the picture of elegant poise and unquestionable humility. Her beauty required no artifice. It was a pleasure, even a gift, to gaze upon her, like viewing a vivid sunset or hearing a perfectly performed song or witnessing the miraculous birth of a newborn.

The Cretan warriors viewed their goddess's arrival as a signal to end the festivities. They took their leave, except for Euboea and her second- and third-in-command. The rest retired to their tents with their cups of wine, spears and shields and armor set outside, ready at a moment's notice.

Demeter shuffled forward to pet the griffin's bushy mane. The beast leaned into her touch and purred. On the back of the griffin was a birdcage that contained several doves.

Aphrodite dismounted and greeted us each by name, beginning with Hades and ending with Zeus. "I'm staying in your old cave on Ida Mountain," she told him. "It has a lot more women's clothes in it than I expected."

Zeus blushed and cleared his throat. "How long have you been here?"

"Too long." Aphrodite turned her attention to me. "I've been waiting on word from our general."

I pointed at myself. *"Me?"*

"She must mean me," Zeus countered.

"I do not," Aphrodite said, so succinctly that he shut his mouth.

I still didn't understand. "But I'm not—?"

"Rhea said you're the legion's second-in-command," Aphrodite stated curtly. "Since her capture, you're the acting general. Was I misinformed?"

"No," Theo replied, taking my hand in his. "Hera is your general."

Aphrodite appraised him. "You must be Colonel Angelos. Prometheus has told me much about you." She stared down at our linked hands and then cast her gaze to the moon.

I spotted the outline of Selene gliding toward us from her throne above. She landed in the clearing and dismounted her winged horse in one smooth motion. I saw her tears and hurried to embrace her.

"Cousin," I said. "What happened?"

Cronus has sentenced Helios to Tartarus.

"He cannot do that. The sun . . . We all need the sun."

Selene buried her face in my shoulder and wept. I relayed the news to the others.

"It's as I feared," Aphrodite said. "Come, I will tell you what we know."

"We?" Hades asked.

"The legion your mother founded—the Wings of Fury—has been very busy." Aphrodite took the cage of doves off the back of the griffin and carried them to the mess hall, which was bathed in the light of the bonfire and lit by torches. A feast had been set out, including ambrosia and nectar, but no one ate or drank, not even Poseidon. On our way, we stopped by our tents to retrieve our weapons. I fetched my sword, and I still had not taken off my glove.

Selene sat with my siblings and me at one table. She had not yet spoken to me again, or to anyone else that I could tell.

Zeus bounced one knee up and down. He was perturbed about Helios's sentencing, and probably also that Rhea had chosen me as acting general. Aphrodite gave him a long, cool stare. I sort of hoped he would push her, because I wanted to see how the goddess of love responded when vexed. Would she kiss someone to death? Hug them until they suffocated? At present, such thoughts were inappropriate, but I was intimidated by my new role as general and had to distract myself.

"Cronus has gone mad," Hades said, pacing in front of us. "The mortal realm cannot survive without the sun."

"He's forcing us to stop running," Demeter replied.

Hestia ran her finger across one blade of her double-headed axe. "He knows we have no choice but to surrender, or everything on earth dies."

"We choose to fight," Zeus rejoined. "We all knew this day would come."

"My troops are ready when you are," Aphrodite said. "I need only send the messenger doves, and they will meet us wherever we choose."

"How many troops?" Poseidon asked.

"Mortals? A few thousand hoplites." Aphrodite gestured at Demeter. "Thanks to Demeter's seeds that grow in any soil, without sun or water, the people of Eleusis avoided starvation. They worship her now."

Demeter's lips spread slyly. "I'm finally appreciated the way I deserve."

Hestia snorted, and Hades appraised her anew.

"How has Cronus not learned of the hoplite army?" Theo asked.

"They kept themselves hidden by moving only at night," Aphrodite replied. "It isn't safe during the day. Cronus has attained the ultimate spy."

"Oh, gods," Hestia said, covering her eyes with one hand. "Helios."

It took the rest of us a little longer to discern her meaning. Poseidon swore under his breath.

"The god of the sun has been Cronus's spy for some time," Aphrodite confirmed. "I believe that's how they found Fort Admiral."

"He finally gave in," Zeus said miserably.

Big, silent tears rolled down Selene's cheeks.

"But why would Cronus send his best spy to Tartarus?" Poseidon asked. "So long as Helios is in the sky, the Early Gods can find us again and again, unless we only come out at night."

"Perhaps they've seen our numbers grow," Aphrodite replied. "And maybe they knew the Upstart Gods would figure out that Helios had divulged where you were and change your movements to occur only at night, as you said."

Without the sun god brightening the world each day, we had to act fast. "How many Titans do we have on our side?" I asked. "First and second generation?"

"Roughly half their numbers," Aphrodite replied. "The Early Gods have settled in Othrys. Cronus directs General Atlas from there."

"That's why he didn't give chase at Fort Admiral," Theo said. "He wants us to come to him. He wants to keep the higher ground."

It would seem Cronus had the advantage in every respect, but as usual, he was letting his arrogance blind him. "We know the city of Othrys well," I said. "My sisters and I grew up there, as did Theo."

Theo shook his head. "The palace has since been rebuilt. We don't know the new layout."

"As far as we know, he rebuilt it the same, except for the sky tower, which is taller," Zeus said. "Does anyone know the layout besides Colonel Angelos?"

"I do," Hestia replied. "When Oceanus restored my memories, he didn't wipe away anything. I have all my memories from the time I was held captive by Cronus."

Demeter squeezed her forearm. Hestia remembered everything, including what Cronus did to her. I hoped they had discussed what happened while I was gone. I didn't want Hestia to suffer alone. Silence wrought by shame could be very lonely.

"We cannot win from the ground," Zeus said, shaking his head. "We saw what they did with the quakes. They'll destroy the whole city and all the refugees in it to open up the earth and drop us into Tartarus."

I closed my eyes and envisioned the Aeon Palace atop the mountains. They would see us coming from anywhere, no matter how we approached. By ground would be the most dangerous. We would never make it up to the city without being detected. When I opened my eyes, everyone was sizing me up, including Aphrodite. They were waiting on my direction, but what to do?

A little voice inside me replied, *Think like a goddess.* Cronus had the high ground . . . unless we swept it out from under him.

We needn't take over the mountaintop. We needed to knock it down.

"Selene, when are they taking Helios to Tartarus?" I asked.

They left tonight.

"We go to Thessaly now," I announced. "Once Helios is gone, it will be night all the time. They will expect us to react tomorrow, after the sun doesn't rise. Selene, you must go back to your station in the night sky, but first, could you go to the Coral Mansion and seek Hyperion's aid?"

I can ask, but my father will not interfere.

"I don't understand," I said, half growling. "How can he stay out of this? Is his agriculture treaty really more important than his son?"

More than wheat and barley are grown in the east. Ambrosia and nectar are also cultivated there. Cronus would spare my father's territory to preserve the food of the gods, but even that can only shield so much. My father is neutral because he must be, for the good of his family and yours. He still cares for Theo's mother and your half sister. Be grateful they have refuge.

"Petition Eos then, or your mother, Theia," I said. "If they still cannot be convinced to join our ranks, ask them to lend us as many winged horses and chariots as possible."

"Hera, what's going on?" Zeus asked. "What's this about winged horses?"

I cranked my neck from side to side to release the tension at the base. "We're going to attack the Aeon Palace from the ground and the sky. We have our wings and our new adamant weapons. With winged horses, our calvary would be a convincing distraction from a powerful regiment of ground troops. I'll leave the ground attacks to Hades and Demeter. Hestia and Zeus, you fight by air."

"And me?" Poseidon asked.

"The water runs into the city through a river outside the palace. You'll enter that way. It should lead you to the dungeons where Rhea and Tethys are being held." I rested my hand on Theo's knee. "And, of course, you're with me."

"Unless you need me elsewhere," he hedged.

"When do we attack?" Demeter asked.

"Day after tomorrow." I beckoned at Euboea, who waited off to the side. "Notify your troops. Everyone else, prepare the trireme for departure. We set out immediately with as many warriors as we can fit aboard."

"What about Cronus's new weapon?" Hestia asked. "The sickle he used at Fort Admiral was not the one he pricked our feet with."

"I don't know," I replied honestly. "I assume the Telchines crafted it for him."

Poseidon tried to mask a grimace. "That's my guess as well. The Telchines infuse sorcery into their smithing. Until proven otherwise, we must presume Cronus's new sickle could destroy a god."

"We will be prepared." Aphrodite stood, drawing all eyes to her. Every time she was within my sight, I was taken aback by her magnificence. She was like a walking dream. "I'll send the messenger doves and summon the troops from Eleusis, and then I'll fly to the Riphean Mountains and ask more griffins to join us. The leader of their pride has been displeased by the drought that killed their grasslands."

"You speak griffin?" Poseidon asked.

Aphrodite did not appear to think this was peculiar. "Love is a universal language. Hera, where do we gather?"

I turned to Theo. "The closest port to Othrys is too visible, and Eleusis is too long a march."

"The temple," he replied immediately.

"Meet us at the Mother Temple down the mountainside from Othrys by day's end tomorrow," I said.

Aphrodite tilted her chin down. "We will be there, General Hera."

Everyone took that as their cue to leave and prepare to depart. Hades stayed after I signaled for him to remain behind, and Zeus lingered outside the mess hall to talk with his daughter, Athena, who had been waiting for us to finish. Aphrodite and Demeter spoke in private, then Demeter hurried to her tent, and Aphrodite began to release her doves. Hestia walked away with Selene, comforting her.

Hades poured himself more wine. "Tell me what you want, Hera."

"Hades," I replied sweetly. "My dearest, dearest brother."

"Don't 'dearest, dearest brother' me. I know who you prostrate yourself in the name of, and he's not worthy of your support."

"Zeus is under a lot of stress."

"He's borderline narcissistic. You're feeding his ego."

I withheld a soul-deep sigh. "We don't have time for this. I need you to decide whether you're with us. Right now."

"Right now? This is the first good wine I've had in moons. Do you know what wine tastes like in the underworld?"

"I don't."

"Piss. It tastes like piss." Hades gulped down the contents of his cup and let loose an admirably loud burp. "Of course I'm with you, and please make that distinction, because Zeus isn't deserving of anything from me at this point. Did you see the reckless way he attacked Father? He gave no thought to the rest of us."

"I'll speak with him," I promised. "By midnight tomorrow at the latest, I need you outside the gates of Othrys."

"By midnight tomorrow," he muttered, mostly to himself. "But I'm drunk."

I took away his cup, which was difficult, because he put up a decent struggle. He couldn't win against my adamant glove, though.

"Sober up," I said. "I have an important task for you." After checking that everyone else was out of earshot, I told him my plan.

His color had gone green. "I'm regretting that last cup of wine. Hera, it's an ambitious idea, but we're talking about a whole mountain."

"Only the top."

"But the timing. Even if I leave now—"

"It will be close, but you can manage. I'll have your troops ready outside the gates. Just be there by midnight."

Hades muttered to himself about how much he was enjoying the temperate weather and the women, and how he was completely unappreciated. Behind him, the camp had come alive with the sounds of clinking armor and voices calling out orders.

"All right," he grumbled. "I'll do it for Mother."

"For Mother," I agreed. Then, seeing everyone bustling about, fulfilling my orders, my heartbeat sprinted. "You know this is insane, all of this."

"That's why it might work." Hades gave me a brotherly shove, then he jammed his hands behind him, strolled off into the woods, and disappeared into the night.

Zeus wasted no time coming to my side. "You should have consulted me before devising such a risky plan."

"Why?" I was tired despite having slept all day and still miffed that he had interrupted my time alone with Theo. "I'm your general. I'm here to serve you."

"Me or yourself?" he countered. "Do you want the throne?"

"When did *you* decide you wanted the throne?" I shot back. "The Zeus I first met here on Crete desired nothing more than to stay in his cave and drink and fornicate and sleep."

"I've progressed."

"To what?"

His face hardened. "Do not compare me to him."

"To whom?"

"I know you too well for you to play dumb with me, Althea."

"Hera," I corrected. "*General* Hera."

Zeus chewed over his next words, and when he spoke, he surprised me. "It was always you and me, Hera. Always."

I finally felt his hope for our success. He understood that I was truly with him. I slapped on a smile. "Only you and me, and every ally we can convince to fight the God of Gods in the next twenty-four hours."

Zeus stepped in closer, as though to touch me, but stopped. "It all comes with a price. Euboea has already asked that she and her warriors continue to live away from the world of men on Crete, undisturbed."

"That seems like a reasonable request." I thought of my sisters, of Theo, of this place. "I wouldn't mind that life."

Zeus's eyes narrowed. "What life?"

"This one." I laughed at him. "I recall you not wanting to leave Crete."

"You made me aware that I had responsibilities elsewhere."

I held myself still, yet my pulse raced. "My sisters and I have always dreamed of our independence. Since we were children, we began searching for somewhere like this to retire and live out our days."

"You were children, and you thought you were mortal. You know better now." Zeus shifted the topic of conversation. "Athena will stay here with Adrasteia. Poseidon needs help readying the ship. I'll see you on board."

He marched off with copious amounts of attitude. At the far end of the mess hall, Aphrodite still released her doves. I arrived as she took out the last one. Cupping it in her hands, she whispered something and released it to the sky.

"How do they know where to go?" I asked.

"They follow their hearts."

I caught sight of Theo off to the side instructing the kitchen workers to load food for our journey. He noticed me watching and then glanced at our tent and shrugged. We would not be able to finish our encounter in the tent tonight. I gave a partial shrug, and he went back to his task.

"When will you admit you're in love with him?" Aphrodite questioned.

"Pardon?"

"I don't need to be the goddess of love to know you adore him."

"I don't see what this has to do with the war."

"War demands that we fight for what we love: our land, our people, our family." Aphrodite closed the empty birdcage. "When we contend with what's in our hearts, we are lost and stand for nothing."

"I know what I stand for," I replied.

"Does he?" she posed. I thought about that as I escorted her back to the griffin. "You love with your whole heart, Hera. You don't give your heart away to anything or anyone unless you are certain they're worthy. This makes you a trustworthy person to follow. Theo will follow you, fight with you, die for you. Love like that doesn't happen often."

Normally I would ignore such silly sentiments, but coming from Aphrodite herself, for whom countless ballads and poems and stories had been written, they were worth considering.

She patted the griffin's side, and it dipped down so she could climb on its back. "I'll see you on the battlefront."

"I'm coming!" Demeter darted across the clearing, her bow and arrows slung across her back. She hopped on the back of the griffin with Aphrodite. "Hera, I'm going to Eleusis. Aphrodite will drop me off. My mortal army of hoplites and I will meet you at the Mother Temple."

"Your army is well deserved," I replied. "You saved those people."

Her cheeks pinked. "Be careful, Hera."

"You too."

Aphrodite's griffin ran across the clearing, spread its wings, and took off. Demeter waved to me until the night sky swallowed them. Selene had saddled up to leave, and Hestia was seeing her off. As I approached them, the moon goddess's voice entered my mind.

I cannot join you on the battlefront, but I will do what I can to assist you. Wait until my signal to attack.

She told me what she intended to do at midnight tomorrow. I thanked her, and she took off into the night, her winged horse charging into the stars.

"Do you think Hyperion will send aid?" Hestia asked.

"I don't know." I did not add that I feared we would fail without him, because I could not think like that. I had troops to lead.

The armed Cretan warriors had gathered in the clearing and awaited further instructions. Compared with an hour ago, their demeanors were very serious. I stood atop a woodpile and addressed them.

"Thank you for heeding the call to arms," I said. "We depart for the mainland immediately. I know most of you haven't left this place since my mother, Stavra, led you here. Stavra believed in love. *Love gives us wings,* she would say. I hope you will entrust her daughters to lead you back to our homeland. Let us choose valor and pride in each other when the shock of combat comes. We stand as one."

I put on a velo that Euboea had given me, with the same design that the cult and Aphrodite wore, and Hestia did the same. The two of us led the way to the beach, where Zeus, Poseidon, and Theo had finished loading the ship. We boarded the trireme and managed to fit every warrior on deck. Once we were situated, Poseidon propelled us out to sea. I didn't need to encourage the troops to rest up. We all knew that whether the sun rose tomorrow or not, a new day would come, and with it, war.

20

The day arrived without a glorious rosy dawn. The sun truly had been taken from us, leaving the moon as the main fixture in the starlit sky.

Our expedition across the Aegean Sea to Thessaly was uneventful, and now all three hundred or so of us marched with torches through a dying forest toward the Mother Temple. The trees resembled the sickly ones I encountered in the underworld. The drought and harsh weather were visible in their scraggly branches and half-dead foliage. This was not the home from my memories.

Though we had slept on the voyage, many of us still yawned and rubbed at our eyes during the hour-long hike. We were very quiet. The perpetual evening played games with our heads, as we were used to associating night with fatigue and rest.

About ten minutes out from the temple, we stopped at the river to refill our water flasks. Poseidon dipped his trident into a shallow portion and shut his eyes.

"These waters flowed down the mountain through Othrys," he said.

"Yes," I confirmed.

"I'll journey to the city from here."

"Alone?" Zeus asked.

"I won't be alone."

Poseidon faced downriver. He had paused more than once along the trail to listen to the dead woods. I had assumed he was being extra cautious, but across the river, a group of men emerged from the trees. In the lead were Lycus and Scelmis, the sons of the chieftain of the Telchines. Zeus lifted a lightning bolt, and Hestia her axe. Poseidon waved for them to lower their weapons.

"Lycus," he called in greeting. "Where's Megalesius?"

"Cronus took him prisoner."

"Was that before or after you betrayed Aphrodite and Tethys?" I asked.

Lycus grimaced. "We had no choice. We meant to trade them for our father, but we only caught Tethys, so Cronus didn't honor his side of the bargain. He's had our father for several moons."

"So now what?" Zeus demanded. "You've come to capture one of us and turn us in instead?"

"We've come to join the Upstart Gods," Scelmis replied.

Poseidon balked. "Bullshit."

"It's true," Lycus said. "Oceanus's daughter Styx came to us with a message. It's the first time we've heard from our god in decades."

"Is Oceanus all right?" I asked.

Lycus answered me quietly. "Styx said he's badly wounded and will have a long recovery. Oceanus asked her to tell us to find you. We monitored your movements across the sea—Poseidon's unnatural currents were easy to track—and followed you here." Lycus fidgeted with the strap of his satchel. "May we join you?"

I pulled Poseidon aside. "You knew they were following us," I said.

"I sensed them back at the shore."

"Do you trust them?"

"Not entirely, but they do worship Oceanus. They will think twice about crossing their god, and I do think they hope to rescue Chieftain Megalesius. They would be an asset in battle."

Hestia glared across the way at Lycus. He appeared properly intimidated, particularly with her shiny double-headed axe.

"We can tell you about Cronus's new weapon," Lycus called out. "Styx told us his sickle is different. We believe our father crafted it, and that's why Cronus took him."

"What else do you know?" Hestia asked.

"Not much," Scelmis admitted. "But if our father melted down the adamant and infused it with sorcery, the sickle would be much more dangerous for you."

Lycus opened his pack, showing us that he had brought along the adamant collars and rope he had made. "We can help."

I didn't want their help, but I didn't feel right about sending Poseidon into the city alone, and everyone else was needed elsewhere. "Swear an oath," I said.

"I swear on Oceanus's life that we are your allies," Lycus replied.

I was appeased, mostly. Zeus was not.

"You harm Poseidon, or defy him, or turn on us, and I will personally summon the Erinyes and cheer as they strangle you to death with their scourges," he said. "But if you join us, and we win, you may live on your island, apart from god and man, undisturbed for as long as I reign."

"You have my word too," Scelmis answered.

"I believe them," Poseidon said.

I trusted his assessment of these sorcerers. They had an air of desperation that had driven them from the shelter of their island and into a war.

"We must go," Lycus said. "The river meanders through complicated tunnels. We may not find our way in time if we do not go now."

"He's right," Poseidon replied.

"Do as we planned," I told him. "Theo will meet you in the palace dungeons and let you in."

"What's this?" Zeus inquired.

"We'll discuss it later," I replied.

He clamped his jaw shut, and his eyes burned like licking fire.

Poseidon waded into the river and crossed. The Telchines marched upriver with him, into the eerie woods. Zeus stalked away.

"You should speak with him," Theo said.

"He's acting childish," I replied. Theo held my stare until I gave in. I caught up to Zeus. Before I could speak, he snapped at me.

"Don't silence me like that again in front of our allies."

"I didn't want them to think we were disorganized and didn't have a plan."

He continued his big strides. "What is this 'plan'? I don't recall hearing about it."

"It was decided last night on the ship, when you were asleep. The tunnel to the underground river is behind a sealed gate. Theo knows the layout of the palace, so he offered to sneak down to the dungeons and open the gate to let Poseidon in."

Zeus halted his angry strides. "When it comes to matters such as this, you should always include me. No matter what time of day. Do not exclude me."

"We weren't excluding you. You were asleep, and we didn't want to wake you."

"Stop coddling me, Hera. If you haven't noticed, I'm not a child anymore."

I folded my arms across my chest. "I noticed."

Zeus glowered quizzically. He mumbled something, and then stopped himself and asked, "What will my role be in this 'plan'?"

"You'll stand vigil for Hades outside the city gates."

Zeus paced a bit away and then came back. "I'm to sit on the sidelines? Hera, I must be in battle."

"You'll get your chance. It's more important that you're safe."

"But *I'm* fated to defeat Cronus."

"You're fated to lead the Titans. All of us are here to make that happen."

Zeus stewed on that. "Whose strategy is this? The colonel's?"

"No, it's mine. And since when did you stop calling Theo by his first name?" I waited, but Zeus gave no reply. "We all agreed to protect you. Trust me, when Hades arrives, the two of you will make quite an entrance."

Zeus stayed silent. His accusation yesterday about my ambitions for the throne rubbed at me. It couldn't be further from the truth.

"When this is all over, and you're secure on your throne, I want to go back to the life I had. I have no ambitions other than that."

His shoulders sank in defeat. "It's been a long journey to get to this point. I know that for you, it's been shorter, but for me, it's been nearly ten years."

"It's almost over."

Zeus made a funny expression, his countenance shining with sudden humor. "So you *did* notice that I'm an adult?"

"Did an 'adult' stomp away and make me chase him down?"

He smirked. "What did you first notice about me? Was it my muscled arms and chest?"

"Ugh."

He tapped his finger against his lips in thought. "It was my shoulders. You definitely noticed my shoulders first."

I laughed. His humor was a welcome break from his anger, though his insistence that he be the best warrior in battle had already led to rash decisions. Last night, while he slept, Theo, Poseidon, Hestia, and I had all agreed that it was pivotal to keep Zeus away from the main battle for as long as possible. For his protection as well as ours.

The Mother Temple had been deserted. It was probably abandoned years ago. The gates were wide open, the courtyard was scattered with leaves, and the window shutters hung ajar. A rat scurried in front of us and disappeared into a cracked door. Hestia released a profound sigh and went straight to the outdoor kitchen, where she began to cut up kindling for a fire. It must have been disheartening to see this place fallen to ruins. For her, the temple had been a true home. Both of us had contributed to the household duties, but Hestia had sincerely loved this place, its resident vestals, and the Guild of Gaea, whereas I could hardly wait to leave. To find myself back here was a twist of fate, indeed.

"Spread out," Zeus said. "Check every corner."

A dozen warriors immediately followed his orders. He was more concerned than Hestia and I were. Our journey from the docks had been depressing. The roads, villages, and fields had all been empty. At one time, this land had been resplendent with evergreen foliage and blooming orchards. Each tree and spring had its nymph, and each field a cow or sheep. The roads had been busy with travelers headed up the mountain to Othrys. The mountaintop city glimmered like a cardinal star in the distance. The moon hung over it like an all-seeing eye. The Aeon Palace glowed brightest among the city lights, an eerie sight at midday, when the sun was usually at its peak of glory.

The warriors came back without anything to report, confirming what I had suspected. No one else was here.

While our troops gathered in the courtyard and mess hall to wait for our allies to arrive, I slipped inside the open door to the temple. The hall within displayed two statues, one of Gaea holding the world in her womb like a woman heavy with child, and a nude replica of Cronus. I stopped before the statue of my father and stared up at him. His abuse of innocent lives burned deep inside me. Cronus was weak and craven, yet without the surety of the three oracles' prophecy, he could rule forever. On the eve of leading countless more innocent lives into battle, with no hint of whether fate would choose our side, I felt certain of nothing.

Hestia entered the temple behind me and slowly walked to the statue of Gaea. "Do you remember the last night we spent in the city?" she asked.

"I do. We put on a play for Stavra."

Hestia pursed her lips pensively. "I thought about that night a lot while you were in the underworld. Mother taught us many lessons, but that night has stayed with me more than any other." Hestia rested her palm on the belly of the statue of Gaea. "You might remember what happened differently, and tell your own version, but I recall wishing to tell my story with confidence and bravery. Since then, I've doubted myself plenty, especially when my memory was in pieces. But never, not even once, have I doubted you."

"I didn't ask to be general," I said in a low voice.

Hestia came to stand with me before the statue of our father. "You serve because it must be done. Our Titan birthright doesn't guarantee we will be good goddesses. Simply throwing thunderbolts or stars doesn't make one a god."

I slipped my hand into hers. "For what it's worth, I remember you always being brave."

"I had my moments."

"You had many moments."

Theo appeared in the doorway. "The others are arriving."

Hestia lifted my hand and kissed the back of it. "Hardship and grief will not be ours alone. We will prevail against our father, and once we do, we will have an extraordinary story to tell."

I kissed the back of her hand and let it go.

We stepped outside with Theo and pulled up short. When he had said the others were arriving, I had expected the army of hoplites that was marching into the courtyard. I had not expected them to be accompanied by Eos, the goddess of the dawn, flying in on her winged horse and bringing with her an entire herd of the marvelous animals. The two groups must have met up during their travels, because Demeter flew alongside Eos, and her troops followed without any wonder at the spectacular sight of the dozens of winged horses soaring above them.

The horses landed one after another in the field outside the compound, Demeter in the courtyard. She dismounted her steed. The hoplites entered behind her, men and women of all ages, and despite the plagues they had suffered for almost a decade, they were astonishingly healthy and well fed. The Cretan warriors emerged from the mess hall to greet the hoplites.

"Liege men of Eleusis!" Demeter called out. "Greet my sister Hera, our general."

I stepped forward, and the hoplites stomped their spears to the ground three times. Their armor consisted mostly of worn leathers, their spearheads were dull, and their shields were dented, but they were here.

"Thank you for joining us," I said. "We will bring you sustenance. We have plenty of food and wine for everyone."

Demeter began to hand out supplies with the help of the Cretan warriors. I stepped back again and faced Theo and Hestia.

"What they lack in gear, they will make up for in heart," Hestia said quietly.

Theo rested his hand on the small of my back and spoke into my ear. "We need them only as a distraction. Gaea willing, they will never see battle."

The hoplites' lives depended on Hades meeting us at the city gates by midnight. After traversing the underworld, I was highly aware of their doom should we fail.

Theo spoke in my ear again. "We will not fail them."

He read my mind so clearly, it was a wonder he didn't live inside my head.

As Demeter tended to her flock, Hestia, Theo, and I went out the gates to greet Eos. The goddess of the dawn loitered among the herd that struggled to find greenery to nibble on.

The rosy-haired goddess embraced me with glowing arms. "This is from your little sister," she said, and then moved on to Theo, hugging him next. "And this is from your mother."

After being gone in the undergloom for nine mortal years, I was grateful to hear that Theo's mother and my half sister were well.

"We were hoping you might bring aid," I said. "How did you get Hyperion to agree?"

"I didn't. My father went to the Aeon Palace yesterday evening to plead for Helios, and he hasn't come home." Eos bit her lower lip in consternation. "My mother stayed home to wait for him, but we think something might have happened. She's lending you the horses. My father's oath to Cronus doesn't allow him to take up arms, but it says nothing about lending you his herd."

"We're very sorry about Helios. Please thank your mother for us."

"She said all the thanks she needs is for Zeus to fulfill the prophecy. My mother and father are both ready to retire their domains and turn over the fate of mankind to the Upstart Gods." Eos searched the crowd, her pink skin and clothes a lovely sight in this dreary landscape. "Where is Zeus?"

"I haven't seen him since we arrived," Theo said.

Eos, Hestia, and Theo began to assign riders to the winged horses. I went in search of Zeus.

Near the back of the compound, the kitchen door was wide open, and Zeus was kneeling outside before a cloaked woman. A hood shielded her face. The second I saw her, she froze. I couldn't see past the shadow of her hood, but her whole demeanor stiffened, and then she vanished.

Zeus rose from the ground slowly as though he were an old man and plodded toward me with his head bowed.

"Who was that?" I asked.

He glanced up and saw me then. "Oh, that was Gaea."

"Gaea?" I stuttered. "As in—?"

"As in the mother of the universe," he finished.

I struggled to find the right words after interrupting such a sacred meeting. "What did she want?"

"To make a bargain."

"A bargain . . . with you?"

Zeus made a motion with his shoulders that was part shrug, part roll. "Gaea has her own agenda." He laughed humorlessly. "Doesn't everyone?"

He was rightly overwhelmed. Everyone in our army was dreaming of life after the war, and they all had expectations of their future leader. What could Mother Gaea want?

"Did you make a bargain with her?" I inquired.

Zeus stared off into the woods. "It's a decision I must make. I have many people's futures to consider."

That was a reasonable answer, except it wasn't the entire truth. He was withholding something. "Since when do you lie to me?" I asked.

"All diplomacy requires placation," he answered.

I had always valued Zeus's honesty with me. Maybe if I was truthful, he would tell me what Gaea wanted. "When this is all over, I really want everyone to know the truth about what Rhea and Gaea have done for the good of humankind. The world should know their stories of victory and sacrifice."

"Rhea and Gaea will be remembered, as will you. Whatever you wish will be yours." Zeus kissed my forehead in a way that was both brotherly and yet strangely not, and then he adjusted his quiver of thunderbolts and lightning bolts and strode inside.

I lingered on the outskirts of the perishing woods, afraid that for the second time since I had known him—and the second time today—Zeus had told me a lie.

21

The trek up the mountain was taking too long. Traversing the steep slopes in the dark of night with troops and riders on horseback had set us behind. We had waited for Aphrodite and her troops for as long as possible, but when they didn't arrive at the temple as planned, we had to leave without them to get into position outside the city wall before Selene gave her signal.

Theo and I rode at the front and set an ambitious pace. Zeus was farther back, with Euboea and the Cretan warriors. Hestia stayed near me, but every so often, she took to the sky on her waspy wings to scout out the road ahead. Meanwhile, Demeter was living her best life. The hoplites consistently asked her if she needed water or if she was hungry. I understood that she had spared them from starvation with a handful of seeds, but she was riding a winged horse while they walked on foot and carried heavy shields and spears. I tried not to roll my eyes when she accepted an apple from a handsome man, which he had peeled and cut into equal slices, all while trudging uphill.

I pulled back alongside her. "Demeter, we need to hurry these people along."

"They're going as fast as they can. They already marched from Eleusis today."

"They can rest outside the city gates. We won't get there in time unless we hurry."

Demeter shoved out a sigh. "Fine, but I'm not giving up the foot rub that splendid young man offered me."

"Keep your foot rub but move your troops along."

As I rode to the front of the party again, Demeter called out, "Let's hurry things along, shall we?"

Our pace improved marginally, enough that we might arrive on time. I grew more optimistic as the afternoon wore on, but then Hestia left for her next scouting loop and didn't come right back.

"Hestia should be back by now," I said, handing the reins of my winged horse to Theo. "I'll be back. See that our party maintains this pace."

I launched into the spangled sky on urgent wings. Flying under the eye of the gleaming moon felt like being home, yet it was eerie knowing that it should have been daytime. As I soared over treetops, I spotted a glint of metal below and swooped down. The narrow roadway was lined on both sides by a dense thicket. Hestia stood utterly still in the middle of the road, her axe raised.

"Hes—"

"Shh. Don't move."

I stopped and listened. The elms and tamarisks were in the bitter throes of drought, their brittle branches parched of life. I heard flapping within a skeletal shrubbery and flexed my gloved hand.

A black-winged creature swooped out of the forest. Hestia launched after it on iridescent wings—maybe they were like a dragonfly's?—and slashed out at the creature. It squawked in pain and plummeted to the ground in a dust cloud. Hestia landed over her twitching victim.

I stalked closer, one ear on the too-still thicket. "What is it?"

"Cronus's pet vulture. He adores the wretched thing."

"Why would he send his pet?" I asked.

"It doubles as his spy." Hestia bent over the vulture and glared into its eyes. "Father knows we're coming."

"We knew this would happen eventually."

"Let him know this," Hestia bit out between clenched teeth, lowering her face to the vulture's. "I'm coming for you, Father, and I remember *everything*."

She stood and shoved the pointed end of her axe into the vulture's breast. Then she yanked it out and struck down with the blade, severing its head. As she picked up portions of the carcass and threw them into the bushes, our party marched into view around a bend. We waited as they caught up to us.

"Cronus knows we're coming," I explained to Theo.

"This doesn't change our plans," Hestia added.

"No, it doesn't," Theo agreed.

We had anticipated that this would not be a stealthy approach, but we had some surprises for him, if we could coordinate them in time.

Hestia and I mounted up. I dug my heels into my horse and hastened for Othrys. We didn't scout ahead again. I kept my attention on the road and tried not to think about what other spies might be nearby.

Before my nerves had settled, the city lights of the Aeon Palace burned through the evernight. The effects of this everlasting evening were visible in the yawns and weighted steps of our troops. We were still a fair distance from the gates, but I could smell death ahead. I held up my hand, bringing everyone to a halt.

"We'll stop here. We have an hour or so until midnight."

The troops stopped and congregated in their respective groups. I had still seen no sign of Aphrodite, nor of Hades, and something else felt as though it was missing too. I hopped off my winged horse and wandered around until I realized what it was.

"Euboea?" I asked, stopping among her warriors. "Have you seen Zeus?"

"He told me he was flying ahead to ride with you."

"When was that?"

"Over an hour ago. Didn't you see him?"

I didn't want to raise alarm, so I feigned forgetfulness. "Oh, right. Thanks, Euboea."

"Hera?" she asked, halting me from leaving. "I'm glad you're back."

Sometimes I forgot that I had been in the underworld for nine years. "And I'm glad you're with us."

"There's nowhere else I'd rather be," Euboea said. "You and your sisters are family. You will always have a home with us."

"Thank you, Euboea." Despite my rising concern about Zeus, I gave her a hug before meandering over to Demeter and Hestia. "Have you seen our youngest brother?"

"Not since we left the temple," Demeter said.

"Same," Hestia replied. "Why?"

"I think he's gone."

Demeter yawned into her hand. "Are you certain? Did you check the cavalry?"

From across camp, Theo waved me over. I rushed off without another word. When I arrived at his side, we spoke at the same time: "Zeus isn't here."

"That fool," I breathed.

"When you flew ahead to find Hestia, Zeus asked me questions about how I planned to unseal the gate to the underground river. Then he flew off back to Euboea, or that's what I presumed. You don't think . . . ?"

"I *do* think." I resisted the urge to punch a tree. "That bigheaded, rash, impulsive, attention-seeking imbecile has gone to the palace."

"I'll fetch him."

"No, I'll go."

"Hera . . ."

"He will only listen to me. You know the plan as well as I do. Direct the troops, Colonel."

Theo rubbed at his beard. "But the plan was for no one to approach the palace until Selene gave the signal. You or Zeus could be seen."

"I won't let him get that far." I spread my wings.

Theo shifted on his feet. "I don't like this."

"I will be back before you know it." On the tip of my tongue rested three little words. I waited to see if Theo would say them first. If he did, I would return them in kind. I wasn't afraid of what they meant anymore.

Theo pressed his lips to mine. "I'll be waiting."

I shook my hands out, my nerves vibrating inside my glove. "If I don't come back, you still better knock the mountain to the ground."

"You'll come back."

His faith in me was heady. After kissing him again, I darted into the ashen woods of sallow cypress trees. A gap opened in the treetops, and I took off through it and soared low over the forest toward the city wall.

The reek of decaying flesh grew sickeningly strong nearer to Othrys. All along the ground were stacked bodies, so many I lost count. My mounting fury helped me tamp down my overwhelming need to land somewhere and vomit into a bush. Even liege men bearing the insignia of the First House, and hoplites who had taken up arms in the name of the Almighty, were among the departed. Cronus had abandoned them all, including their wives and children.

My eyes burned with unshed tears. I swallowed them, saving them for when I could fathom the terrible apathy of any being, god or mortal, allowing even one soul to suffer starvation unto death. I remembered all the souls in the land of evening crammed along the riverbanks, packing the bridge, and filling the fields, all waiting for entrance into the underworld. These bodies had belonged to some of those dead. I wished I could have done more for them. Even now, I was sorry I couldn't stop to bury them properly and offer blessings over every body.

I refocused on the city wall ahead. It had been renovated with higher ramparts and watchtowers, as well as the catapults General Atlas relied on. I landed in the shadows outside the gate and surveyed for guards. The reek of death was nearly intolerable. I hoped to see Zeus skulking around, but he was nowhere in sight.

Then I saw it—a gap in the wall. I crept to the opening and crouched to the ground. Tiny shards of a lightning bolt were scattered about my feet.

Zeus, you fool.

I slipped through the gap in the wall. Zeus didn't know the layout of the city, so I traveled the most direct path to the palace, the one I thought he would take. Every business was shuttered or closed. Taverns were in disarray, and the agora had shrunk from many streets' worth of merchants' tents to a handful huddled in one small courtyard. At one time, the bustling outdoor market had been a colorful place of rich smells and booths packed with crates of vegetables, fruit, baked pastries, and freshly caught fish. Now even the stray dogs were so famished and emaciated that they had no strength to growl at me.

I clung to the shadows, darting down alleyways and past huts and shacks with boarded windows. I paused in an alley across from the Aeon Palace. The rebuilt home of the Almighty did not resemble the last one. The former palace had exuded immaculate grandeur, but this fortress was utilitarian, with tiny rectangular windows and fewer balconies and exterior doors, which meant fewer ways to sneak inside.

I searched the wall surrounding the palace and discovered another hole and shards of lightning bolts. My anger for Zeus more than doubled. The stormking was frustratingly unstoppable. His behavior was not brave, it was reckless. I had to find him and get back to the troops before Selene gave her signal.

I slipped through the wall into the palace grounds. The wide-open area had no benches, hedges, trees, or decorative fountains or statues, all of which the previous garden had boasted. Even a sheep would be bored with the flat and empty grounds.

Two guards patrolled ahead. I darted out behind them and ran to the palace. Once they were gone, I flew up the side to the closest balcony. I could see all of Thessaly, including the moonlit Aegean Sea. The entry's door handles had been sawed off. What remained was still hot from the lightning bolt Zeus had used as a blade. I crept into the vacant chamber.

"Zeus?" I whispered.

I padded out of the chamber and down corridor after corridor. The palace was disturbingly empty, with no furniture, wall hangings, or floor coverings anywhere, nothing to admire except a glossy floor and bright wall sconces. It did not resemble a dwelling befitting of any god, let alone the God of Gods.

Since Zeus would be headed to the underground river in the catacombs, I took the grand stairway downward. The next two levels were also bare, but when I finally reached the main floor, maroon tapestries with the Almighty's alpha and omega symbols draped the walls, and sturdy chairs and side tables were set here and there. At the far end of the entry hall, another stairway led to the underground levels. I took the steep steps down the narrow stairwell, into the depths of the palace. The descent was long and arduous. How far below the palace was the next level?

A shadow blocked the stairway. His molten amber eyes shone in the dim.

"Helios?" I asked.

"Yes."

I hurried down the next few steps, rushing to give him a hug. He drew a sword. It wasn't his flaming sword, but he held it with a sneer and unmitigated aggression. I stopped a half-dozen stairs away from him, and my chest fell. His silky tresses had been shaved off, and he had scars across his scalp. His ear piercings were gone, and he had lost so much weight he was gaunt.

"Helios? What happened to you? Selene has been really upset. We were told you had been taken to Tartarus. We've all been so worried."

"Shut up, brazen bitch."

I slowly lowered my gloved hand toward my sword. "I'm Hera. Do you remember me?"

"Don't move." Helios climbed the next stair. "Put your hands up."

"Oh, Helios," I breathed. "What did they do to you?"

He ascended another two steps in a quick lunge. "I said shut up."

"Do you remember Selene? She's your sister. And I'm your—"

Helios whipped his sword up so that it pricked me in the throat. I lifted my hands above my head. His eyes blazed with a hatred that broke my heart.

"I tried to save you," I said. "I don't know what they did to you, but I'm so sorry."

"You will be sorry, but not to me." Helios's smugness was so unlike him. I had to conclude that his mind had been tampered with, or maybe after years of captivity, it had shattered.

Footsteps came down the stairs behind me. Menoetius blocked the way back up to the main floor. The bullish god of warcraft disarmed me of my sword and grinned menacingly.

"Hera, welcome home."

22

Helios held me at sword point while Menoetius took my helmet, breast-plate, and glove. He took special note of my adamant glove, which I pretended didn't bother me, but I could have throttled him when he tried it on. His meaty hand was too big, of course, but that didn't stop the imbecile from shoving his fingers in it several times before putting it in his pocket.

"Where's the rest of your band of brutes?" I asked.

"My brothers-in-arms are no longer required." Menoetius smacked his lips together obnoxiously. "The Almighty has a shiny new guard to help out."

"Bring her to me," Cronus called from below. His soft voice echoed chillingly up the stairwell.

I stared into Helios's daggered glare and saw no part of him that I recognized. He was pure malice. "What did Cronus do to him?" I asked Menoetius.

"Cronus didn't do anything," he replied. "Mnemosyne and Helios had a couple long visits to make the sun god more agreeable. The goddess of memory has an unmatched gift."

Menoetius shoved me down the stairs, with Helios leading the way. I felt as though I was sinking into the earth. I had never heard Menoetius speak so many words at once, and for most of them to be praise for Mnemosyne, who on behalf of Cronus had hurt Hestia, and now Helios, was repulsive.

The Almighty waited for me in a windowless, well-lit throne room devoid of any of the character or nuance that I had come to expect from the God of Gods. This floor was more furnished than the ones above us, though much of it was still plain and functional compared with the grand abode my siblings and I had knocked to the ground. The Early Gods had taken shelter in the lower floors, probably to prevent Selene or Eos from spying on them.

Cronus's stature was precisely as I recalled: medium build and height, with a trim figure and the undeniable air of a seasoned performer that made him impossible to unravel. White flames shone from the Almighty's hair, and his inky, calculating eyes smoldered with the voraciousness of a bird of prey. His intense, penetrating stare emitted no emotion, like a vulture hovering, waiting for its victim to expire. I could never get a true sense of what Cronus was after, and he was *always* after something.

"Menoetius, you may go," Cronus said.

His bullish guard took a step back. "Will Mnemosyne be available soon? She agreed to have a chalice of nectar with me the other day. I haven't seen her since. I was hoping tonight we might—"

"Not tonight, Menoetius." Cronus shooed him. "Go now, and stop asking about Mnemosyne. She's a very busy goddess. When she wants to see you, she will."

Menoetius reddened, then ducked his head and stomped out.

"Hera," he bellowed grandly. "I knew you would come."

"Where are the others?" I asked.

"Others?"

"Hyperion, Iapetus, Coeus, and Crius. I've been told they're here."

Cronus paced over to the wine cask on a table in the corner and poured himself a sizeable portion. "My guards are here, and General

Atlas is never far away." He placed his arm around Helios's shoulders. "I'm especially proud of my new personal guard."

Helios glared at me without blinking.

"You had to compel him to serve you. I pity you when he figures it out."

Cronus released Helios with a breathy chuckle. "Helios is formidable, but in the end, everyone has a cause for surrender. Care for a drink?"

"No." How could he behave as though this were a social call?

"I'm glad to see you've embraced your patronage and no longer go by that mortal name. You held on to it longer than I thought you would." Cronus sipped his drink, his praise fully mocking. "I expect my other children will arrive soon . . . at midnight. Isn't that when Selene said she will give you the signal to attack?"

My heart banged so loudly, I could scarcely hear myself inhale.

"The moon goddess was reluctant to heed me until I threatened to throw her brother into Tartarus. I offered Selene a fair bargain. Helios is spared from Tartarus, and she gets to visit him whenever she wishes. All she had to do was nudge you to come here."

I pried my heavy tongue off the bottom of my mouth. "Selene wouldn't make a bargain with you."

"She would for her brother." Cronus sipped his wine again, his stare fathomless. "Midnight isn't far off. You must be thinking through your strategy: Poseidon arrives from the underground river, Hestia and Zeus swoop in by air, and Demeter and Hades rise up with the ground troops. General Atlas assured me all of your efforts will fail."

The palace could have been sinking down on top of me for how leaden I felt.

Selene had betrayed us. That was the only way Cronus could know our strategy. She had told me once that she would do anything for her siblings, but this? She might as well have sold us to a slaughterhouse.

Cronus drained his cup, his lips stained crimson. "I thank you for finding your missing brothers. You saved me great trouble. Rhea was reluctant to give up their locations."

"Where is my mother?"

"She's your mother now?"

I refused to let him bait me. "I want to see her."

"Spoken like a true goddess." Cronus set down his cup and clasped his hands together eagerly. "Come along, Hera. I'll show you."

Helios accompanied us down a corridor, his fist on the hilt of his sword, and opened a door to a prison cell. The room was full. Rhea, Mnemosyne, and another goddess—Tethys, I presumed—were chained against one wall. Shackled to the opposite wall were the four pillars of the sky—Hyperion, Coeus, Crius, and Iapetus. Their limbs were flimsy, skin pallid, and physiques distressingly frail. They bore ragged burgundy slashes down their forearms, and none of them was conscious. Helios gave no indication that he was aware his father was present, let alone incapacitated. He wore the same irate expression that was so unlike the formerly cheerful god of the sun.

I didn't understand. How were these first-generation Titans being held here? Their chains were not made of adamant. They were made of regular iron, like the ones the Cyclopes and Hecatoncheires wore.

"What have you done to them?" I asked.

"The best smithy in the world enhanced my adamant sickle with sorcery." Cronus touched the wound on Hyperion's arm. "One cut of my sickle can now drain a Titan of their strength . . . and make them mortal."

"Impossible."

"Actually, it is very possible. A Titan's strength cannot be destroyed, only transferred to another mighty vessel."

A warning jabbed my soul. Cronus had done more than divest the Titans and Titanesses of their godliness. He had brought them to their knees.

My voice rattled. "They're your family."

"They're also my subjects." Cronus petted Mnemosyne's head, smoothing down her voluminous red hair. "I've done us all a kindness. Now that they're mortal, we can be a true family under one ruler, one Titan, one god. They will no longer be tempted to compete for my throne. They can live a simple life, a mortal life, without eternal responsibilities or obligations. Toward the end of his service, Helios begged me not to put him back in his chariot. Don't you think Selene would rather spend her evenings at home, sleeping in her bed? And wouldn't the goddess of the dawn prefer to exist for herself, instead of as a bridge between two gods mightier than she is?"

"That's not your choice to make." I had always respected Helios's, Selene's, and Eos's dedication to their domains. The heavens were beloved by all the world, yet Cronus described their duties as a noose around their neck.

He glowered in dissatisfaction. "I thought you would understand the freedom I've given them. They can do as they wish, live where they wish, love who they wish. They are the narrators of their own stories, rather than performers doing destiny's bidding."

I refused to admit that I saw the appeal. I had a choice . . . didn't I? My story was mine to tell, but how much of it had already been dictated?

"What do you desire, Hera?" Cronus asked earnestly. "You don't want someone seated on a throne to assign you a domain and force a mantle of duty on you for the rest of time. Let me take that away. Let me spare you a life of servitude. Let me give you the choice I never had."

Iapetus moaned. I thought the god of mortality might wake, but he remained comatose.

"Did you give your brothers a choice?" I challenged.

Cronus was as remorseless as a scavenger. "My brothers wouldn't confess it, but it was only a matter of time before they all turned on me like Rhea."

"Your paranoia blinds you. You don't know how to be part of a family."

"Is that one of the lies your mother told you?" Cronus grabbed Rhea by the face, squishing her cheeks. "My dear consort, your favorite daughter, Hera, has come to rescue you, but she's too late. You're as mortal as the woman that raised her."

Rhea groaned. Cronus dropped his hold on her, and her head lolled to the side.

"My lioness," he said with a cruel twist of his lips. "Sedated by a simple tonic. How powerful are you now?"

"Rhea is stronger than you'll ever be."

The Almighty nodded once, solemnly but not in agreement. "I imagine you see me the same way I saw Uranus—rash, arrogant, paranoid." Cronus wagged his finger at me. "Don't make the mistake of underestimating me. Oceanus thought I couldn't defeat Uranus. He believed I was incapable of winning."

"Oceanus thought you were incapable of *ruling*. You were never his leader."

Cronus chuckled knowingly. "Always? Never? You reveal your youth by speaking in absolutes. Always and never don't exist. There is only now, and who holds the power."

"Your power has corrupted you," I countered. "You take what you want, and whomever you wish. Even your own daughter."

"Ah, you mean Hestia," he replied, again guiltlessly. "I never partook of her, but I knew it would humble her if she thought I did, so I asked Mnemosyne to plant that lie in her mind."

I wanted to strangle him. "Is that what you were doing to the people you let starve to death? You were teaching them humility?"

"I am the God of Gods. I decide their happiness. That is my role as their ruler. I helped mankind thrive in a true Golden Age."

"And then you plagued them to death."

"No, *you* did. You and your siblings had a choice." Cronus fisted his hands, his façade cracking. "The role of a god is to choose what's good for our subjects. We decide mankind's fate. They worship us, and they follow us, and they die for us. That's the plight of a god."

Cronus reached behind him and drew his sickle from where it was sheathed between his shoulder blades. The shiny, jagged-edged weapon stabbed a spike of fear through me. "Do you really think Zeus would be a better ruler? I would spare you and your precious demigod. Will Zeus? You are not his equal. You are his plaything. He will always seek to control you."

"Is this how you convinced Rhea to fight for you? You pitted her against everyone else?"

Cronus went very still, his nostrils flaring.

"I know she helped you defeat Uranus. You would be nothing—absolutely nothing—without her."

Cronus raised his sickle. "Hold her."

Helios's arms came around me from behind. He squeezed as Cronus strode to me and lifted his sickle to my throat.

"You will always be Hera, daughter of the Almighty, but once you are mortal, you will be as fragile as a lamb."

He backed away with his blade still raised. I shoved uselessly against Helios's grasp as Cronus redirected his blade toward Rhea. He yanked my mother's head back with his free hand. Her eyes remained closed, but her lips parted.

"Do you know how to kill a god?" Cronus posed. "The first thing you do is make them a god no more."

He swiftly drew the blade across Rhea's throat. Her eyes shot open, and she gaped right past him at me.

"Her-a," she gurgled, blood pouring down her throat.

Cronus let her go, and her head drooped to the side.

"No!" I wrestled against Helios, but he held me as my mother's blood spread down the front of her. "No, no, no."

Cronus wiped the blade off on his boot. "You've now lost two mothers because you were too weak to save them."

My lungs hurtled against my ribs so hard, I thought they might snap them. Or perhaps that was my heart, expanding and shrinking, breaking over and over again.

Cronus came before me. "Do something independent for once, Hera. When your siblings arrive, convince them that mortality is the only path to happiness for our family. Do this one final act as a Titaness, and I will let you and your demigod go free."

"Another bargain," I uttered lifelessly.

"Another *choice*."

I summoned my mother's mettle and glared at the Almighty with the heat of a thousand suns. "It doesn't matter how many of us you shrink down so that you can feel bigger, or how many lies you tell yourself. You will never be worthy of the throne."

"You have my temper." He sighed. "This will make you very angry, but as your god and your father, I promise it's for the best. You will be happier as a mortal."

While Helios held me, Cronus stretched my arm out between us and lowered the ragged blade of his sickle toward my skin.

A boom rattled the foundation of the palace, and then a scuffling noise came from outside the door. Another louder explosion blew the door down, and all three of us went stumbling. Poseidon stood in the raining dust and debris. He slammed his trident against the ground, and the earth buckled beneath us. Cronus went reeling again, and Helios and I toppled to the floor. Zeus appeared in the doorway, a thunderbolt in each fist. He cast one at Cronus, who rolled out of the way. The thunderbolt hit the wall, exploding and opening a hole through it. Zeus heaved the second bolt, and it struck Cronus in the chest, throwing him backward through the hole in the wall.

More booms shook the palace.

Poseidon ran to the hole. "He's fled," he said, slamming his trident against the floor.

"Cousin," Zeus exclaimed in relief.

Helios waited until Zeus was close, and then drew his sword and slashed at him. Zeus jumped back too late and took a blow to his chest. The god of the sun rounded on me next. I slowly pushed to my feet.

"Helios, this isn't you," I said. "Cronus tampered with your memory. Your sister Selene bargained with him to save you from Tartarus. We aren't your enemies."

He picked me up by the throat so my tiptoes dangled over the floor and then tossed me. I rolled to a stop, gasping. Poseidon ran at him, but Helios knocked him aside and loomed over Zeus.

"Cronus tortured you," I rasped. "He held you in chains. You lasted longer than any of us would have. You're the strongest of us all. Helios, please don't let him win now."

"Cousin," Zeus said, cradling his wound. He put his bloodied hands out between them. "I won't fight you."

Helios arced down at him with his sword. Poseidon slid in front of Zeus, his trident lengthwise across his chest. Helios's sword struck the adamant and shattered. I jumped on Helios's back and wrapped my arms around his neck. He twisted and squirmed, trying to throw me off. I wrapped my legs around his chest and then opened my wings and flapped hard. The force threw him forward, headlong into the wall. He hit his skull and staggered over, falling to his side, unconscious.

Poseidon sank to his knees before our mother. "How?" he scraped out.

"Cronus's new sickle can turn a god mortal," I explained. "He did that to her . . . and then he did this."

Zeus surveyed the other prisoners, tears gathering in his eyes. "He stole all their Titan strengths?"

We were joined by others. Scelmis and Lycus came in, supporting their father, Chieftain Megalesius. The chieftain appeared as battered as these prisoners.

"We found him in the cell down the corridor," Lycus explained. "He was sedated."

Megalesius let go of his sons and shuffled closer, resting a hand on our mother's head. His chin trembled on withheld tears. "Dearest Rhea. What have I done?"

"Cronus forced you to enhance the sickle," Scelmis said. "It isn't your fault, Father."

The foundation of the palace trembled like the rumbling belly of a beast.

"We need to move the prisoners to safety," I said.

Zeus, Scelmis, and I broke their chains, and Lycus shook them awake, though they remained groggy and confused from the sedative.

"Get them out of the city," I told the Telchines. "They've been through enough."

"I'll conjure a barrier so we can leave unseen," said the chieftain.

Scelmis passed me his satchel. Inside were an enchanted rope and the two adamant collars the Telchines had crafted. "You won't feel the effects unless you touch them."

"Thank you." I put the satchel crosswise over my shoulder.

Poseidon picked up Rhea and passed her to Lycus. "Take our mother too."

"We'll take care of her," Lycus promised.

A loud huffing noise came from behind us. Menoetius stood in the doorway, his chest puffing up and down, his face inflamed. At first, I thought he was preparing to charge, but then I saw the tears in his eyes as he scanned the prisoners.

"The Almighty told me Mnemosyne was preoccupied," he growled. "Did he do this? Did he put her here?"

"He did," I replied. "He captured them all and took their Titan strengths."

"Even Mnemosyne's?"

"I believe so. You were probably next."

Menoetius removed my glove from his pocket. He offered it to me without making eye contact. "This is yours."

I took it back and put it on. He stalked past me, and I tensed as he brushed against my shoulder, but his focus was elsewhere.

"Mnemosyne," he said, pulling her into his big arms.

"Menoetius?" she croaked. The goddess of memory cozied against him and shut her eyes. He held her with tender care.

"I'll help get the prisoners out," Menoetius said. "Mnemosyne is coming with me."

"What about your allegiance to Cronus?" I asked.

"I'll leave his punishment for what he did to his 'allies' to the Upstart Gods," Menoetius replied, stroking Mnemosyne's head.

Zeus slung Helios over his shoulder. Our cousin's true memories were still buried in his mind, and I trusted that, like Hestia, he could be healed.

Poseidon, Zeus, and I climbed to the main floor and out the open front doors. The booms and blasts came from the city wall, where General Atlas and the liege men of the First House contended with Demeter's army of hoplites. We stayed in the shelter of the portico, out of sight. I saw no sign of our air troops, but what I did see caused me to freeze. The midnight sky had no moon.

Across the courtyard, Cronus stood before Selene. He lunged, and his sickle impaled her straight through the chest. She crumpled to the ground, and her voice filled my mind.

Tell my brother and sister that I'm sorry.

The moon goddess's silver radiance dimmed until she was a shadow. A bluish light drifted out of her. Cronus caught it in his fist and shoved it in his mouth. Her Titan strength glowed from inside his cheeks. He swallowed, and it dropped into his chest. There the luminosity spread and brightened his veins until they resembled bolts of lightning.

Cronus rolled his neck from side to side. His arms began to stretch, and his chest expanded. His legs lengthened, and his head swelled. He doubled in size in a heartbeat, and then doubled again . . . and again. His sorcery-enhanced sickle changed proportions to fit his hand, scaling with him, until he reached his apex.

The Almighty towered over the city of Othrys, the top of his head higher than the tallest spire of his palace, his enormity incomprehensible, more immense than any of the Gigantes or Titans. He was no longer just a god. He was a colossus.

23

Cronus's chest heaved as he recovered from his frightful growth spurt, but I doubted his sedentary state would last. We needed to evacuate Othrys now.

"Poseidon, sound the alarm for the refugees to flee the city," I ordered. "They need to get off the mountain as quickly as possible. Then fly to Demeter, outside the city wall, and tell her troops to hold their ground."

"Yes, General." Poseidon flew off into the relentless evening.

"Zeus, we're going to need everyone on our side. Wake Helios."

"What if he still wants to kill me?"

"That's a chance I'm willing to take."

He set our cousin down near the palace doors and patted his cheek. "Wake up, big boy. We need you."

Helios roused. He scowled at Zeus with more bewilderment than ire and then spotted Selene's body across the courtyard.

"Sister," he groaned.

"She tried to save you," Zeus said.

My bones felt hollow as I searched the sky, still half expecting to see the moon. Selene had been a constant in my life. Day or night, she had been there, ever vigilant, ever present.

"I will avenge my sister," Helios choked out.

"*We* will," I replied. "First—do you have an overwhelming desire to kill Zeus?"

"You mean more than usual?" Helios answered. He rubbed at his grief-stricken face. "Except for an awful headache, I feel myself."

"Hera threw you headlong into a wall," Zeus said, hoisting Helios to his feet. "So if you're interested to know who your favorite cousin should be—"

"Another time, perhaps?" I cut in.

Cronus's panting had lessened. He tipped his head up in wonder, examining the sea of astral lights from his new, heavenly height. He tapped a star with his finger. As though cut from a wire, it fell from the sky and plummeted into the cold, bleak Aegean Sea.

The Almighty's chuckle rang out. "No more do the four pillars hold up the sky. I am Cronus, alpha and omega. The heavens are mine to fell."

Helios gripped me for support. "Great Gaea. He's finally done it. He possesses more power than even his father had."

Cronus pinched a constellation, peeling it from the firmament, and let go. Six stars dropped to the earth like autumn leaves on a frosty morning. One star collided with the courtyard, and a blast of heat lashed at us. The others struck the city, where people were fleeing into the night with torches.

Cronus opened his giant black feathery wings, knocking into the palace towers and breaking the tops off several spires.

"Zeus?" I asked, drawing my sword.

"Ready when you are."

We opened our wings and shot into the sky. A star landed in my gloved hand as I drew level with Cronus's face. He squinted as though he couldn't see us properly. Zeus chucked a lightning bolt as I heaved the star, each aiming for one of his eyes. Cronus folded his wings around him in a protective shield. The force of them flapping open again threw us pinwheeling away.

The night sky filled with the whinnying of horses. From across the city, the Cretan warriors descended on winged steeds with their swords raised. Euboea rode at the front, driving her warriors into battle with bloodcurdling fury. Hestia soared with them on her own wings, leading the way, her double axe extended in front of her.

Our cavalry circled Cronus's head. Some hacked and sliced at his ears and nose, while others shot arrows into his cheeks. He swatted at them like pesky gadflies. They circled back with increased vigor and unshakeable spirits.

I reentered the fray. Cronus roared and flapped his wings. They were too small to lift him now, but they whipped up mighty gusts that scattered us. I bounced across the courtyard, crashing into the palace wall. Euboea sailed overhead on her ivory steed, flying headlong into the winds with her sword to the stars. She banked and sliced at Cronus's hand that held his sickle. He smacked her, and she spun off her saddle and plummeted to the ground.

"Euboea," I said, landing at her side. "Can you move?"

Blood pooled behind her head. Her skull was cracked in the back, and death surged in her eyes. She closed them. "Hera?"

"Yes, my friend?"

"I'm sorry."

"You have nothing to apologize for." Hot tears brimmed over my lashes. "You're going where the heroes rest. I've seen the sparkling gates and golden meadows. I imagine there's lots of dancing."

"And wine?"

"No afterlife would be complete without it."

With a gut-shaking roar, Cronus called upon more stars to crash down around us. I shielded Euboea with my wings as cinders pelted us. When I lowered my wings again, she had passed on.

I bowed my head and let my heart speak. "Goddess Gaea, receive thy dutiful daughter. Guide Euboea by hand through the gates of Elysium, and offer her rest in the fields of gold."

More stars streamed down from the heavens in a rain of fire. The sky lit up like midday as they bombarded the city and mountaintop in endless blasts.

Cronus was going to bring down the mountain all by himself.

Oceanus had warned me that the prophecy was a farce, yet I had led my family and my people into war. Every life lost on this battlefield was my torment.

Warm arms closed around my shoulders. I blinked up at Zeus. Ash and soot rained down, blanketing us both. Fires raged across the city, their light reflecting in his earnest eyes.

"It isn't over," he said. "We're fated to win."

My only thoughts were of despair.

"Hera, Cronus had to steal the strength of over half a dozen Titans to call upon the heavens." Zeus rested his forehead against mine. "But the stars always belonged to you."

Hestia shouted a warrior's cry and dive-bombed Cronus, raking her double-headed axe down the back of his neck. Demeter had arrived, and she shot bronze arrows at his throat, called them back, and let them loose again. Poseidon had come with her. He flew low, dragging the end of his trident across the ground, ripping up the earth beneath Cronus's feet. The mountain quaked and split with a monumental groan, and Cronus wobbled as he swung his sickle at my siblings darting around him.

My soul would have me stand and fight.

I rose on unsteady feet, bidding the earth to give me strength.

"I'll see you up there," Zeus said. He launched himself upward on alabaster wings.

Helios had joined the battle with his fiery sword. Mounted on his sister's winged steed, he attacked Cronus's hand that held the sickle, cutting at his knuckles. In a rage, Cronus raised the sickle over his head and swung down, straight through the center of the main tower of the palace. One half toppled down the mountainside toward the sea, scattering my siblings. The second leaned toward Othrys, where refugees were still fleeing for the city gates.

I ran underneath the lilting tower and caught it with my back. My Titan strength propped it up, but it still threatened to crush me.

General Atlas entered the courtyard, his golden armor gleaming in the firelight. He marched in my direction as the tower grew heavier. I shoved against it, trying to tip the wreckage the opposite way, but it tilted further, casting me deeper in its shadow.

The giant general loomed over me. My grip slipped, and my feet skidded across the ground. He raised his sword, and then a spinning shield cuffed him in the back of the head.

He turned around slowly. Theo, in full body armor, galloped at him on a black warhorse. Atlas aimed his blade at Theo, swung, and cut the steed down at its front knees. The animal collapsed forward in a heap of dust and rolled over onto Theo, pinning him.

Atlas strode toward him as Theo struggled to pull his weight out from under the crippled horse. The tower inclined further against me. I couldn't move to help Theo, or it would fall on the city. I gritted my teeth and pushed with all my might.

My feet stopped slipping.

"Hello, little bird."

Gyes stood over me, his hundred hands bracing the weight of the tower. Behind him, his brother Cottus had set a foot on Atlas's chest. The general squirmed and shoved, but he was pinned. Theo had pulled himself out from under the horse and was catching his breath. Obriareus helped Gyes with the tower, and together, the two Hecatoncheires pushed it over the side of the mountain and into the sea.

High above, on Gyes's shoulder, next to his fifty heads, sat Hades.

"Good timing, don't you think?" he asked.

I stood and brushed myself off. "Actually, you're late."

"Forgive me," he replied dryly. "I didn't mean to miss all the excitement."

Theo got up. I tossed him the satchel Scelmis had given me.

I indicated the general caught under the foot of one of the Hecatoncheires. "Let him up."

Cottus lifted his foot. Atlas rolled away and clambered to his feet. I picked him up by the throat with my adamant glove.

"Is that all you've got?" he rasped.

I squeezed harder. He pushed at my arm and tried to pry himself away, but I held on. "You attacked the man I love."

Atlas's face turned several shades of red. He slammed his forehead into mine. I did not let go. The glove had a mind of its own, crushing and crushing.

"Theo, put the collars on him wherever you can reach."

Theo slapped an adamant collar around one of the general's big wrists. He put the second collar around Atlas's other wrist. The general quit struggling. I lowered him to the ground, and Theo tied him up.

Our aerial assault was waning. Less than half the winged riders remained, and we still hadn't seen any sign of Aphrodite and her legion. Demeter and Hestia were nursing wounds, and Poseidon was flying back from where he had been thrown out to sea. At the city wall, our ground troops were locked in heavy combat with the First House's army, which was breaking our lines with pelting volleys.

Zeus fought tirelessly. He assailed Cronus with a rapid flurry of thunder and lightning bolts. Our father batted most of them away, and a few were redirected toward us, while the rest struck buildings in the city.

One lightning bolt whizzed past Hades's head. He glowered at Zeus. "My turn," he said. He spread his wings and disappeared.

One of Cronus's ears tugged sideways. He snatched at the air. Hades reappeared, lying on the ground in front of us with his helmet crushed. Cronus lifted a foot to stomp on him, but the three Hecatoncheires stepped between them. The hundred-handed monsters were less than half of Cronus's colossal size, but they balled their dozens of fists and growled, undaunted.

Cronus forced a laughed. "My foolish children, you released the Gigantes? They are twice as stupid as they are hideous. Send them back to Tartarus where they belong."

Suddenly, the ground began to shake. Lumbering over house-tops came the Cyclopes. Arges, Steropes, and Halimedes lunged over the crumbling palace wall and stood behind their brothers, the Hecatoncheires. Each one held a smithy hammer.

The tide of war had turned.

24

Never in my dreams did I imagine such a sight. The Cyclopes and the Hecatoncheires had emerged from the pits of Tartarus to join us in the fight against the Almighty, who as a colossus dwarfed even the Gigantes, a force unlike any the world had seen.

"Cronus," Arges said by way of greeting. "You promised Mother Gaea you would release us after Uranus fell. Did you forget, little brother?"

Cronus sneered. "Gaea has always been blind to your worthlessness. How she could ever think of you as more than a mistake is beyond me."

My siblings, Theo, Helios, and I regrouped behind the Gigantes. Poseidon scooped up Hades and brought him to us. All of us were smudged with ash, and even Helios's once-ivory steed was heathered from the smoke and soot. We were terribly worn out, yet Cronus had fared no better. He no longer wore his smug smirk. His feathered wings were in tatters, he bled from countless cuts, and his face and limbs were riddled with burns.

"General?" Theo asked, mounting a winged horse. "What's the plan?"

"Get the sickle," I ordered. "Gigantes? Stay clear of the blade. It's deadly to a god, so I'm certain it could harm you."

"Send them back to the pits of Tartarus," Cronus shouted over me. "I only ever agreed with my father on one topic: the Gigantes are monsters. They don't belong in the mortal realm."

"Neither do you," I growled.

My tired and battered liege men valiantly raised their weapons. Zeus pumped his arm overhead and, with a guttural cry, took flight. My siblings and I followed him, along with Helios and Theo on their winged horses.

The Cyclopes and the Hecatoncheires roared in chorus and sprinted at the Almighty. Cronus raised the sickle and jammed the blade into the earth, and a zigzagging crack opened between us. The cracks that Poseidon had made split wider and longer as the last of the erect section of the palace crumbled. From my vantage point above, I could see down through the opening to familiar stormy skies, crimson mountains, and the pits of Tartarus. Cronus had carved a hole through the earth, straight down to the underworld.

Steropes jumped over the divide and fell short of the other side. Clawing for purchase, he slid down and disappeared into the pit. Halimedes bounded across and clobbered Cronus in the chest. Cronus twisted and threw him backward, and Halimedes, too, plummeted into the pit.

Arges was the last Cyclops standing. He halted while the Hecatoncheires leaped, all in a row. They jumped short, but they used their hundred hands to climb and pile on top of Cronus. The monsters held him down, dangling his head over the pit. Only then did Arges leap across the divide, shoving his hammer against Cronus's chest.

"Cut his hand off!" Helios yelled.

They had no sufficiently sizeable blade, so Arges began to hammer at the Almighty's wrist.

"Theo," I called. "Could you . . . ?"

"I can try." He soared closer to the pile of monsters and spoke with his persuasive voice. "Cronus, let go of the sickle." The Almighty continued to struggle against the four Gigantes. Theo concentrated harder. "Go to sleep, Cronus. Go to sleep. You *must* sleep. You wish to rest above all else."

The Almighty's eyes glazed over. His lids grew heavy.

"It's working," Gyes said.

Something didn't feel right. Even with Arges smashing his wrist, and Theo's efforts of persuasion, Cronus's hand was still tight around his blade.

The Hecatoncheires loosened their grip on the Almighty.

"Wait!" I cried.

Cronus sat up, yanking free of most of Cottus's hundred hands. He threw Cottus into the pit and then flipped over so he was on top of Arges. The Cyclops dropped his hammer as he struck the ground. Cronus lowered the sickle to his gullet and spit in his one eye.

"You don't belong here," he snarled.

Gyes picked up Arges's hammer and slammed it over Cronus's head. He drooped to the side, dazed. The two remaining Hecatoncheires grabbed him again, but he kept wrenching from their grasp.

"There has to be a way to stop this," I muttered. I glanced at Helios. "Ready for your revenge?"

He raised his fiery sword and dived at Cronus, then leaped from the saddle and landed on his wrist. Then he burst into flames.

Shining like a beacon, Helios slid down to Cronus's fingers and began prying them off the sickle one by one. Cronus shouted in pain and released his grip, and Helios leaped forward into his palm and pushed the sickle free.

Cronus closed his fist around Helios, and the god of the sun made a loud snapping noise. When Cronus opened his hand, Helios's limp body fell.

A cry went up into the evernight, and Zeus dived after Helios.

I flew at the sickle.

The weapon shrank as it spun downward. Although I was as likely to grab the blade as the handle, I extended my gloved hand and took the chance. When the sickle was still three times the size of any sword I had held, I snatched it out of the sky, and it shrunk to suit me.

Zeus landed safely away with Helios in his arms. The god of the sun resembled a twig snapped in two. Arges flipped Cronus over onto his back and pinned him across his chest with his hammer. I flew down to hover over Cronus's sneering mouth. He gnashed his teeth at me.

"Brazen bitch. You've no future without me as your ruler. I am alpha and omega. The whole world will fall into disarray without my reign. The Golden Age can never be repeated. My rule will never be outdone."

I aimed the adamant sickle at his nose. "This was your choice, Cronus. You sealed your own fate. Your story ends here."

"You will never achieve any glory, Hera. You will always be in the shadow of those who see the world more clearly."

"I see the monster that you are very clearly, Father. The heavens will shine a little brighter without you." Holding the sickle in my outstretched arm, I banked downward toward his throat. "This is for every goddess and every woman you harmed."

I dragged the sickle across his gullet. The jagged blade sliced deeply, but instead of blood spewing out, a forceful blast shot at me. I dropped the sickle and held my glove out for protection. The stream of light poured into my palm and amassed into a ball that grew and grew. Its weight forced me to the ground, but I landed on my feet with my gloved hand above my head. My legs trembled as they slowly gave way. I sank to one knee under the weight of the light and braced against the earth with my other hand. The heavier the radiance weighed, the more Cronus shrank. My vision blurred, blinding me to everything except the massive star growing above me, resting in the palm of my hand, made of all the Titan strengths that Cronus had stolen. Their combined power rivaled the sun.

Demeter came beside me and steadied my outstretched arm. Hestia joined us, and my sisters buoyed me together.

"It's too heavy," Demeter groaned.

Hestia gritted out a reply. "Not for us."

Cronus shrank faster. My bones smoldered like brittle tinder in a flame. My skin shone with the light of a thousand stars, emanating from my soul. I leaned heavier into the earth, pleading for Gaea's support.

Then, out of the corner of my eye, I saw Aphrodite land on her griffin with another rider. Eos jumped off and dashed to us.

"Hera, get up," shouted the goddess of dawn. "Demeter and Hestia, don't let go of your sister. It will take all of us to put this sun where it belongs."

"On three," Hestia said. "One, two, three!"

I pushed into my knees, rising to my feet, my sisters supporting me. We opened our wings and launched upward, flapping them as rapidly as our racing hearts. Our ascent was painstaking as we pushed up against what felt like the weight of the entire sky.

After an eternity of climbing, we crested midheaven.

Eos called out beside us from the saddle of Selene's winged horse. "Higher! We must fly higher than the stars!"

We flapped harder and rose into a web of constellations. My arm shook. My chest ached. My gloved hand burned. The strength of my wings was faltering.

"We can do it, Hera," Hestia gasped. "For Rhea and Stavra."

Our mothers' names were the impetus I needed to reach into the deepest core of my being—what made me both mortal and a goddess—and fly.

The stars gradually fell below us, sparkling at our feet, the constellations mapping shapes and figures and lost memories.

Eos slowed her steed to a weightless stop. "You can let go now."

Demeter and Hestia immediately obeyed, but now that the Titan strengths were safely away from Cronus, I wanted to weep.

"It's all right, Hera," Eos encouraged. "You can let go."

"But who will move the sun?" I asked.

"The combined strength of all those Titans needs no master. The sun will move itself. Its light will shine down on earth for countless millennia to come."

I lowered my shaking arm. My luminous skin lost its luster as the sun gently drifted off into the blue-black firmament until it arrived at heaven's ceiling.

My sisters wrapped their arms around me.

"I'm ready to go home," Demeter said.

Eos lingered, her attention on the sun. Her rosiness was fading, her hair lightening to white. Her skin took on a silvery sheen.

"Are you all right, Eos?" I asked.

"The heavens have their sun, but they need their moon. As the goddess of the dawn, I'm the only Titan left who can touch both." She started to fade into the nothingness. "I always wanted a real throne in the heavens."

"I can think of no one more deserving," I replied.

Eos continued to fade until only her crescent smile could be seen, and then it widened and widened until she disappeared into her smile's pale effulgence. My sisters and I witnessed the dawn of the new moon tearfully. As we bathed in its silver gleam, Eos's voice entered my mind.

The reign of the Titans has come to an end. I will watch over you and your sisters always, Hera.

Demeter sniffled. "Do you think we'll ever see her again?"

I thought of the constant presence of the ever-fluctuating moon. "As often as we want."

Hestia hugged us both closer, and the three of us hung there, suspended in the peaceful silence of the uppermost heavens, like newborn stars.

25

Flying back to earth was a speedy yet somber journey. The sun rose steadfastly over all the world as we drifted down through gilded clouds. Dawn would never be the same without Eos.

As Mount Othrys came into view, or what was left of it, smoke plumes rose in ashy pillars all over the city. A huge pit had swallowed up the palace, and the uppermost peak of the mountain had been decapitated by the barrage of exploding stars.

We rode the salty winds across the sparkling blue Aegean Sea and up the steep mountainside to what was left of the palace grounds.

The remaining Gigantes had contained Cronus once he had shrunk to his mortal size. Zeus, Poseidon, and Hades were filthy and sweaty but whole. They conversed with Aphrodite and several of the surviving Titanesses, the members of Rhea's precious legion, Wings of Fury. They were a small but mighty bunch, including Metis, Asteria, Leto, and Styx. Aphrodite's cult of Cretan warriors rested amid the rubble, exhausted from the nightlong battle and mourning the loss of their captain. Theo sat among the women instead of with the gods, which made me curious about what I had missed.

Aphrodite was the first to greet us.

"I'm sorry we were late," she said. "Metis made it very clear that we needed Eos, so we had to fly to the Coral Mansion and get her before we could come."

"I understand," I replied quietly.

Theo strode over, his pace more patient than I had time for. I rushed to him and jumped in his arms. "You're safe," I breathed.

"Me? Everyone saw what you did. Hera . . . a sun?"

"It had to be done." I buried my face against his neck and breathed in his leathery scent. "The heavens are restored."

He sucked in a short breath. "Your glove is still hot."

"Sorry." I tried to tug it off, but it wouldn't budge. "I'll try again after it cools."

Theo gripped my hips. "Do you remember where we left off in our tent on Crete?"

"How could I forget?" I moved closer, my pelvis against his. "Why do you ask?"

"I'd like to finish that tonight."

I would wander off with him right now if I thought we wouldn't be noticed. His touch was the only balm that could soothe away the aches of battle.

Theo kissed me lightly, his lips tight. "You need to speak with your brother."

From his tone, I knew immediately that he meant Zeus. I glanced across the courtyard, where he was midconversation with Hades and Poseidon, though staring back at us.

"What is it?" I asked.

"I'll let him tell you." Theo took me by the hand—the gloveless one—and walked with me to my brothers. Upon our arrival, only Hades offered a smile.

"Well done, Hera," he said, elbowing me playfully.

"I wasn't gone long. What did I miss?"

Poseidon gestured at Zeus. "You tell her."

He gripped the handle of the weapon at his waist—Cronus's adamant sickle. "We've been discussing how best to deliver Cronus to the underworld. We thought that since you survived there once, you could take him."

"Me? Hades lived there and knows it far better than me. Why not him?"

"Hades has another assignment," Zeus replied.

I waited for him to go on, but no one explained.

Hades kicked at a piece of rubble. "I told you this was a bad idea."

"What's a bad idea?" I asked. Their silence grew into unbearable awkwardness. "Enough," I pleaded. "Someone tell me what's going on."

Zeus maintained a forcibly calm demeanor despite the color rising in his cheeks. "As my first order as Ruler of the Titans, I would like you to deliver our father to Tartarus. As my second order, Hades will guide the Gigantes back to their home."

"Their home . . . as in the underworld? No. I told them they were welcome here with me."

"You shouldn't have made a promise you couldn't keep," Poseidon said.

"But I did. Gaea wants them here too. She's been waiting for someone to let them out since Uranus locked them away." I glanced across the way at the Gigantes. They ogled the sun rising in the morning-blue sky, their expressions marked with pure bliss. "They are happy. They aren't hurting anyone. Why send them back? Do they even want to leave?"

"Zeus hasn't asked them," Hades answered shortly.

"Then I'll ask them. They lived in the mortal realm long before any of us were even born. They deserve a choice." I turned to go, but Zeus grabbed my arm.

Theo took a weighted step toward him. Zeus glared but released me.

"They cannot stay here, Hera," Zeus said. "Consider how the mortals will respond. We have to think of them. They won't see Gaea's children. They only see monsters."

"I thought the same until I got to know them, and then I realized how extraordinary they are. It doesn't matter that the Gigantes are different than us. It's not our place to decide where or how anyone should live."

Zeus gave no indication that he even heard me. "They don't belong in the mortal realm, Hera. No one is choosing that for them. We're simply accepting what they are."

"The Cyclopes made our adamant weapons. We could not have prevailed without them."

"And we will be forever grateful," Zeus replied.

I would have rallied Demeter and Hestia to defend the Gigantes with me, but they were far enough away that I didn't wish to make a scene. I also wasn't certain they would side with me. They didn't know the Cyclopes and the Hecatoncheires as I did, and I could tell by the distance they kept that they hadn't yet seen past their hideousness.

"Does everyone feel this way?" I asked, searching each of my brothers. "Poseidon? Gyes carried you when you were more pus and blood than skin and flesh, and Hades, dare I say they're your friends? They trust you. They trust *me*."

Hades threw up his hands and marched away.

"The Gigantes weren't out of place in the underworld," Poseidon replied. "Down there, they aren't monsters."

"But I told them they could stay," I repeated, more weakly.

Zeus gripped the hilt of the adamant sickle. "They need to go home, Hera, where they are meant to be."

Seeing him standing there so defiantly, and with the sickle, I no longer saw the brother I had fought alongside. I saw Cronus and Uranus. Disgust filled my voice. "You sound like your father."

"*Our* father," Zeus corrected. "And like *our* father, I'm now your ruler. You will do as I say."

I stepped up to him and tapped my gloved finger against his chest. "Who's going to make me?"

A rumbly voice called out from behind us. "We will take Cronus to Tartarus," Gyes said. The two remaining Hecatoncheires, Gyes and Obriareus, and the Cyclops Arges stood near the open pit. "We can find our own way home."

I hung my hope on Zeus again, my pride burning the back of my throat.

"Please," I begged. "We can find them their own island, like the Telchines and the cult of Aphrodite have. Surely there's somewhere secluded in the southern isles that isn't—"

"I've made my decision, Hera." Zeus's hard voice left no quarter for further argument. "If the Gigantes wish to deliver Cronus to Tartarus, they may do so with my thanks. But they are not welcome in my domain."

I shook my head in disbelief, seeing him anew. "Who *are* you?"

"Your god."

I fell back a step. All the exhaustion from the last several days hit me at once. Theo touched my elbow, bracing me, but he did not let me appear weak as we walked away.

"Theo? This is wrong. Zeus's first decision as our ruler is wrong."

"He thinks he's doing what's best for everyone." Theo's tone was doubtful, as though he disagreed with his own assessment.

"The Gigantes fought for us."

"They knew there was a chance they couldn't stay, yet they came in support of you, of your mother Rhea, and of Gaea."

His assessment only made things worse. The pits of Tartarus were for beings like Cronus, the rottenest souls alive. The Cyclopes and the Hecatoncheires were like the dead. They had no ambition or artifice. They served the gods they loved with their whole hearts.

"I don't want to say goodbye," I said.

Theo released my elbow. "You're sister to the Ruler of the Gods now. You have duties."

"Not to his throne," I snapped.

"No, to your own throne. You're the goddess Hera." Theo planted a sweet kiss on my cheek. "No man or god can tell you what to do. You always do the right thing."

"Doing the right thing is the worst," I grumbled.

"Sometimes it really is."

I straightened my posture and glided over to the Gigantes.

The temperature was much warmer by the pit. The heat from Tartarus wafted out of the hole in waves that stunk of sulfur. Cronus was bound in chains—metal, for he was weaker than a demigod—and gagged. I peered up into the Gigantes' faces with a distraught frown.

"We will miss you, little bird," Gyes said. "You're welcome in the underworld anytime."

I laughed emptily. "You're all mighty warriors deserving of your own Elysium."

"Maybe we will see you there one day," Arges replied. The Cyclops threw Cronus over his shoulder, dangling him upside down so his face was level with mine.

My father mumbled something presumably uncouth against his gag. I leaned in and recited the first challenge he ever gave me.

"So you think you're a god? Then bring me the stars."

He shot me a red-hot glare. I stepped back as Arges climbed into the pit and descended, followed by Obriareus and Gyes. It was then that it occurred to me that they had left a prisoner behind.

"Theo, where's Atlas?" I asked. "Shouldn't the general be locked up in Tartarus too?"

"He's gone, sentenced to another prison."

"Another prison? Where?"

Theo scrubbed at his beard, and tiny flecks of ash fell. "Zeus condemned Atlas to replace the four pillars and carry the weight of the heavens on his shoulders. He will hold the sky up from the land. A guard of Cretan warriors flew Atlas north, to a place wrapped in clouds and darkness, where night and day never greet one another. There he will serve out his sentence for the rest of time."

Atlas was a mighty Titan, arguably our strongest enemy left. An eternity in Tartarus was a horrible sentence, but bearing up the heavens, alone in the twilight, was an equally insufferable punishment.

Poseidon joined us at the pit. "Stand back, Hera. It's time to close the gate."

I peered into the hole to make sure that the Cyclops and the Hecatoncheires had finished descending. They were gone.

Poseidon drove the end of his trident into the ground. The earth shook, and the gap began to seal. Before it had shut, the quaking quit.

Zeus stormed over. "Why have you stopped?"

"I didn't." Poseidon stared at his trident, perplexed. "It did it on its own."

"Well, finish it," Zeus ordered. "I'd like to get off my feet."

A guttural roar rose from the pit, sending Poseidon and Zeus retreating. My sisters did the opposite. Demeter and Hestia wandered over with Aphrodite and the other members of the Wings of Fury. Theo grabbed on to me as a mightier tremor rattled the ground. Along with it came an equally angry sound, a voice like spewing lava.

"Zeus, god of thunder, you betray our bargain?"

My brother paled and backed farther away from the pit.

"Zeus?" I said. "What did you do?"

He stuttered indecipherably.

"Did you make a bargain with Gaea?" I demanded. "What was it, Zeus? What did you promise her?"

"I couldn't allow those m-monsters to stay in the mortal realm," he stammered. "The Gigantes belong in Tartarus. She asked me to let them out in exchange for supporting me as the next ruler of the gods. I said I would consider it, but I couldn't let her monstrous aberrations threaten the order of my world."

"*Your* world?" I retorted. "Oh, Zeus. You fool."

The ground quaked in mighty rolls, and we all went swaying. Theo and I held on to each other tighter.

A second roar rose from the underworld, and then a spine-tingling shriek.

"Great gods," Hades said. "Close the pit! Quickly!"

Poseidon began to reseal the opening, but two gargantuan, hideous winged serpents burst out, and hot rocks sprayed down on us. The beasts flew so high they blotted out the sun and moon, and I swore when they breathed fire, the stars bled.

Typhon and Echidna were loose.

26

Typhon hissed like a hundred snakes, and his mate, Echidna, roared like a hundred lions. Their sinuous, scaled bodies dived down from the heavens, straight into the earth, where they leaped in and out of what was left of the mountain as though it were the ocean and they were jumping waves.

Those of us on the ground took to the sky on wings, either our own or a steed's. The Cretan warriors ran to evacuate the city before Typhon and Echidna buried the former God of Gods' great stronghold. Theo rode a griffin, the steed of choice for Aphrodite and her legion of Titanesses. The Wings of Fury were armed and, unlike the rest of us, not fatigued from the battle against Cronus, yet they did not attack. The serpents were nimble, and spent as much time above the earth as they did underground, making them impossible to track.

I joined Theo on his griffin to rest my wings. We sought out Zeus, who hovered above the savage serpents wreaking havoc underground and in the sky.

"What was your bargain with Gaea?" I asked.

Zeus gripped a lightning bolt in one hand and a thunderbolt in the other. "I told her I would consider releasing the Gigantes if they helped us win the war, but I made no promise."

"Did you learn nothing from your father?" Theo growled.

Zeus appeared properly chastised. "Hera, I swear I made no bargain. I didn't."

And that was the third time Zeus had lied to my face.

"It doesn't matter now," I snapped. "Typhon and Echidna won't stop. They will bring down the whole mountain."

The pair of otherworldly creatures moved in sync, up and down, in and out of the earth. Demeter shot her entire quiver of arrows at them, and they all bounced off. Zeus tossed his bolts, one after the other. They struck Typhon's back, but the great beast paid them no more mind than he did the new sun. I called to the stars. Six of them came, one after the other. Each one struck the beasts, but they were immune to the fiery explosions. Nothing penetrated their hides. Neither one sustained so much as a scorch mark.

We were lesser gods, and this was no longer our domain. The creatures were not here to destroy us. They were here to destroy everything.

"What about the sickle?" I asked.

Zeus unsheathed it from his waist and dived at Typhon. The serpent's sapphire wings flapped furiously. As the beast rose from the earth in a torrential wave of rubble, Zeus sliced at his back. The serpent roared as it rolled and kicked Zeus into the clouds. He caught himself on ash-stained wings and soared back to us. We waited for the adamant to divest the creature of its strength.

Nothing happened.

Hades soared over to us. "You cannot defeat them with that little toy," he shouted. "Do you know how much adamant it took to cage them in the first place? Three times their body weight. Each! That took centuries and centuries of mining, and cost thousands of souls. So unless you can mine that amount of adamant and form it into a weapon immediately, they will fell this mountain and then move on to the rest of the world until it is entirely desecrated."

"I'll speak with Gaea," Zeus said. "She cannot want this."

"Choices have consequences!" Hades cried. "Want has nothing to do with it. Even Gaea cannot call them back to their cages now. Typhon and Echidna were created for one purpose, and one purpose only—to obliterate."

All our troops, battle worn and frayed, watched helplessly as more homes were smashed to ruins.

Theo wrapped his arms around me from behind. "I love you, Hera."

I sank back against him. It had been inevitable, admitting how I felt about him. I was done fighting fate. "I love you too. I always have and always will."

He leaned so far forward against me, I thought, *This must be how it feels to hold up the sky.*

"I'm sorry," Theo said, and then he pressed his lips to my ear. "Hera, do not stop me."

His persuasive voice put me on alert. I recognized something was wrong, but I could not resist. I found myself going very still. "All right, Theo."

He raised his voice and again employed that irresistibly persuasive tone. "Every god, goddess, or warrior who can hear me, cover your ears!"

We immediately did as he ordered.

Theo opened his mouth and sang. His voice was muffled by my hands, but the vibrations of his chest were familiar from all the sleepless nights when he had sung me this very lullaby.

The tune was soulful, achingly soothing. Typhon and Echidna finally took notice of us, of Theo. They rose from the earth to listen to his song.

The beasts weaved through the air on spiny wings toward him. Seeing them cow to him drove another warning to the deepest chamber of my heart. My tongue wanted to scream for him to stop, but I could not break free of his command.

He climbed off the back of the griffin and onto Typhon's shoulders. The winged serpent gave the hiss of a beast that had detected someone was attempting to tame it.

Theo opened his mouth wider, and his chest pumped harder, while he sang the sweet, sweet melody to the growling beasts. As he coaxed them toward the opening in the earth from which they had escaped, I realized that Theo would have to go back with them to where they belonged, far below, in the underworld, to see that they fell asleep in their prisons. And I could not stop him.

My heart screamed louder, tearing me free of his persuasive voice. My hands shook over my ears. No one else had broken his spell. They were still mesmerized, held by the strength of his will. But my will was as mighty as his, if not mightier.

A battle commenced between my heart and my soul. It wasn't Theo I wished to fight. I had been told this would be his fate, and I could try to stop him. I could let the mountain fall and spite the sun I had set in the heavens. For another day with him, I would do all that and more.

I would let the world crumble.

His head snapped to me, and those honey eyes I loved so dearly begged me to let him go. I hated him for it, but this was not my choice. It was his, and whether I was a goddess or not, I would never take that away from anyone. God or mortal, everyone had a right to agency.

The damage to the mountaintop had left it unstable. The pit to Tartarus was collapsing in on itself. Theo continued his lullaby, charming the serpentine monsters back into their home. Like an asp hypnotized and coaxed into a basket, Echidna dived through the sinkhole first. Typhon, transfixed by Theo's transcendent voice, slithered nearer to the hole. Theo gazed up at me again, his eyes full of love and gratitude. They were more beautiful than any two stars in the heavens, warmer than any sun, and they saw me more clearly than any sentinel moon.

"Goodbye, Theo Angelos," I whispered.

He held on to the neck of the beast as it descended back into the belly of the earth.

The second that Theo's song could no longer be heard, I dropped my hands and screamed with the entire strength of my soul. My siblings shook themselves out of their stupor, and I saw their shock when they comprehended that the pit to Tartarus had sealed shut.

I launched off the griffin and flew to the ground. Sinking to my knees, I pressed my gloved hand over the tiny crack that was left of the pit.

"He may come back," Hades said behind me.

We both knew that was impossible. Theo had been warned by the greatest Titan healer in the land that he could never reenter the underworld or else his soul would die and he would be Forgotten.

A hand rested on my shoulder. "Hera."

I whirled and stood in one motion. Grabbing Zeus by the throat, I squeezed hard with my glove. "I could crush your windpipe. You would survive, but the next few years of your life would be very unpleasant."

"I'm sorry," he rasped.

"Hera," Demeter said. "Don't."

I dropped Zeus, and he stumbled back, clutching his throat.

"Don't ever speak to me again," I snarled.

Spreading my wings, I took off for the sun. I didn't know how long I flew across the heavens, or where I would eventually land, and I didn't care, because I no longer existed in the same world as Theo.

27

Demeter and Hestia hissed and roared and flapped their arms like wings. The audience of girls gasped. I deepened my voice and continued narrating from memory.

"The two giant winged monsters rose from the earth and dived around the mountaintop, like sea dragons in and out of waves. The gods didn't know what to do, but one man—a demigod—with a singing voice unmatched by any minstrel, knew a lullaby that would hypnotize the monsters. He sang to them more exquisitely than anyone had ever sung before."

My voice cracked. I swallowed my rising tears and ignored the ones building at the corners of my eyes. My sisters continued to act out Typhon and Echidna, the wicked winged serpents.

"Our hero sang with all of his soul as he rode the biggest monster down into the center of the earth and locked both of the sleeping beasts back in their cages, saving every living thing in the mortal realm from the wrath of Gaea."

Demeter and Hestia lay on the ground and pretended to fall into a peaceful sleep.

The girls applauded, some of them standing and clapping. The oldest girl at the front, our half sister, Delphine, raised her hand.

"Hera?"

"Yes, Delphine?"

"What happened to the demigod?"

Demeter peeked one eye open.

I played with the hem of my chiton, my fingers restless. "Our hero fell into a peaceful sleep too."

"Will he ever wake up?" asked a younger girl.

My throat grew hot and itchy. "I . . ."

Hestia jumped up and clapped her hands. "Who wants a honey-and-walnut pastry?"

Our small audience forgot all about the unanswered question and ran across camp to the mess hall with Hestia.

Demeter came over to me. "How about next time I narrate, and you act out Typhon?"

"No." I dashed away a stray tear. "I should be the one to narrate."

"You shouldn't punish yourself, Hera. It's been a year. Theo wouldn't want you to keep doing this to yourself. Even his mother has moved on and found happiness in Thessaly."

"You don't know what Theo would or wouldn't want for me."

Demeter released a singsong sigh. "I know he would want you to answer one of the messengers from our brothers. Hestia and I will do as you ask, but they're family too. We cannot ignore them forever."

"You know my feelings on the matter. I won't speak of it again." I exited the schoolyard. "I'm going for a walk."

I left the cult of Aphrodite's camp and took the trail up Ida Mountain. In private, I allowed myself to cry. The path ended at the cave where Zeus had lived when I found him. Some days I wished I had never listened to the oracles, but that meant I would also be wishing away my first kiss with Theo.

A voice called from the woods: "Hera."

A hooded figure stepped out of the ancient forest of cypress trees. I flexed my adamant glove, now permanently fused to my skin, and backed away.

"You needn't be afraid, daughter."

Oh, but I should fear her. The last time I heard Gaea, she released Typhon and Echidna on the mortal realm. That was the worst day of my life.

"I understand your fear," she said, "but I need to speak with you. You must go home."

"This is my home."

"No, Thessaly is your home. Your brothers are building a palace on Mount Olympus."

"So I've been told."

"You were also told the prophecy was never about Zeus." Gaea lowered her hood, revealing her face, and I gulped down a sob. "It was always about you, my shooting star."

"Stavra?" I stuttered.

My mother smiled. I missed her so much. "Stavra was the mortal name I chose, but I've always been Gaea."

My mind reeled, forward and backward and upside down. "But you . . . I saw you die."

"You saw a body die," Gaea said. "I am the soul of the earth. I will live forever. I may take a mortal body anytime I wish, in any form I wish. Every living thing ever created is me, and I am them. I forget none of my own."

Tears stung my eyes again, unbidden. "Is Theo . . . ?"

"Theo rests from the cares of the world. His soul lives on, as long as we remember him." This gentle promise, although obscure, gave my soul a brief reprieve from the torment. "Now that you know who I am, will you trust my advice? Go home, Hera, and claim what is yours. If you do not, you will live to regret it."

"I regret many things. Not serving *him* isn't one of them."

Gaea bowed her head. "Your fury will be your undoing."

"It's done me well so far."

"Bitterness doesn't suit you."

"Theo is dead because Zeus—the god that never lies—lied. Three times, Mother."

Gaea raised her hood to hide her face. "That was only the beginning. Don't go to Mount Olympus if you don't wish, but what transpires next is beyond my control. I cannot reason with my sons any longer. They do not respect me as their equal. Like you, I seek peace and happiness. I will not persuade you to leave yours when I am retiring to find mine."

The breadth of my ingratitude struck me. I raised my gloved hand and pressed a fist over my heart. "Thank you, Mother. For everything."

The Mother of All Living Things bowed to me, teaching me more about humility than anyone ever had, and wandered off into the woods.

Her words haunted me on my walk back to camp, but when I returned and saw my sisters dancing and singing in the clearing, any desire to leave Crete fled. I joined them, spinning and twirling, desperately trying to break free from the sorrow weighing down my heart.

The decree came several moons later. I had mostly forgotten about Gaea's visit. I spent my days putting on plays for the girls and hiking through the woods alone, and I spent the nights drinking and dancing myself into a stupor. Sometimes, when I drank too much, I could hear Theo singing to me. I would tell him I loved him, mumbling to myself in the empty shadows. It was a cycle of forgetfulness and indulgence, anything to keep my mind off the hollowness inside me.

Soon after the messenger arrived, Hestia, Demeter, and I gathered in the outdoor mess hall in the late-afternoon sun, the smell of roasted lamb thick in the air. I heard the messenger recite the decree and then told him to repeat it five more times. Each time, my anger mounted. The parameters of the decree were clear and completely infuriating.

"This is absurd," I said. "Tell Zeus we're perfectly happy here."

"Wait," Hestia replied, halting the messenger.

"What?" I asked.

"Hera," Demeter said. "It's time."

"For what?" I snapped.

"We're goddesses. We can't hide forever."

"Hide?" I jerked my chin backward. "I'm not hiding. I chose this life, and I'm living it to the fullest."

Hestia addressed the messenger. "Thank you for coming. Please tell Zeus that we will come see him. Give us a moment."

The messenger scurried out of the mess hall.

"I'm not going!" I called after him. "You two go and pander to your ruler, but I'm not interested in hearing any more from him."

Hestia sat on one side of the bench beside me, and Demeter sat on the other.

"Your story isn't over because Theo is gone," Hestia said.

Her utterance of his name put an immediate lump in my throat.

"Theo believed in you, as a woman and a goddess," Demeter added. "He would want you to live your story to the fullest."

"You're really going to go put up with Zeus's new rules?" I asked.

"Our brothers need us," Demeter said. "I've missed them. Well, Hades. I've missed Hades. Zeus needs our help to rule, obviously. We should hear him out."

Hestia took my gloved hand in hers. "Will you come with us?"

"No."

She sighed. "Please think about it. Zeus said he will always save a place for us on Mount Olympus, and he's respected our wishes to remain independent so far. It would be good to discuss his vision for our future."

"And drink his fancy nectar," Demeter added.

Their persuasions were well intentioned, but I could not bring myself to agree. "So you're leaving me," I said curtly.

"We've done some good here," Demeter said. "I'd like to find out what else I can do. Maybe visit Eleusis and see what sort of shrines they've built in my honor. I'd like the chance to fall in love one day too, and Crete has a decided lack of men."

Had I been selfish, keeping them here with me? I realized that I had, and now that I recognized it, I couldn't in good conscience stop them from living as they wished. "I hope you have a wonderful visit to Mount Olympus," I said vacantly. "Give Hades and Poseidon my love."

"We will." Demeter kissed my cheek and hurried off.

Hestia lingered at my side. "I was never interested in falling in love, and seeing your pain these many moons solidified my choice."

"Oh, Hestia." I tipped my forehead against hers. "I'm lost without him."

"You're not lost. You're wandering. You'll find your path when the time is right." She kissed my cheek and left to pack for her journey.

The messenger came forward again, clearing his voice.

"What?" I demanded.

"His Excellency would like to speak with you."

I shot to my feet. "Zeus is here?"

"He's waiting for you in his cave."

I threw open my wings. I had not flown since the worst day of my life, but I would make an exception for this.

The messenger cleared his throat again, louder. "Um, Goddess Hera? Remember restriction number one of the decree?"

"I remember all of the restrictions: no more flying, no adamant weapons, no mentioning Wings of Fury. Lie, lie, lie." I took off from the camp and flew up Ida Mountain, landing outside the cave. I called ahead, warning Zeus, because, good stars, I hoped he would put up a fight.

"Zeus! Where are you, you terrible liar?"

I stormed inside with my wings open. He turned from where he had been viewing the five pairs of wings that our mother, Rhea, had painted on the wall the day he was born so he would remember his family.

"What's this about you rewriting history?" I demanded. "Or what I hear about you drawing lots with our brothers over domains? Since when do you have only two siblings?"

"I drew lots with the two siblings who are actively participating in rebuilding Thessaly and erecting our new home on Mount Olympus. I hope you will come see it. The palace is magnificent. Bigger and better than any ever built."

"You sound like a proper ruler of the Titans," I said sourly.

Zeus raised a finger to silence me. "Now remember, dear sister, we don't use that term anymore. We're known as gods and goddesses. It's best that we sever all ties to the old gods, so they may enjoy their retirement in peace."

"And the decree about our wings?" I flapped mine, perhaps a little dramatically. Performing in plays had made me more theatrical. "Am I forbidden to fly?"

"Our wings are from our past. I'm looking toward our future. From what I hear, you've given up on both."

"What does that mean?" I tossed my hair back, suddenly aware that I couldn't recall the last time I had washed or combed it.

Zeus swept out an arm, indicating our surroundings. "You once accused me of hiding here. Now you're doing the same."

Hearing this for the second time in one afternoon did not help my mood. "I'm living the life I chose," I countered.

"You're a goddess. Quit pretending to be mortal and come home with me. You have a domain waiting that you cannot shirk. I've assigned one to all of our siblings. Drawing lots helped me decide for Hades and Poseidon."

"What was decided?" I asked.

"Poseidon is god of the sea, and Hades is the ruler of the underworld."

"Poor Hades! It's not fair to send him back to the underworld. He's already served there."

"Which makes him better suited than anyone else. Hades has regenerative healing. The rest of us would suffer, even perish, and you cannot deny that he has a soft spot for the dead. I told him he's always welcome on Mount Olympus."

"I'm certain that made a world of difference when you kicked him out of the mortal realm."

Zeus ignored my sarcasm. "He was eventually convinced of the merit of his assignment. Since you haven't asked, I'll tell you about our sisters. Demeter's domain is obvious: she's the goddess of the harvest. They threw another festival for her this year in Eleusis, you know." His voice took on a note of sadness. "You didn't come to the festivities on Rhodes. Helios would have wanted you there."

The invitation—to attend the opening celebration for the colossus statue he had built on the isle of Rhodes, in Helios's image, to commemorate his sacrifice to defeat Cronus—was an honor that Zeus had never given Selene, Eos, Euboea, or Theo. Naturally, I did not go.

"And Hestia?" I asked, revisiting the subject at hand. "Did you honor your promise when you gave her a domain?"

"Of course," Zeus rejoined. "Hestia's is as she requested—the virgin goddess of hearth and home. She may remain a virgin spinster, if that is her wish." He gave me a sly smirk that I used to find endearing. Now I wanted to smack his face. "Would you like to know which domain I've given you?"

I was anxious to inquire, but it didn't really matter. No matter what the assignment was, I wouldn't do it. I was finished with goddess duties and responsibilities. They had given me nothing but a broken heart. "You can tell me, but I'm content where I am. Every joy I've ever had was in mortality."

"Then why, if you're no longer interested in being a goddess, do you care if we revise the history about the War of the Giants, omitting the Wings of Fury and your role as my general?"

"What about Theo?" I growled. "Did you cut him out of 'history' too? Will you forget his sacrifice?"

Zeus waved a hand. "Nothing either of you did is forgotten. I've simply adjusted the narrative to accommodate your current choices. You're the one playing at being mortal."

"But you're not telling the truth. You couldn't have prevailed without Theo or me."

"That's debatable."

"Debatable?" I screeched, my voice echoing in the cave. "Theo died following me."

"Us," Zeus corrected.

"No, me."

"Don't diminish his sacrifice with your selfishness," Zeus countered.

I flexed my hands open and shut, imagining how it would feel to grab his throat.

"Don't think about it," Zeus warned, sidestepping me.

Suddenly, as though a wind swept through me—or perhaps it was my pounding headache from drinking too much last night—I was depleted. I tucked my wings away and let my shoulders droop. I had been fooling myself to think that I could dance and drink and narrate my life away. Any life without Theo was lonely, but I needed to move on.

"What do you want, Zeus?" I asked, my tone lifeless. "You want me to lie for you? Fine. You want me never to fly again? Done. I'll pretend you triumphed over our father on your own. I don't care, as long as you leave my sisters and me alone."

"The messenger already told me they're coming to Mount Olympus to join my new circle. We'll no longer be known as the Upstart Gods. Now we're the Olympians."

My jaw clenched. "Hestia and Demeter won't stay. They're going for a visit."

"They will join me. They're needed, as are you." Zeus took my ungloved hand in his and raised it to his lips. "I've missed you, dearest Hera. Marry me."

"You've lost your mind. Aren't you already married?"

"Metis and I are long over. It's always been me and you."

I yanked my hand from his grip. "I swore I would never marry."

"I can wait for you to change your mind," Zeus promised. "You saw our union. I've seen the vision in the throne room too. You're sitting beside me."

His faith was galling. "I didn't fight for my independence to end up shackled to you."

"You fought in my name."

"I have my own name. You force me to marry you, and I will despise you until the end of my days."

He scoffed. "You will not."

"I will. The war changed us both."

He ground his teeth. "I'm offering you a throne of great power."

"You're offering me a prison."

"You saved me from this place and raised me up," Zeus said, glancing around. "You stood with me through the hardest days of my life. We're not finished, Hera, and you know it."

I placed my face right up to his. "I was never responsible for saving you. You're responsible for saving yourself."

He recoiled. "Why must you be so angry?"

"Angry? This is rage, and you deserve it all." I refused to engage him any longer, so I reiterated my original statement. "Should you force my hand, I will ruin you. Choose wisely, Ruler of the Gods. I will never succumb. I will make your life miserable."

"You only hurt yourself by making promises like that. The world will remember you as a shrew."

"They will remember you as far worse," I rejoined.

"Me?" He rested a hand over his chest. "I'm a hero."

"I *made* you a hero."

"Then stand with me," he challenged, taking my hand again. "You belong at my side. Hera and Zeus. It's fate."

"I will never stand at your side again. You may force me there, but if you do, I will stand *against* you until the end of time. I will never lie for you. I will tell the truth of our past, so long as divine blood flows through my veins."

"We're well matched, Hera." His voice held unyielding determination. "One day you will accept that you're mine. I will see to it that you do."

I tugged my hand from his. I had vowed not to lie, yet he had not lied either. He wanted me, and he would not give up until he had what he desired. I couldn't say which of us would win, only that I had a story left to tell.

I marched out of the cave, my fists trembling against my sides, and stared up at the stars veiled by the sun. I would never let anyone forget the truth of the fall of Cronus. I would recite every sacrifice, by every warrior, male and female, that brought about the end of the Golden Age. In plays and poems and songs and dances, I would teach the true story, no matter how it made me appear. No one would forget the real heroes who had stood up to the Almighty with their wings of fury.

ACKNOWLEDGMENTS

Warmest regards to these Titans:

Adrienne Procaccini, for taking me under your editorial wing at 47North and becoming my goddess and queen. You would have flown with the Wings of Fury. Guaranteed.

Jason Kirk, for your omnipotent eye. Your capability to improve a story globally is equally as astounding as the fine-tooth comb that you take to each and every page. I never stop learning from you. As I've established more than once, everyone needs a good editor like you.

Marlene Stringer, for championing me every single damn step of the way.

To the gang at APub: Kristin King, Ashley Vanicek, Brittany Russell, and the marketing team. Also, my copyeditor and proofreader. You all make one helluva team.

Clarence Haynes, for continuing to educate me about the best stories out there through movies, TV, and comics. Your friendship has brought me much brightness during a historically bleak year.

Michael Makara, for telling me to slow down and take my time. I listened to you . . . 31 percent of the time. I love you, handsome. Thank you for being my muse.

John, Joseph, Julian, Danielle, Ryan: you saw me through another book and COVID twice! The real prize goes to you, folks. Love you, my dears.

Kate Coursey, Kathryn Purdie, Sara B. Larson, Veeda Bybee: my friends, confidants, cheerleaders, and the best women a girl could have. Titanesses and goddesses, you are.

My parents and sisters for never giving up on me. My Dungeons and Dragons group for showing me what magic can do. My readers and book bloggers for your endless support. And last but not least, Hera, the goddess of marriage, for teaching me I can be myself—unflinchingly.

ABOUT THE AUTHOR

Photo © 2015 Erin Summerill

Emily R. King is the author of the Hundredth Queen series and the Wings of Fury series, as well as *Before the Broken Star*, *Into the Hourglass*, and *Everafter Song* in the Evermore Chronicles. Born in Canada and raised in the United States, she is a shark advocate, a consumer of gummy bears, and an islander at heart, but her greatest interests are her children and three cats. For more information, visit her at www.emilyrking.com.